Haven Island PD

Protecting Paradise

CHIEF
Alejandro

Neri Lopez

Chief Alejandro
Haven Island PD: Protecting Paradise

Neri Lopez

Siren Book & Craft LLC

Copyright © 2025 by Neri Lopez
Publisher: Siren Book & Craft LLC
Editor: Michelle Zammataro
Cover Designer: Neri Lopez
Cover Model: Jose L. Barreiro – Model, Actor, former Ranger, and MMA fighter
Cover Model Photographer: Wander Aguiar Photography
Cover background image: Neri's beach photo and Vecteezy.
Maps are fictional and designed by Neri Lopez with images from Vecteezy

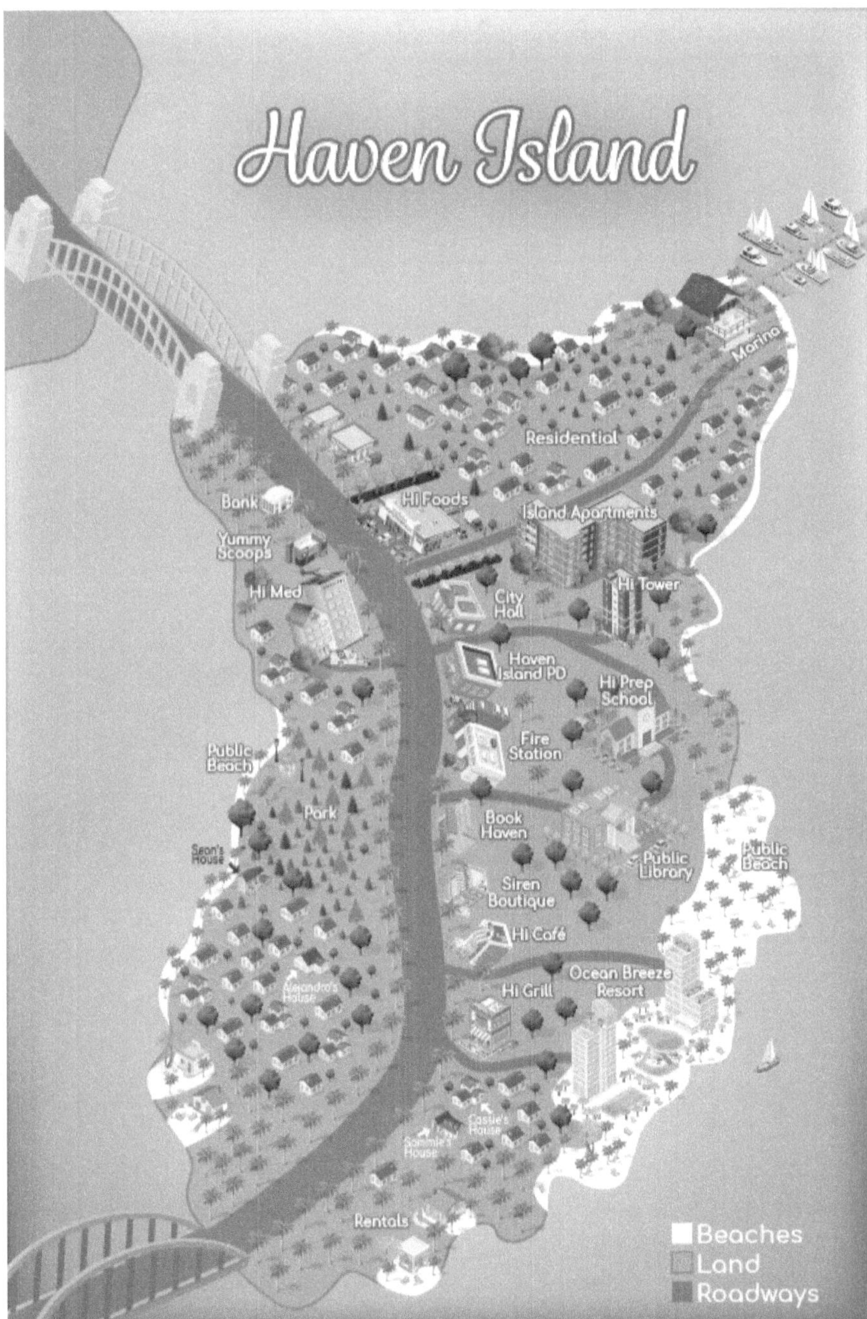

Haven Island
Marina
Residential
Bank
Yummy Scoops
Hi Foods
Island Apartments
Hi Med
City Hall
Hi Tower
Haven Island PD
Hi Prep School
Fire Station
Public Beach
Park
Book Haven
Public Library
Public Beach
Sean's House
Siren Boutique
Hi Café
Alejandro's House
Ocean Breeze Resort
Hi Grill
Castie's House
Sammie's House
Rentals
Beaches
Land
Roadways

Contents

Chapter 1

Crazy Ex

Sammie

"You need to leave...now!" I screamed at Lincoln, my ex-husband and baby daddy of my triplets.

With every ounce of strength I had, I pushed against the door, desperate to close it, but his foot blocked the way. He forced it open, and I stumbled, slamming against the wall.

"I want to see my kids," Lincoln growled at me as he stepped inside.

"Why now?" My chest heaved with each breath as I stared into his crazed eyes.

Lincoln and I had dated for only six months when he convinced me to move in with him on the mainland and leave the island. He was so charming and loving, I couldn't imagine my life without him. We packed up our cars with all my stuff and drove to his two-story house in an affluent neighborhood in Jones County.

"Where have you been for the last nine years while I've been raising our children alone, because you couldn't be bothered with child support? Hell, you never answered my calls. And now you want to see them. Again, I ask you, why now?"

"I have a right to see them."

"You lost that right when you abandoned us."

How dare he? Having a quickie marriage at the courthouse after learning I was pregnant was bad, but abandoning me when he discovered I was carrying triplets was beyond awful. During my pregnancy, I called Lincoln multiple times to update him. Even though the doctor placed me on bed rest and I lost my job, I still continued to reach out. The silence was deafening. My calls remained unanswered. I told him the exact date of my cesarean, yet I still didn't get the Lincoln I wanted. That was the last straw.

If he didn't want to meet our beautiful children and help me raise them, that was his loss. I steeled myself against him, embracing the reality of a single mother. I moved back to my parents' house, prepared to raise my children with the support and love of my family and friends.

I stared out the front door and gawked at the shiny black BMW sitting in my driveway. Pointing out the door, I said, "Did Daddy buy you a new car?"

"Jealous." Lincoln smirked and walked around looking in the front rooms like he owned the place.

Entitled Asshole. I grabbed his arm. "I need you to go."

His bursting into my house was not the best way to introduce him to the kids. Deep down, I didn't want them to meet him at all. He didn't deserve them. He left us, not the other way around.

"Daddy?"

Shit! I spun around, startled by the sound of Hollie's sweet voice echoing from the kitchen. *Oh no, my time had run out.* My girls were standing in the living room with my mom, Eleanor. Mom steadied herself, leaning against the couch, as she and Hallie gaped at Lincoln. Not my sweet Hollie. Her eyes sparkled with hope.

"Hey, sweetheart. Give Daddy a hug." Lincoln's behavior shifted completely from being an asshole to acting the part of a loving father. *Jackass!* He lowered himself into a crouch, ready for his daughter's embrace. Hallie, being the protective older sister, glared at Lincoln. She wrapped her arms around Hollie, stopping her from going to Lincoln. *Go Hallie!*

Over the years, the kids asked about their dad. I told them he wasn't ready to be a parent, but I promised to let them meet him when the time was right. A child should never have to feel as if their parent didn't love them. I never expected Lincoln to show up on my doorstep after his Houdini act. A phone call would've been nice. I still had the same number.

The way my trio asked about their father was as diverse as they were. Hollie, the youngest, was my compassionate child. Kindhearted and always willing to give someone a second chance. She spent years asking the most questions about her father, hoping to learn as much as possible about him to build a closer relationship when they met. Hallie, my realist child, was wary of wanting to meet him. She didn't understand why he didn't want them. The eldest Holden considered himself the man of the house, altogether eliminating his father from the equation.

Lincoln stood when he realized they weren't running toward him. *Did he think the kids would run to him like a normal dad when they had never met him?* My kids don't approach strangers.

"Where's your brother?" Lincoln strolled into the living room.

"He's not here!" Hallie screamed. "Hollie, let's go." Hallie grabbed Hollie's hand.

"But it's Daddy?" Hollie screeched.

I grabbed a pad and pen from the foyer table and wrote my cell number. Lincoln and I needed to discuss his intentions with the kids. I didn't want him making promises to our kids that he would not keep.

"Here's my number in case you deleted it. It's still the same." I handed him the piece of paper. "Call me and we'll meet somewhere to go over when you want to meet them, but not now."

"No." Lincoln headed toward my mom, who was now blocking the entrance to the kitchen. "I want to talk to my kids now." Mom's arms wrapped around the girls, pulling them toward her chest.

"Get out of my house or I will call the police!" I hollered at him.

"Nice try." Lincoln spun toward me. "But this isn't your damn house."

"You're right." My dad appeared behind my mom, his hands on her shoulders. "It's our house, and I need you to leave."

My father distracted Lincoln, giving me enough time to pull out my phone and dial our police chief, Alejandro Reyes. Alejandro, whom I called Alex to tease him, was married to my childhood friend Annie. When I moved back to town after Lincoln left me, Annie, who was also pregnant. She sat beside me and kept me company throughout my entire bed rest. We were so eager to raise our kids together. I pressed the speakerphone so Alex could hear everything Lincoln said.

"Hey, Sammie," Alejandro answered. "What's going on? Who's your dad shouting at?"

Gasping to control my breath, I rambled. "Lincoln is at my house, and he won't leave."

"Who's on the phone?"

"The police. So you'd better leave." I glanced at my dad. "Dad, take the kids outside!"

"You called the fucking police! Give me that fucking phone?" Lincoln stalked toward me, his face bright red. His hand grabbed my phone, but I pulled it away.

"Please hurry!" I screamed.

He backhanded my hand so hard I lost my grip, and my phone skidded across the floor down the hallway. Lincoln raised his hand, and I cowered. *Was he going to hit me?* He'd never hit me before, but I didn't know this crazed version. With a frustrated yell, he swept the crooked multi-colored vase my kids made me off the foyer table, the ceramic shattering as it hit the floor. I stepped back, clutching my throat. Lincoln never looked back. He slammed the door on his way out. I ran for my phone.

"Are you still there?"

"I'm on my way."

I peeked out the front window that overlooked the driveway.

"Alex." I placed my hand over my racing heart. "He's leaving."

"I'm two minutes out. Don't hang up." His voice vibrated with anger.

"Okay." From the side of the window, I kept myself hidden from Lincoln's view. Lincoln glared at the house from the driver's seat, his jaw clenched, before he sped off. The sound of his screeching tires echoed down the street.

"Is Holden with you?" A chill snaked up my spine as I mumbled the words, imagining danger lurking at every corner.

"No, I was at my mom and dad's house. The boys wanted to go fishing with my dad, so I left them there."

"Thank God," I sighed and placed my hand over my heart.

My mom burst into the living room. "I heard a car pull out. Did he leave? Is that Chief Reyes?"

"Yes." I stepped back away from the window. "He's on his way."

"But, Mommy?" Hollie squeezed past her grandparents. "It was Daddy, and I wanted to talk to him," Hollie whined.

"Oh, baby." I approached Hollie and squatted in front of her, placing my phone on the floor to hold her. "Not tonight, but I'll talk to Daddy and get it all sorted out so you can get to know him another time."

I hated agreeing to any kind of get-together with her miserable excuse for a father. My lawyer fought his lawyer in court during our divorce proceedings, and the judge granted me sole custody but gave him monitored visitation rights.

A loud bang erupted on the door, making everyone jump. Alex's voice crackled through the phone.

"Sammie, it's me at the door. Let me in."

Chapter 2

Helping Out a Friend

Alejandro

"Lincoln is at my house, and he won't leave."

What the hell was Lincoln doing at Sammie's house? It had been years since I'd heard that name come out of Sammie's mouth. I covered the phone and mouthed to my mom, "I gotta go."

"Please hurry!" Sammie said before she screamed.

Those words followed by her bone-chilling scream made my blood run cold. I bolted from the kitchen, snatching my keys as I flew out the door. I kept Sammie on the phone so I could hear everything going on at her house.

When I met Annie, I also met Sammie. Wherever one went, the other followed, and I was happy with that arrangement, since Sammie was the reason Annie even considered dating me. Being with the 75th Ranger Regiment under the U.S. Army Special Operations meant a long line of deployments, which I'd never minded—until Annie. My focus shifted to having a family and living out my second dream of becoming a local police officer on Haven Island. I loved my hometown.

I never liked Lincoln from the first time I met him—arrogant, entitled asshole acted like his shit didn't stink even though several of my brothers in blue had busted him for drug possession. Sammie told Annie they were moving to the mainland, and he was getting clean. The day Annie called to tell Sammie she was pregnant, Sammie was also pregnant with triplets, and Lincoln was nowhere to be found.

When Annie died, Sammie helped me through those dark days. I had to help Sammie, considering I failed Annie.

I sped through the island with my lights and sirens blaring like a bat out of hell to her parents' house. I pulled into the driveway and slammed on my brakes. Sammie's car was the only one in the driveway. I heard Hollie's muffled cries. They were breaking my heart. I had grown to love those kids as if they were my own. I called out to her, identifying myself, and paced the porch waiting for her to let me in.

Sammie threw the door open and ran into my arms. "I'm so glad you're here."

Her body shuddered in my arms, making me fear she would fall if I released her. I looked over her shoulder and saw the girls with her mom and dad.

Easing her backwards, I closed the door, and stooped to her eye level and said. "Let's have a seat, and you can tell me what happened."

She bobbed her head, hugging herself with her arms. She turned toward her parents. "Mom, Dad, can you take the girls out back while I talk to Chief Reyes?"

"Sure. Come on, ladies." My mom hustled them out of the room.

"He just showed up and demanded to see the kids." Sammie blurted.

"When was the last time you saw him?" I reached out and grasped her hands.

"The night I told him I was pregnant with triplets. We fought because he said he wasn't ready to be a father, let alone to multiples. He accused me of tricking him into getting married. He grabbed his clothes and stormed out. I haven't seen or talked to him since that night."

I rubbed the back of Sammie's hand. "Was he in court during your divorce proceedings?"

"Neither of us was there. As the primary caregiver, it was difficult for me to leave them, and his lawyer said he was in rehab. I'm not sure if that was an excuse or if he really was getting help for his drug addiction. I got sole custody, but the judge gave him supervised visitation rights if he ever got clean."

"He's never asked to see them before today?" I couldn't believe a dad could act like his kids didn't exist for nine fucking years.

"No." Sammie shook her head. "Not once has he contacted me about meeting his kids."

"Did he seem high when he came over?"

"I don't know!" Sammie bolted from the couch. "His eyes were bloodshot, and he looked like he was about to punch me, but I didn't stare at him too long. I just wanted him gone. Ugh." Sammie threw her arms up in the air and began pacing. "I should've paid better attention."

"Hey." I stood and held her elbows to stop her pacing. "You had a lot on your mind since the girls were home. Don't beat yourself up. He surprised you, that's all. Now you know he's in town, and I'll help you set up a game plan. I will not let anything happen to you or your kids."

Sammie's watery eyes looked into mine. "I have to talk to him and let my babies be around him. How could I have been so stupid when I dated him? I ignored every red flag. Hell, Annie warned me so many times, and I didn't listen. Oh God," Sammie dropped her face into her hands and sobbed. "I was so stupid."

I pulled her into my arms. One hand gently soothed her back while the other nestled her face against my chest. I held her close, listening to the heartbreaking echo of her sobs. Her body trembled, and I felt her warm tears soak into my shirt. The embrace was a gesture of friendship to comfort Annie's best friend, no strings attached. Because I buried my heart with Annie, nothing else would ever be possible—especially with her best friend.

Chapter 3

The Weight of the Past

Sammie

My life was turning into a damn made-for-TV movie. Just when I felt I could do this triplet mom thing, that jerk had to come back into my life. Blubbering on my best friend's husband was not the way to go, even though being held by him shot a burst of warmth through my body—like coming home.

Wasn't it wrong to crave Alex's touch, even though Annie had passed seven years ago? We had become friends during that time. Alex and I would call each other anytime we needed an extra pair of hands with the kids. Even though I was living at home, Alex always helped us fix stuff around the house or the boutique.

If you gauged the closeness of his son Cody and my Holden by their frequent visits and friendship, they might as well have been siblings. The two were inseparable when they weren't in school. We honored Annie's dream of raising our kids together. While we were expecting, Annie and I spoke about setting up Cody with one of my girls so we could combine our families forever. I'm sure we weren't the first parents to get the crazy idea to set up our kids. Stepping back and out of Alex's arms, I wiped my face.

"Sorry, I didn't mean to cry all over your uniform."

"It's fine. Nothing the dry cleaners can't fix." Alex grinned at me.

Oh, Annie, I thought, *you picked the right man as opposed to me.* With a smile, I turned away from Alex, trying to hide my thoughts of how things might have been if I hadn't introduced him to Annie. *What a terrible thought!* I was a horrible friend for thinking of my best friend losing out on the love of her life for her last years on this Earth. And I wouldn't have my amazing children. Everything happens for a reason, and Lincoln was my cross to bear because of my stupid decision to follow him to the mainland and have sex without a condom. I must've had an interesting look on my face because Alex reached out.

"Hey," Alex grasped my hand. "I'm not worried about my uniform. It's just water."

"And makeup." I released his hand and brushed the dark, wet spot on his chest. "What if it doesn't come out?" I needed to stop rubbing it. I was only making it worse. "I'll pay for the cleaning."

"Sammie, look at me." Alex lifted my chin with his hand.

I gazed into his smiling eyes. He wasn't mad at all.

"It's not a problem," he whispered.

As we got closer, I nodded, and his warm breath brushed against my face. His beautiful brown eyes held my gaze. That moment captivated me, and I finally understood Annie's infatuation with Alex. He was powerful, dependable, and kept his promises.

His face lowered to mine. I closed my eyes and smelled his woodsy aftershave. My heart raced, and my lips parted. *Oh God, he was going to kiss me. Finally, I would be his.* But at the last second, he angled his head and kissed my cheek.

"Sammie!" My mom's voice jolted us apart like we were two teenagers caught in a compromising position. "Should we go get Holden?" She appeared in the kitchen doorway.

I cleared my throat and glanced anywhere but at Alex.

"He's fishing with Cody and my dad," Alex spoke up, since apparently the cat had caught my tongue. "I can bring him home after we're done at the station."

"I..I... We what?" I stared at Alex. "Why do I need to go to the station?" I already told him I didn't want to file a report. *Why was he being so damn stubborn?*

Alex crossed his arms. "I want you to fill out a police report that states how he forced himself into your house and slapped the phone out of your hands."

"Why?" I squinted. "Can you arrest him?"

Alex rubbed the back of his neck. "No, but it will show that he's not above hurting you to get to the kids. Unless you want to place a restraining order on him?"

"I can't do that," I sighed. "He has a right to see the kids, and if it has to be supervised, I want to be there when he's with them."

"Okay, but if you think for one minute, he might get violent or is high when he asks for a visit–" Alex pointed at me. "–you call me, and we'll find a social worker or some other person to supervise those visits. He will not hurt my wife's best friend."

"Thanks." I nodded. "You and Annie were so lucky to have found each other."

"Lucky would have been if she were still here with me, helping me raise our child, but I'm glad I had the time I did with her."

"Yeah, I get that." I patted his shoulder. "Mom, I'll go with Alex now and bring Holden home when we're done."

"Okay. I'll see you later." Mom locked up behind us.

Chapter 4

HiPD

Alejandro

"**C**ome with me to my office and I'll take down your statement and add it to my report." I placed my hand on Sammie's lower back as I guided her through the police station. Several of my officers glanced in our direction, while others who knew Sammie, greeted her.

"Hey, Sammie," Officer Charlotte Spencer got up from behind her desk and gave Sammie a hug. "What are you doing here?"

"Uh—" Sammie glanced between Charlotte and me. "—trouble with my ex."

"I'm sorry. Let me know if I can help." Charlotte left and headed toward the lounge.

We always kept a full pot of coffee in the lounge for all the officers. We were coffeeholics. When we entered my office, I shut the door for privacy.

"Do you want anything to drink? Coffee? Water?"

"No, thank you." Sammie sat in the chair facing my desk, fidgeting with her hands in her lap. "I just want to get this over with and get Holden. I'll feel better when he's with me."

"Gotcha." I sat and woke up my computer. "I'll fill out my part before I put in your statement. Just give me a minute." I opened the file and added my report. I didn't have to start a new file on Lincoln, because he already had a report a mile long from before he left the Island. He had several arrests for drug possession, but money talks, and his daddy always got him off.

"Okay, tell me exactly what he did, and I'll type." I typed in every word Sammie said. When she finished, I submitted my report.

I pulled out my cell phone and called my dad.

"Mijo, is everything okay?"

"Si Papi. I'm with Sammie at the station. Are you, Cody and Holden, still fishing?"

"Nah, the boys were so hot, we went out for ice cream and now they're just watching a movie."

I squeezed the bridge of my nose with my fingers and closed my eyes. I should've told my dad to keep the boys away from Main Street in case Lincoln recognized Holden.

"Okay, keep them inside. I'll be there shortly with Sammie."

"What's going on, mijo?"

"I'll explain everything when I get there."

I heard some rustling and footsteps. Then my dad's voice got low when he whispered, "Why is Sammie with you at the station? Is she okay?"

My parents loved Sammie and her kids. They worried about her as much as they worried about me.

"She's fine. We'll be there soon."

I hung up and took a deep breath because when Sammie found out the boys were in town; she was going to blow a gasket.

"Are they okay? They're done fishing?"

"Yep." I shut down my computer and came around the desk. I had never lied to Sammie, and I wouldn't start now. "They finished early, so Dad took them out for ice cream."

Sammie bolted out of the chair and screeched. "They were in town!" I put my hand on her arm.

"Calm down. Holden is okay."

"Alejandro Reyes, don't tell me to calm down after what happened to me today." Sammie paced in front of my desk like a wolf watching its prey. "Why didn't you call your dad and tell him not to take Holden out in public? I thought they were fishing out of their backyard?"

"Sammie." I blocked her path and held her shoulders. "They're okay. Remember my dad was ex-military. He would protect those boys with his life."

"I know," she sighed and placed her palm on her forehead. "I trust your dad. I'm a mess. Lincoln is turning me into a paranoid psycho."

"Come on, you're not paranoid." I chuckled.

"Gee, thanks." Sammie swatted my chest.

My choice of words distracted her and lightened the mood. If I kept her calm, we could discuss the problem and find a solution. That's how I attacked every problem I encountered. Find the source, fix the problem. I didn't want her going after Lincoln half-cocked. If his behavior today was a sign of his growing anger, she might not be so lucky next time. Lincoln could become aggressive enough to hurt Sammie if he felt she triggered his anger. In my line of work, officers encountered various forms of domestic violence daily. I'll be damned if I wanted her on the opposite side of that anger.

"You'll feel better once you see Holden. I'm done here. Let's go."

We left the station, walked to the patrol vehicle and drove off. I was ready for this day to be over. Here I thought I was getting off a few hours early to go fishing with the boys. Instead, I was protecting my wife's best friend and filing a report against her crazy ex. Cody and I had been looking forward to today for quite some time, especially since Holden could come with us. That's okay. We would find another day. All was not lost. We still had a couple of weeks before school started. I'm sure I could leave work early another day or take them on the weekend.

Chapter 5

Just Want to Hold My Boy

Sammie

I remained silent for most of the trip home. I wasn't angry at Alex, only unable to find words that didn't reveal my deep longing to embrace my son and know he was safe. In my heart, I knew Roberto would protect him, but I needed to see him with my own two eyes. The moment we pulled up at his house, I leapt from the car and knocked on the door. Milagro opened it and embraced me in a warm hug.

"Hola, Sammie." She said in her broken English. Alex's parents were Cuban. Both families migrated to the United States in the sixties and became citizens.

"Hi, Milagro. Where is Holden?" I loved Milagro and Roberto, but I couldn't wait to see Holden.

"Come with me. He's in the living room with Cody."

Even though I was following Milagro, the instant I saw Holden, I sprinted towards him, yanked him off the couch, and wrapped him in a loving embrace, relishing the scent of his sweaty skin.

"Hi, Mom." Holden hugged me back. "Are you okay?"

"I'm good now." I released him and kissed his cheek. "Let's get your stuff and go home."

"Can I finish watching the movie?"

"No, not today. We need to get home. I need to talk with you and your sisters."

"Oh...kay." Holden looked at Cody. "Can we finish it another day?"

"Sure." Cody shrugged. "Can you stop it, abuela?"

"Sí." Milagro clicked the button on the remote.

"Thanks, bro." Holden said to Cody, and they fist-bumped.

I walked to the door and remembered I didn't have my car.

"Hang on, Holden." I pulled my phone out of my purse. "Let me call your grandfather and ask him to come get us."

"Where's your car?" Holden's head tilted.

"It's at home. I came with Chief Reyes." I always used his proper name with my kids. They needed to respect their elders.

"Sammie." Alex placed his hand over my phone. "I can drive you guys home."

"We both won't fit in your police car."

Alex held a set of keys and jingled them. "We can go in my SUV, not the patrol vehicle."

My mind must be spiralling if I forgot about the car Alex drove when he wasn't working. I needed to get it together before we had a family meeting and talked about Lincoln.

"Oh right, sorry." Remembering my manners, I turned to Alex's parents. "Thank you both for taking care of Holden."

"We love having him," Milagro said, and Roberto nodded.

"Bye, Holden." Cody shouted.

"Later," Holden blurted over his shoulder as I nudged him with my hand out the door toward Alex's SUV.

As soon as we stepped outside, Alex's eyes darted up and down the street. I appreciated his watchful gaze. Holden sat in the back seat behind me. The click of the seatbelt confirmed he was ready. I settled into the front seat.

"How was fishing?" I asked Holden

"It was fine, but hot. We asked Mr. Reyes if we could have ice cream, and he drove us to Yummy Scoops. I had chocolate."

"I'm sure it was good. Did you thank Mr. Reyes?"

"Yep." Holden nodded. "What's your favorite ice cream, Chief Reyes?"

"Uh...I don't really have a favorite." Alex drove down Main Street, his eyes glancing everywhere.

"So what do you order at Yummy Scoops? Mom orders cookies and cream. Right, Mom?"

"I sure do." I nodded. "That's my favorite."

"Chief Reyes, if you had to pick one. What would it be?" Holden was not letting Alex off the hook.

"I would get mint chocolate chip." Alex glanced at Holden with a smile.

"Oooh, that's a good one?"

"It sure is." Alex nodded.

"Mom, can I get that one next time?"

"What if you don't like it?" I liked mint chocolate chip, but I wasn't sure I could eat two bowls of ice cream.

"Can Chief Reyes take me so I can try his?"

"Sure, buddy," Alex offered. "I'll take you and Cody this weekend if it's okay with your mom." His eyebrow lifted in question.

"Yay! Ice cream twice in one week." Cody was hooting and hollering. "But wait, what about my sisters? I bet they would like to go out for ice cream."

"Holden, where are your manners?" I reprimanded. "You can't invite yourself and your sisters on an ice cream trip with Al... Chief Reyes."

"It's okay." Alex chuckled. "I'll take your sisters and your mom."

"Awesome! I can't wait to tell Cody, Hollie, and Hallie." Holden burst out of the car as soon as Alex parked in our driveway.

"Thank you for offering to take us to the ice cream shop, but I work all day Saturday and Sunday. If you want my help with the kids, you'll have to go on Sunday after I get off work at five."

Alex leaned his left arm over the steering wheel and watched Cody before he turned to me. "That's up to you. I don't mind taking them myself. It's not like when they were babies. But if you want ice cream, we'll do it on Sunday."

"I'll let you know. With school beginning next week, I'm attempting to maximize my time with them before homework and activities begin." If Alex took them on Saturday, I'd have them all to myself on Sunday.

"Sounds good. I'll do whatever you prefer. I'm free all weekend."

"Okay." I placed my hand on his shoulder. "Thank you for the save today. I really appreciated it."

"Of course." Alex leaned in and whispered. "Let me know if you have any more issues with Lincoln." His eyes roamed over my face.

"I will." I said breathlessly.

His beautiful brown eyes seemed to stare into my soul, drawing me closer to his face. My heart was racing in my chest.

"Mom!" Holden screamed from the door, and I flinched. "Are you coming?"

Thank you, Holden, for breaking me out of my lovesick trance before I made a huge mistake and kissed Alex. I smiled wistfully, wishing we could be together.

"I...I'll talk to you later." I scrambled out of the car and waved before I entered the house.

"Mom, Dad, kids!" I hollered in the foyer. "Where are you? We need to talk."

"In here," came my dad's deep voice from the living room.

Mom and Dad were on the couch while Hallie and Hollie sat on the floor in front of the cocktail table playing Jenga. Holden joined them.

"Mommy—" Hollie's voice cracked as she crossed her arms and hmphed. "I just... I wanted to talk to Daddy. Why did you make him leave?"

I wish the kids knew how toxic Lincoln was, but to be honest, I never said anything negative about him. For all these years, I tried to be the better person. I told them things didn't work out between us and that it had nothing to do with them. *Ugh! Why now?* Let the tough questions begin.

"Your dad surprised me. I want to talk to him in private before he comes to visit you guys."

"But why?" Hollie whined.

"Because you guys have never met him before and I think it would be best if we meet at a park." That explanation was murky as hell.

"I don't understand," Hollie frowned.

Well, here goes nothing. "I don't want to speak for your dad. It's best he tell you where he's been when he meets you. Since you guys like the outdoors, I thought a park would be better than a restaurant."

I struggled to conceal the truth. Their father was a terrible person, who favored drugs over his children, but I couldn't tell them that. At a park, I could redirect them away from him more easily than in a restaurant.

"Can I see him tomorrow?" Hollie's eyes sparkled with excitement.

"Holls, stop," Hallie yelled at her. "Mom's being nice. Dad didn't want us. He's a druggie."

"How do you know?" Hollie frowned.

"Whatever." Hallie stood and stormed out of the room.

How the hell did Hallie know Lincoln was a druggie? She must've overheard a conversation with my parents because I never told my kids Lincoln used drugs.

"But Hallie!" Hollie spun around watching her sister.

After Hallie left, Hollie turned to me, her face streaked with tears, her voice choked with emotion. "I miss Daddy."

"How can you miss someone you've never met, Holls?" Holden hugged her. "Don't cry." Holden helped her off the floor. "Let's go play another game with Hallie in our room."

God bless Holden. He embraced his job as the man of the house, shouldering the responsibility with a sense of duty. It's clear that he doesn't resemble his dad, thank heavens. I slumped in my seat. Holden was growing up so fast. He's always looking out for his sisters. One reason I enjoyed Holden's playdates with Cody was so he could escape and be a kid playing or fishing, free from all responsibilities. It pained me that his childhood had been, in part, sacrificed to help with the girls.

I knelt in front of the table to clean up the game pieces left behind like a train wreck.

"Are you going to let him take the kids out?" my mom shrieked.

My parents hated Lincoln. They suspected his drug problem, but I sugarcoated it. Maybe they could have forgiven Lincoln if he got clean. They would never forgive him for abandoning me pregnant with triplets, nor could they understand how he could vanish from our lives without a backward glance.

"I wish he'd never shown up." I placed all the pieces into the box. "I can't keep them away from him per our divorce agreement."

"That sucks," Mom snarled.

"Yes, it does." I chuckled because I rarely heard my mom curse. "I'm just glad they have to be supervised visits. If I'm there, I can make sure he's nice to them and not high as a kite. I don't trust him."

"We don't trust him either. We think he was on something when he barged in," Dad grumbled. "I'll be happy to supervise those visits when you can't."

"Me too." Mom added.

"Thank you both." I stood and put the box on the bookshelf cabinet. "I'll talk to Lincoln and set something up. I'm gonna go to bed after I read to the kids."

"When are you gonna talk to Lincoln?" Mom stood in front of me.

"When he calls. I handed him my number. Not that it's changed." I sighed. "I don't know if the number I have for him is current, so I'll wait until he calls me. In the meantime, if he shows up here while I'm at work, call me."

I left my parents in the living room and made my way to the kids' room. They were all playing another board game.

"Hey, do you guys want a story?" I asked from the doorway.

"I can do it." Holden smiled at me. "Go relax, Mom, you've had a hard day."

"I love you guys." I stepped in and gave each of my kids a hug and a kiss. I felt blessed. "Come get me if you need anything."

"Okay, Mommy," the girls said in unison.

Chapter 6

Whiskey Night

Lincoln

"How did it go? Did you get to meet your kids?" My wife, Ava, blurted out as soon as I walked into our apartment.

"How the hell do you think it went?" I growled at her. "I need a minute."

I dashed into our bedroom and locked the door. Bursting into my closet, I pulled every fucking shoebox out of my way so I could get to the one that offered me my white powder relief. My trembling hands fumbled with the lid as sweat poured into my eyes. The box tipped over, and a photo along with several items fell out. I stared at my reflection in Ava's small makeup mirror. *Fuck! I looked like shit.*

Not the time to self-analyze. I grabbed the powder and made two crooked lines with a sharp razor blade. I snorted up one side and down the other. Damn, that felt good—instant nirvana. I leaned back against the closet door and closed my eyes. I took several deep breaths before opening my eyes and seeing the current photo of Sammie and my kids on Haven Island Beach lying next to the box. I downloaded it from Sammie's social media account, which took some doing since she blocked me after the babies were born. *Fucking triplets, damn I was good.*

I checked my stash in the box. *Shit, two packets left.* I had used Ava's monthly allowance from her parents, who were loaded like mine, for that last buy. *Where had it all gone? I had bought six packets.* Those meager two packets would not last more than a week at best. It's a good thing I stopped to place a bet with my bookie. I wagered on a player beating the record in today's game—a solid bet. I was confident the player would win, which would buy me a few more days.

My father kept pestering us about grandkids, and Ava had been struggling to conceive. Just my luck that my strong-ass sperm hit its target with my poor ex instead of my rich wife. I had to tell my parents about my triplets. Sure, my father would be furious, but he would eventually jump for joy and return to being my cash cow.

I picked up the photo and stared at Sammie. She had always been beautiful, but now she glowed with a mother's love. Damn, she was still hot even after having triplets. I wasn't expecting Sammie to welcome me with open arms today, but I didn't expect her to shut the door in my face. Those were my fucking kids, and if I wanted to see them, she shouldn't stop me. Who cares if it took me years to meet them? Or that I needed them to help get me out of a bind? I'm here now. That's what should count.

The banging on the bedroom door jolted me from my thoughts.

"Lincoln! Are you okay? Unlock the door!"

"Dammit," I whispered and threw everything back in the box, hiding it in the back. "I'm fine!" I opened the closet door and screamed. "I'll be out in a minute." I stripped and put on a t-shirt and pajama bottoms before I swung the bedroom door open.

"Are you okay?" Ava reached out and touched my arm. "I kept knocking, but you didn't answer. I was worried about you."

"Sorry, my stomach was acting up," I mumbled and walked past her into the kitchen for a beer.

After popping the top off the bottle, I flung myself onto the couch. Without taking off my shoes, I rested my legs on the cushions and crossed my ankles before taking a long drink. Lying back, I got comfortable, enjoying my cold beer.

"Can you please take off your shoes? You're getting the couch dirty."

I despised the way her voice dripped with condescension. She didn't have the right to reprimand me like a child. I was a grown-ass man. Still, I needed her and her trust fund. Several times I tried to double our money with bets, but I didn't always win and had to get creative with our funds—her funds. I cared about Ava—she epitomized beautiful eye candy and was decent in bed—but if I was being honest with myself; I cared more about her money than being married to her.

"Fine." I kicked my shoes off. "Better?"

"Yes, thank you." Ava nodded. "What are you gonna do?"

I reached into my pocket, took out the piece of paper Sammie had handed me, and entered the number into my phone.

"Sammie gave me her number. I'm gonna call her tomorrow and find out when I can see my kids."

"You don't have her number?" Ava frowned.

"No. I deleted it and blocked her number when I left her.

"Wow," Ava's mouth dropped. "Okay. Let me know if I can help. I can't wait to meet them." Ava scooted to the edge of her chair.

"Don't get too excited." I smiled wryly. "Sammie wasn't exactly happy to see me." I grumbled. The last thing I wanted was for Ava to want the kids to be over all the time.

"I'd like to be with you when you meet them. I would love to take them bowling and to the movies. Oh, and we can have sleepovers!" Ava clapped her hands.

"Whoa there, slow down." I put my hand up. "I can handle this myself. Besides, I'd rather be there alone when I meet them because they don't know I'm married."

"Oh." Ava's chest caved, her shoulders rounded as she stared at the floor. "Okay."

I guzzled my beer and stood before walking around the island into the kitchen for something stronger. Whiskey sounded good.

"Lincoln," Ava's voice carried into the kitchen. "I was looking over the business accounts, and we are almost at zero on our bank balance. I thought you said we were okay."

Nag, nag, nag, that's all she ever did. "We're fine," I said over my shoulder.

"How?" Ava stood on the other side of the island staring at me.

"I haven't transferred all the money from our business account."

I grabbed the whiskey bottle because why dirty up a glass when Ava didn't drink whiskey. She hated the aroma and the burn as it went down her throat. More for me.

"From where? Which account?"

Why couldn't she leave it alone? I'm the man. She should shut up and mind her own business, taking care of the cooking and cleaning. I would have left Ava ages ago, but her trust fund let me continue living the comfortable life I enjoyed.

"I have it under control, okay!" I yelled at her and shoved past her into the living room with my bottle. I didn't need her crap today. I'd taken enough shit from Sammie.

I picked up the remote and settled back onto the couch. Propping my feet up on the coffee table, I watched the player who was going to win me my next stash. Ava sat in silence next to me as she scrolled through her phone. She hated football. I didn't care. I just needed the fucker on TV to break the record. *Thank fuck Ava kept her mouth shut. I'd had enough of her questions for one day. Was she back on the banking app?*

"Ava Grace, stop fucking checking the account!"

"I'm not." Ava turned her phone around and showed me her social media account.

"Good." I nodded. "I'll transfer money this week to that account."

"Okay."

Ava wasn't aware of my multiple accounts. She didn't need to know I transferred small amounts of her money into my personal offshore bank account. That was my get-out-of-town emergency fund. If things went south, I planned to move to the Maldives. They didn't have an extradition treaty with the U.S.

Chapter 7

The Nights were the Hardest

Alejandro

"Cody?" I called out when I got home.

Despite the gnawing urge to return to work and research Lincoln Rogers, I drove home. I could investigate the scumbag tomorrow and uncover any unlawful deeds from the last nine years.

"He's in his room." My mom walked out of the kitchen, drying her hands on a dishrag.

"Hola, Mami." I wrapped my arms around her and held her close. My mother was the best. With a heart of gold and comforting guidance, she was always ready to step in and help me.

"Come get a cup of coffee." She pulled me into the kitchen, pushed me into a chair, and poured me a cup.

"Where's Papi?"

"He's with Cody in his room." She placed the cup of coffee in front of me before she sat. "How's Sammie?"

"She's in a tough spot." I took a sip.

"What happened?"

"Remember Lincoln, her ex?" Mami nodded. "He resurrected today and barged into her house demanding to see his kids. She got scared and called me."

"Why now?" Mami frowned. "He hasn't seen those kids since before they were born."

"I don't know." I sat back and spread my legs out. "But I'm going to find out as soon as I figure out where he's living. There has to be a reason he's showing up now after so long."

"Maybe the guilt of not knowing his kids was bothering him?" Mami stared at me.

"I doubt it. But tomorrow I'm gonna see what he's been up to. I don't want him upsetting Sammie or her kids. She has enough on her plate."

"You like Sammie, don't you?" Mami quirked her eyebrow at me.

"Of course I do. She's a good friend." I nodded and took another sip.

"Just a friend?"

"Well, yeah. What else?" I frowned.

"Be careful, Alejandro, with Lincoln and your feelings toward Sammie."

"What are you talking about?"

"I think you feel more for Sammie than friendship. You call her all the time when you need to ask her opinion about something with Cody. You're both raising those kids together. I can't believe you're so blind that you don't see that."

"What? No. I'm just honoring Annie's wish."

"I'm sure it started out that way, but if you didn't like Sammie, this so-called friendship wouldn't have lasted."

"Okay, but like I said. She's a good friend."

I didn't want to have this conversation with my mom, so I guzzled the scalding hot cup of coffee as fast as I could and regretted it when the hot liquid burned all the way down. My mother made me think about things that could never be. I stood, and she placed her hand over mine, stopping me from leaving.

"I think there's more to it, and I want you to know I'm happy for you. I love Sammie and her kids."

"Yeah, okay." I squeezed her hand, walked to the sink, and rinsed my cup. "I'm gonna go hang out with Cody so Dad can take you home. Thank you for watching him today."

"It's always my pleasure to watch my grandson. Maybe someday you'll give me more." She winked at me.

That was not happening anytime soon or ever, but tonight wasn't the night to burst her bubble. I placed my hand on her shoulder as I passed her toward the doorway. She gripped my hand.

"You need to live again, Alejandro. Annie loved you. She wouldn't want you to be alone for the rest of your life. You and Cody need the love of a good woman."

"I'll get Dad." I cleared my throat and left.

Cody lay next to my dad on his bed listening to him read Harry Potter. Papi always knew when to take Cody aside and make things easier for me. They were like two peas in a pod. Annie's parents had died early on, so my parents were Cody's only grandparents. I tapped on the door to get their attention.

"Hey, guys. I'm back. Papi, I can finish the story if you're ready to take Mami home."

"Sounds good." Papi kissed Cody's forehead and scooted off the bed. "I'll see you tomorrow, Codyman."

"Night, Abuelo."

My dad slapped my shoulder on his way out. "Buenas noches, mijo. We'll lock up."

"Gracias, Papi." I grabbed the book my dad had been reading and sat on the bed, leaning against the headboard. "I see your grandfather was reading about the wizarding boy. I love those stories."

"Is Miss Sammie going to be okay?" Cody sat up and faced me.

"Yeah, she is."

"What happened? She seemed upset."

"It's their story to tell, but if Holden wants to tell you, then that's between you guys. How about going out for ice cream this weekend with them?"

"That would be great!" Cody bounced on the bed.

"Here, take my phone and call Holden while I shower and change. When I come back, I'll read you another chapter." I handed him my phone.

"Thanks, Dad." He hollered before calling Holden.

I left the room. I could have showered and changed after Cody went to bed, but I wanted him to talk to Holden before it got too late. Right now, I bet Holden would be eager to chat with Cody. Holden was going to need a friend if Lincoln was back in town.

I finished thirty minutes later. I checked all the doors and windows in my house, police officer habit, and headed for Cody's room. He was still on the phone.

"Hey, it's time for bed. You can talk to Holden again tomorrow. Your grandparents will be here while I go to work."

"Okay." Cody nodded. "Holden, I gotta go. Talk to your mom and see if we can play tomorrow. Okay. Bye."

"Listen, if you want to hang out with Holden, I'll talk to your grandparents and see if they can figure something out. Maybe Holden and the girls can all come here." I would love for Sammie's kids to be here tomorrow because if Lincoln made a return appearance, they wouldn't be home. I'll text Sammie tonight."

That's great, Dad. Thanks."

Cody gave me back my phone and scooted under the covers. I read another chapter but stopped when he yawned. Closing the book, I set it aside and got up. I tucked him in, gave him a kiss on the forehead, turned off the light, and went to my room.

Lying in bed with my nightstand light on, I looked around the bedroom. Memories of Annie filled the room. The top of our dresser was still full of her floral body sprays, jewelry, and a photo of the two of us hiking before we had Cody. Her nightstand held the last book she read along with a photo of the three of us at Cody's first birthday party, when he grabbed a piece of cake and shoved it into his mouth.

It had been six years since her death, but I still couldn't bring myself to box up her clothes and items. Hell, I still wore my wedding ring. I lifted my hand and stared at my wedding ring. Annie had wanted to buy me something with a diamond, but that wasn't me. I just wanted a simple gold band to show our love and commitment.

I shut off the light. The nights were the worst because in the darkness I could imagine Annie lying next to me like we used to late at night before we made love. She would tell me about her day, and I would regale her with stories of mine. Mine were always crazier than hers, but she always wanted to hear them.

Then she would slide over me, our lips would meet in a fervent kiss that heightened until the barrier of clothes felt unbearable, and we longed to be intertwined. On some nights, my dreams were so vivid that I'd have to find release with my hand. More often than not, my hand would reach for the other side of my empty bed as tears traced paths down my face into my pillow.

No matter what, I couldn't let go of Annie. During our brief marriage, I hadn't been the best husband, always putting my job before her needs. Then, God took her away from me, and I had to live without her, with no way to make it up to her.

Cody barely had three years with his mom before she became one of God's angels, and I blamed myself. If only I'd spent more time with her, God might've given us more years together. Deep down I knew that wasn't true; my God was a loving God. But I couldn't seem to get those thoughts out of my head. I deserved to be alone because I'd been a lousy husband to a loving wife. *I begged and pleaded with God while Annie was sick. Why Annie? Why not me?* I lived a dangerous life between the military and being an officer. It should've been me. Mami told me everything happens for a reason. I didn't know what could possibly be the reason for Annie to lose her life. *Fucking Ovarian Cancer!*

Chapter 8

Waiting for the Other Shoe to Drop

Sammie

I set my alarm extra early today. I needed to get to the boutique and change out the window displays. With school starting in a week, I had to create back-to-school outfits, accessorizing my mannequins to draw in customers.

I showered, dressed, and checked to make sure the kids were still sleeping. The girls were in Hallie's bed together, and Holden was on the floor next to them. I eased the door shut and followed the sweet smell of coffee into the kitchen. My mom and dad were early birds. They were probably already on their second cup. I was pouring my coffee into my to-go cup when my mom walked in.

"You're up early." She reached for the milk in the fridge.

"I wanted to update the window displays before I opened the store. Are you okay with the kids today?" Mom usually went into the store with me during the school year, but in the summer, she always opted to stay home, and we hired several student workers.

"We'll be fine. Thank you for updating the displays."

"I love doing them. I might move around some of the other displays inside the store." I had gotten my degree in fashion merchandising, and I loved working in retail stores doing things that attracted customers.

"I'm sure whatever you do will look fantastic." Mom refilled her cup. "Do you want something to eat?"

"No, I'll just get a bagel." I grabbed a resealable bag for my bagel when my phone buzzed on the counter.

"Who's that? It's early."

"It's Alex."

> Alex: Sorry for the early text. Cody wanted to know if your kids wanted to come over today and hang out with him. It would be good for them to not be there in case asshole shows up at your house again.

"Cody wants to have a playdate with the kids today."

"You mean with Holden and the girls?" Mom asked because normally only Holden got invited over.

"Yeah, with all of them."

"Okay. I'll call Milagro later and set up a time."

> Sammie: No worries. I'm up. Gotta go into work early. My mom will set something up with your mom.

> Alex: You're going to work now?

> Sammie: Yep.

> Alex: I'll meet you there.

> Sammie: Why?

> Alex: Because I want to make sure you're safe.

> Sammie: You know I have been taking care of myself for my entire adult life.

> Alex: Humor me.

> Samme: Fine.

> Alex: Perfect. See you soon.

> Sammie: Whatever.

"Alex is going to meet me at work.

"Of course he is." My mom mumbled.

"What is that supposed to mean?" I glared at my matchmaking mom and leaned against the kitchen counter.

"It means that I think he likes you."

"Of course he likes me. We're friends." I shrugged. "Alex is good with you calling Milagro to set up a playdate." I grabbed my purse, bagel, and coffee. I did not have time to discuss my love life. "I gotta go, but I'll check in later."

"Sammie," my mom called out, "let me know if you hear anything from Lincoln."

"I will!"

The drive to work was especially short at this hour because there weren't many cars on the road. I pulled into the parking lot and saw Alex leaning up against his patrol car, cool as a cucumber. He lived closer to the boutique than I did, so of course he'd get there sooner.

"How long have you been standing there?" I asked when I exited my car.

"A few minutes." He pushed off his car and strolled toward me. "So why are you here at the ass-crack of dawn when your store doesn't open for another two hours?"

"I have to get some displays done." Alex followed me to the back door, waiting while I unlocked it and turned off the alarm.

Placing his hand on my arm, he said, "Wait here while I look around."

I sighed, but waited. If he wanted to make sure everything was safe, who was I to stop him? He came back a few minutes later and gave me a thumbs-up.

"Was that really necessary?" He'd never met me at the store and looked around before. Granted, it was early in the morning, but still.

"After yesterday's visit from Lincoln, yes."

"Whatever." I grumbled.

"What displays?" He followed me through the store to the front.

"What?" His presence this early in the morning, without my java jolt, was throwing me off my game.

"You said you had to work on displays. What displays?"

"Oh." I set my stuff down on the back counter and walked to the front of the store. "These." I pointed at the mannequins in front of the windows.

"Nope." He shook his head. "Not those."

"Alex, I don't have time once the store opens. I need to get them done now."

"Fine, I'll keep you company until the sun rises and there's more movement outside." Alex propped himself against the wall and crossed his ankles.

"That's ridiculous. Don't you have work to do?"

He checked his watch. "Nothing that can't keep until it's daylight."

"But you're dressed—" I said, pointing at him, "—in your uniform. Surely, you were up because you needed to get to work early too."

"It can wait." He moved his hand around. "Go do what you came in early to do. I'm fine."

"Why don't you help me, and I'll get done quicker?"

"Sure. Why not?" Alex stepped away from the wall toward me. "What do you want me to do?"

"Follow me." I walked around the store grabbing shirts, pants, skirts, backpacks, purses, and anything that looked cute for back-to-school. As I chose an item, I tossed it at Alex, and he draped them over his arms like a pro.

"This is a lot of stuff," he grumbled.

"I have four mannequins to undress and redress."

When I had everything I needed. I grabbed the items from him and placed them on top of a display close to the windows.

"Now, I need you to undress that mannequin so you can put a new outfit on her." I pointed to the other mannequin next to mine.

"This is so awkward," he mumbled.

"What? You've never undressed a woman before?" I smirked at him.

"You know I have." He glared at me. "But they're not usually so stiff."

"That's what she said." I laughed.

"Ha, ha, funny." He struggled to pull the t-shirt over the mannequin's arms. I should've shown him, but it was far more enjoyable to watch his frustrated expressions. To his credit, the mannequin's arms were bent, creating the illusion of a natural, casual posture.

"Aha!" he screamed when he finally got the shirt off.

"Not so fast, Chief, now you have to put this shirt on." I handed him a cute, short sleeve top.

"Really?" he grumbled while he tugged and pulled the shirt over the mannequin. "Why can't we put a bikini on them and call it a day?"

"Uh," I said, my hands on my hips, turning to him and trying to suppress my amusement at his awkward attempt. "If you had a daughter, would you send her to school wearing a bikini?"

"Fuck, no." He got one sleeve on.

"Well, there you go." I watched him put the head through the neck opening before he went to the other sleeve. It's a good thing the material was stretchy or he would've ripped the seams.

"You're doing great," she said, a smile spread across her face. "Bet you've never dressed a woman."

He made the wrong buzzer sound. "You'd be wrong. I dressed Annie many times after she was sick."

I stopped and glanced at him. He stood frozen as he gripped the bottom of the shirt and stared at the mannequin.

"I'm sorry." I stepped over to him and placed my hand on his shoulder. "I shouldn't have said that."

Alex flinched and dropped his hands from the mannequin. "I'll go stand by the counter until you're done."

Shit. I didn't mean to bring him down. She wanted to help Alex move on and follow through with her promise to Annie. But Alex held it all in and pretended he was okay for Cody's sake.

"Alex," I grabbed his arm before he walked away. "If you want to talk about Annie. I'm always here to listen."

"No." Alex pulled his arm away from me. "I'm fine."

"She was my best friend. I miss her every day." I shouted at him. His eyes wandered over my face. *What was he looking for? My anger? Sadness.?*

"I'm sorry," he mumbled. "I wasn't trying to upset you. I know how much you loved her. I'm just not ready to talk about it."

"Alex." I stepped up to him and cupped his face. "It's okay to grieve, but you have to live your life. Annie wouldn't want you to be alone. She loved you too much for that. Your mom told me you still have all of Annie's clothes. I can help you with that. We can go through them together."

"You've been talking to my mom?" Alex pulled away. "Why?" Alex threw his arms up in the air. "This is none of your business."

"Look." I held my hand out, pleading my case. "Those last few days before Annie died, she made me promise to look after you. She wanted to make sure you were okay. And sometimes when I pick up Holden, your mom and I talk." I winced.

"Stop, just stop." Alex lifted his hand, freezing me in place. "I'll take care of Annie's things when I'm damn good and ready. And stop gossiping with my mom about me."

"Okay." I stared down at the ground and mumbled. "I'm sorry. Let me know if you need help."

"I don't need anyone's help. Besides, like you have room to talk. When was the last time you went out on a date?"

My head jerked up. "That's different." Now he was picking a fight. "Lincoln didn't die. He left me high and dry. I'm doing the best I can to raise my kids. Don't be an ass. I'm only trying to help."

"Sorry." He rubbed his hand over the back of his neck and turned away from me, staring outside. "Well, look at that. The sun is rising, and I need my morning cup of coffee."

"Thanks for helping me." I nodded and followed him to the back.

"Lock this door behind me." He said before he stepped toward his car.

I did as instructed and leaned back against the door. Oh, Annie, I'm trying to help him, but it would be easier to move a ten-ton boulder off a cliff. He misses you so much, and I don't know how to reach him. But for you, I'll keep trying.

I walked back to the front and continued dressing my mannequins. Lindsey would be here soon, and I needed to be ready to open the store.

Chapter 9

Leave Me Alone

Alejandro

Why can't everyone stay out of my business? Everyone grieves in their own way. So what if it took me seven years to get over my wife's death? Who the hell cared? It's my life, and if I want to keep all my wife's things, then so be it. Screw what anyone else thinks.

I turned my head and stared at Hi Cafe. The thought of Cassie's delicious coffee made my mouth water, and I'd give anything for a cup. But Sammie and Cassie were close friends, and with my luck, Sammie had already speed-dialed Cassie and told her how I reacted to her helping me with Annie's things. *Fuck!* Damn this small town. I loved it, but when I felt raw, I didn't want anyone psychoanalyzing my feelings. I shook my head and drove to the station. If I was lucky, someone from the night shift had already made a pot, and I could grab a cup and go wallow in my misery alone in my office.

Storming through the front door, I waved to the officer at the front desk and went straight to the lounge. *Ka-ching. The coffee gods were smiling down at me.* The pot was full, waiting to be devoured. I poured a cup and went to my office, greeting several officers along the way.

Booting up my computer, I took several sips and stared at the framed photos on my desk. One was of Annie tickling Cody. The other was from when I came home after my last deployment from Afghanistan. I met Annie before that deployment and fell head over heels in love with her. I couldn't wait to get home and marry my girl. We spent a year blissfully in love before we created our beautiful baby boy. The last picture, taken earlier this summer, was of my father, Cody, and me, fishing on the small lake behind their house.

Married life had been amazing. I'd felt so blessed to have survived the war and come home to my beloved. Then the grenade went off, and my life blew up into a shit ton of scattered pieces I was still trying to put together. My phone beeped with a text.

> Sammie: Sorry about this morning. Mom is taking the kids to your parents' house after breakfast. I'll pick them up when I get done with work. Just wanted to let you know.

> Alex: Thanks.

I didn't know what else to say. I'd said enough this morning. I sighed and set my phone on my desk. My incoming emails were never-ending, so I tackled them first. Once that was done, I searched Lincoln's record.

If Lincoln was going to insert himself in Sammie's life, I needed to see what he'd been up to. *Damn!* Lincoln's rap sheet was long and included several overnight stays in jail, but all his incidents were low-level arrests. Possession of 10 grams of pot. Public fights with proprietors, but no weapons. Drunk in public, but no fights. At the bottom of the list, I opened Lincoln's sealed file from when he was a minor and looked into those incidents. They were more of the same. Scrolling back to the top and most current files, I saw a drunk in public arrest from a few weeks ago.

Lincoln's actions could still escalate into more violent crimes, even though he had never been arrested on assault charges. I noticed that his residence was on the mainland. I wasn't as familiar with Jones County, but my fellow Rangers, Captain Jay, and Griffin, aka Cain when he worked undercover, were brothers in blue in the Jones County Sheriff's Office. Griffin was always on the road early. He had trouble sleeping after the war. I'd try him first.

"Hey brother, what's going on?" Griffin picked up. "Kind of early for you." I could hear the radio and road noise in the background.

"Yeah, it is." I sighed. "Can you do a drive-by for me?"

"Absolutely, what or who am I looking for?"

"It's Sammie's ex-husband, Lincoln Rogers. I'll text you his address."

We officers were always multitasking as we drove. Nothing new there. Half the time we were running a tag on the computer, answering our work cell phones, listening to dispatch, keeping our eye on the road, and sometimes eating or drinking. All part of the job.

"I'll head over now. What do you want me to do? Did he do something wrong? Can I arrest the scumbag?"

Griffin had never met Sammie, but he knew all about her. Jay, Griffin, Lucian, and I met up in town for a drink on some nights when Cody slept over at Holden's. Lucian's loose lips gave away my relationship with Sammie, making it out to be more than it was.

"No, I don't have probable cause yet. I want to know if he is living at that address, if he's alone, the type of neighborhood, and shit like that."

"Done. I'm almost there. I'll do some recon and get back to you."

"Thanks, brother. I owe you one."

"Hah, you owe me many, but who's counting?" Griffin laughed.

"Apparently, you," I said wryly.

"True that. I'll collect when I'm ready."

"I'm sure you will."

I hung up and texted Sammie.

Alex: Have you heard from Lincoln?

Sammie: No, why?

Alex: Just checking.

Sammie: I'm not your mission. You don't have to babysit me.

Alex: Right

Sammie: Fine

Detective Lucian knocked on my door and stepped inside before I let him in. He always did that; no biggie. I set my phone down to give him my full attention.

"Hey, Chief." Lucian sat in the chair opposite my desk. "Turn that frown upside down, my friend. It's almost the weekend."

"Sammie's ex made a reappearance and scared her." I blurted.

"Shit." Lucian's eyes got round as saucers and he scooted to the edge of the seat, ready for action. "Is she okay?"

"Yeah." I pointed to my computer. "Asshole has a shit ton of incident reports, but no prosecution or arrests. And to make it even better, he has sealed records from when he was a minor."

Lucian leaned over my desk to see my monitor and whistled. "He has sealed juvie records?"

"Yep, he's a real gem."

"What the fuck?" Lucian leaned back in his chair with his mouth hinged open. "How the hell does someone like that not serve time?"

"Daddy moneybags. I remember Annie telling me she hated Lincoln when Sammie started dating him because he was a rich snob."

"Shit, I can see why Sammie's scared. Let's hope he doesn't escalate."

"My thoughts exactly. Have you heard about any recent robberies, fights, new dealers?"

"The usual pickpockets on the beach, some break-ins in empty homes, but no robberies. No new dealers that I know of, but I'll put my feelers out."

"Thanks. I want to make sure he stays clean while he's here." Lucian's keen observations made him the best detective on Haven Island PD. Every case was a puzzle to him, and he loved the challenge of discovering how everything fit.

"Will do. You know, you could take Sammie out and distract her from this crazy ex." Lucian wiggled his eyebrows.

"Not you too?" I sighed.

"It's been a long time–" he shrugged. "–just saying. It's okay to go out on a date. If something happens great, if not, then you guys stay friends. What have you got to lose?"

"Our kids are friends. I don't want it to get awkward." I glared at him.

"Oh, so you have thought of it," Lucian smiled.

"Not really. I still love Annie." I grabbed the photo of me hugging Annie in my fatigues. I ran to her after I disembarked from the plane, so happy to see her waiting for me with a sign that said "Welcome Home."

Lucian stood and pulled the photo out of my hands, waving it in my face. "Alejandro, you're always gonna love Annie, but you're too young to live the rest of your life alone. Make peace with it and move on. It's okay." Lucian slammed it down on my desk. "I'm gonna get to work. Think about what I said."

Lucian flung the door shut on his way out, the glass rattling, breaking the silence in the room. I'm sure Sammie didn't think of me like that. Sure, sometimes she gave me her flirty smile, but she gave those to a lot of men. She was just being her sassy self. *How could I fall for my wife's best friend? Wouldn't that be wrong? Wasn't there a sister code like the men's bro code or did it not count if someone was deceased? Why was I, for the love of all that is holy, considering that now when I should be focused on work? Fuck, my head was all screwed up.*

I should hook up with someone from the mainland and get laid. Lord knows Jay, Griffin, and Lucian were constantly trying to set me up when we went to the bars for a drink.

Chapter 10

Siren Boutique

Sammie

I ran around like a chicken with its head cut off at Siren's today from the moment the doors opened. Thank goodness Jenny, one of our part-time workers, and Lindsey, my exceptional full-time worker, were on shift with me.

Our island had one main road that ran north and south. As you walked on Main Street, you could smell our saltwater taffy and see them making their fresh fudge through the window at Salty's. Stop in at Book Haven and choose from an array of genres—Rowan, the owner, loved to direct her customers to new authors. Open the door to Hi Café and inhale the delicious aromas of Cassie's specialty coffees. Near the end of the block, visit Hi Grill. Where Cassie's parents cooked the perfect burger. Siren Boutique, my parents' shop, was nestled in the middle of Main Street between Book Haven and Hi Café. The perfect spot to shop before getting a cup of coffee or after, depending on which direction you came from.

My parents always wanted a store on Main Street, so when the previous owners moved out, they bought it and restored it to its natural beauty. They redid the floors and added a welcoming red and white awning to the front facade. Our Back-to-School Event was one of our biggest, second only to our Black Friday Holiday Event. Main Street became a flurry of excitement the week before Thanksgiving, with holiday decorations being put up everywhere. From wreaths to menorahs and Christmas trees, we had all sorts of decorations.

Siren was the only boutique on the island where you could buy men's, women's, and kids' clothes and accessories. We assisted all our customers in creating a perfect look with individual customer service. Parents and their children streamed through our doors shopping for back-to-school clothes, shoes, hair accessories, purses, and backpacks, buying anything their child needed to feel confident walking into school on their first day.

I had finished ringing up a customer when she inquired about my watch. Tilting my watch toward the client, I looked at the time and realized Lindsey and I had missed taking our lunch breaks. Jenny always ate lunch on time. She'd track me down at noon on the dot and let me know she was leaving, but Lindsey and I, as fellow workaholics, always lost track of time.

"Lindsey." I tapped her shoulder while she straightened a rack of dresses. "Go take your lunch break. It's slower now. Jenny and I are good."

We both walked to the checkout counter. I had another customer waiting for me, ready to check out.

"Okay." Lindsey grabbed her purse from under the counter. "I won't be long. I'm gonna run next door and get a cup of coffee and a muffin. Do you want anything?"

"I would die for Cassie's Latte. Wait a second, and I'll give you some money." I finished ringing up my customer's purchases and gave her the total.

"No worries. You can get the next one." Lindsey waved on her way out.

I finished the sale and handed my customer her bag. "Have a nice day."

"Excuse me, can you help me?" A lady came over with several shirts, pants, skirts, and dresses draped over her arms.

"Of course." I walked around the counter to where she was standing. "What can I help you with?"

"I'm starting a new job as a paraprofessional at Hi Prep, and I wanted to buy an appropriate outfit for my first day. I want to make a good impression on the kids and my new boss." The lady covered her mouth. "Oh my gosh, I sound like a teenager." She giggled.

"Not at all. For a new job, everyone should treat themselves to a brand-new, confidence-boosting power outfit. My name is Sammie."

"Hi, Sammie. I'm Grace. I'd shake your hand, but I'm not sure I could get it out from under all these clothes." Grace gave me a wry smile.

"No worries. Follow me." I chuckled and walked her to an empty rolling rack near the back of the store. "Let's see what you have there." I helped her put all the clothes on the rack.

"I appreciate your help. I grabbed so many items I've confused myself. My husband didn't come with me, and I would love another person's opinion when I pair them."

"Of course, I would love to assist you. What grade will you be helping with?"

"Third through fifth."

"Hey, my triplets are going into fifth grade at Hi Prep."

"Oh my gosh, that is so wild. Maybe I'll get to meet them."

"That would be cool." I smiled. "I think you need to go with pants because you'll be walking around the classroom, crouching down to help students." I wheeled the rack next to the changing rooms. I chose a pink, round-neck blouse. "How about this one? It looks professional and is easy to wash in case it gets messed up. These pants are extremely comfortable, and black goes with everything."

"Sounds good." She took the outfit.

"Try those on, and I'll continue to create more outfits with the items you chose. When you get back, you can see if you like them." Grace hurried into the changing room, while I bundled outfits on the rack for her to try on.

The changing rooms were next to the register, making it easier for me to help Grace and keep our customers happy when they were ready to check out. We never trained Jenny on the register since she was part time, and only worked summers while she was home from college.

"Sammie!" Grace came out and spun around. "I love it!" She hollered.

"I'll just be a second." I told my current customer and peeked around the clothes rack. Grace spread her arms out and spun around, looking in the mirror, checking out her new look. "It looks amazing on you. Try the other outfits and see which one you like better. They are all paired off." I pointed to the rack.

"Okay. I'll come out and show you."

"Sounds good," I grinned and finished checking out my customer.

Every few minutes, Grace came out and praised my pairings. Her excitement inspired my customers, and I made several pairings for them as well. Grace plopped the pile of clothes I had paired onto the checkout counter.

"Thank you so much, Sammie. I'm gonna take everything except the dresses." She beamed. "I can't thank you enough. I'll get out of your hair now."

"You're not in my hair. I loved helping you."

Grace left my store carrying several bags with a huge smile on her face. My customer's happiness meant everything to me. The radiant glow that illuminated their faces as they looked at themselves in their new clothes filled me with an amazing sense of satisfaction and excitement.

I was ringing up another customer when I heard Lindsey's voice before she placed my latte on the counter next to the register.

"You want to take a few minutes?" She asked as she rounded the counter.

"Nah, too busy." I put the receipt in the bag and handed my customer her bag. "Have a wonderful day."

"Thank you, you too." She grabbed her bag and smiled.

I took a sip, savoring Cassie's delicious coffee. It never mattered what flavor I got; her coffee beans were ground to perfection. Best liquid lunch when I didn't want to stop working because my store was overflowing with customers—like today. My phone buzzed.

"Excuse me for one moment," I said to the next customer in line. "I need to see if it's my kids texting me." I grinned and pulled my phone out of my pocket.

"I got this." Lindsey shoved me out of the way and began ringing up the purchase. "Take a break."

> Lincoln: I'd like to see my kids tomorrow

> Sammie: I work tomorrow

> Lincoln: so

> Sammie: I want to be there when you meet them for the first time.

> Lincoln: I don't want to wait any longer.

> Sammie: You've already waited nine years, what's another day?

> Lincoln: No. Let one of your parents come. They can meet me at the park tomorrow at 2.

> Sammie: Fine. I'll talk to them tonight and get back to you.

I shoved my phone into my pocket and let out a low growl.

"Are you okay, Sammie?" Mrs. Hammell, one of our best customers, who was shopping with her grandkids, reached out and touched my arm.

"Yes, ma'am," I forced a smile. "Nothing I can't handle."

Mrs. Hammell had lived on Haven Island as long as I could remember. She was a dear friend of my mom and always brought her grandkids in for their clothes.

"Okay. Let me know if I can help you."

"Thank you, Mrs. Hammell. I appreciate that." I darted into the back room before I said something nasty about Lincoln in front of a customer.

The scalding coffee did little to warm my trembling hands as I leaned against the wall. Why was Lincoln here after all this time? Deep down, I didn't give a shit about him or his feelings. I stopped caring the minute he left me literally, barefoot and pregnant, in the kitchen. He couldn't leave us fast enough.

For my kids, I would do anything, even if it meant sucking it up with my ex so they could get to know their father. Only Hollie wanted to meet him. Maybe Hallie and Holden would come around, but I wasn't forcing it. I needed to calm down before I talked to my parents about meeting him tomorrow. My phone buzzed again, and I jumped, throwing a silent prayer to the man above that it was Lincoln changing his mind.

> Alex: I'll feed the kids tonight and then drop them off at your house.

> Sammie: Thx. I have to work until eight.

> Alex: No problem.

How did I ever think I could raise my triplets alone after Lincoln left me? It takes a village, and I'm so grateful for my tribe.

Chapter 11

Shifting Debts

Lincoln

I sat on the couch waiting for Ava to come home and make me dinner. Sammie had better figure out a way to get my kids to the park tomorrow. I didn't give a shit who came with them. I could make it work. I needed to get them on my side. My funds were running low, and Grandpa needed an additional incentive to pay up.

I had gotten my bachelor's degree in finance and all the industry certifications, including the CFP (Chief Financial Planner) before I started dating Sammie. So after Sammie, I went to my dad with the woe is me act, and he helped me set up my branch of his investment company two floors down from his office floor. He made me promise to stop gambling and doing drugs or he'd take the company away. Like God, he could giveth or taketh my company away. I still had the occasional issue, but he always had his lawyers bail me out. Then I met Ava. He made me marry her—again with the threats.

He referred his fellow lawyer friends to me. At first, I invested their money like I was supposed to, but when I noticed they had an endless amount of funds, I got greedy and I began making fake investments. For years, no one asked for their dividends; they continued to keep their money invested. Then the market crashed, and they wanted to pull out their money. I accommodated the first few and placed a few bets, but as they continued to ask, I went into the red.

Using my kids was an incredible idea. Triple the money. How had I not thought of it before? This year I could grant my father his Christmas wish to be a grandfather—in triplicate. Sammie and the kids were a secret I planned to take to the grave. The thought of raising triplets sent shivers down my spine. Never in a million years had I considered meeting them, especially after I married Ava.

We had been trying to have kids for a couple of years and then found out she had issues with her ovaries. It devastated Ava, but I was ecstatic. I didn't want kids. I married Ava only because my parents wanted to improve their social standing in the community. My scandalous behavior and other flaws were a source of shame for them.

A few days ago, I manned up and told Ava about the triplets. We'd just had sex, and I wore her out.

"I need to talk to you." I lay flat on my back and placed my forearm across my face. I didn't want to look at her while I dropped this bomb on her. I loved Ava, but I wasn't in love with Ava.

"You sound serious."

Might as well rip the band-aid, so I blurted. "I had triplets with Sammie."

"That's not funny, Linc." Her voice got low.

"I'm not being funny." Ava knew about Sammie. She just didn't know I had impregnated her and left.

"What the hell?" She jolted upright, turned toward me, and flung my arm off my face. "Are you fucking kidding me? You had kids with another woman and never told me? You know how much I wanted to give you kids. You, asshole!" Ava smacked my chest.

I grabbed her wrist and pulled her into my arms while she pounded on my chest until she got tired. Then the tears began. In that moment, I felt like the asshole that I was.

It had taken several days to calm Ava down before she wanted to meet them. All I could think about now was the saying about what a tangled web we weave when we practice to deceive. *What the hell? I had to step up and become a father to triplets. Fuck, I hoped I liked them.* At least the baby stage was over. *Thank fuck!* The thought of changing all those diapers and calming three screaming babies made me want to throw up.

Ava came in and sat with me on the couch.

"Did you call her and set something up for tomorrow?"

"She's going to bring the kids to the park at two."

"I'm so glad you are finally going to see them. I can't wait to meet them." Ava bounced in her seat.

"I don't want you there tomorrow." I glanced at her frown.

"But–" I interrupted her. "I need to build a relationship with them first, Ava. You can meet them later, like we discussed."

I scooted closer to Ava and put my arm around her to ease the blow about not wanting her there. "I promise you'll meet them soon."

"Next time?"

"Sure, next time." I side-hugged her.

"Do you want to see the clothes I bought for my new job?" Ava stood and grabbed her bags.

How did I not notice all those bags? "How much shit did you buy?"

"Not that much."

"Did you go to Siren's?"

"I did, and I met Sammie. She was so nice. I think she liked me."

"Why the fuck did you go there? Did you tell her you're my wife?" I bolted off the couch ready for a fight.

"No." She backed up. "I told her my name was Grace. I didn't say anything about you or the kids."

I grabbed her arm and shoved her away from me. "You better not have. Go make my dinner. I'm starving."

"O...okay."

I dropped back onto the couch. Ava better be telling me the truth.

Chapter 12

Recon and Robberies

Alejandro

The morning flew by fast between reviewing reports and researching Lincoln. It was lunchtime. I hadn't brought lunch since I bolted out the door when Sammie said she was going to the shop early. My cell rang, and Griffin's name flashed on the caller ID.

"Hey, did you find him?" I asked.

"Yep, meet me for lunch. I'm at Jim's Crab Shack."

Jim's was our favorite seafood place on the mainland just over the bridge.

"I'll be there in twenty."

"See if Lucian wants to join. I'm bringing Jay."

"Roger that." I hung up and headed for Lucian's desk.

"Hey." I knocked on Lucian's desk. "Lunch with Jay and Griffin?"

"Sounds good. I'll meet you at your car."

I nodded and headed out. Lucian wasn't far behind. We got to Jim's and found Jay and Griffin at a table.

"Hey brothers, how's your day been?" I grabbed a chair and sat.

"Ours is a hell of a lot better than yours." Griffin grinned.

"Fuck," I groaned. "What did you find out?"

"The asshole lives in a ritzy part of town in a two-story colonial-style house. Looks like fucking Tara from Gone with the Wind."

"How the fuck do you know about Gone with the Wind?" Jay snickered.

"Hey, I watch the classics. Just cause I look like the people I arrest doesn't mean I'm as stupid as them."

"That's true." I nodded. "He was the one on our team who always quoted the classics."

"See." Griffin pointed at me. "Someone appreciates my intelligence."

"Frankly, I don't give a damn." Jay said wryly and Lucian chuckled. "Just tell him what you found out other than the house looking like Tara."

"Anyway," Griffin rolled his eyes at Jay and turned to me. "I didn't see anyone else enter the house, but I'll go back several times and check it out. His family still has money, and he's married to a rich chick. Her name is Ava. No other kids that I could find."

"Thanks, I appreciate your help."

"Anytime."

We ordered and changed the subject. After lunch, I went back to my office and called my mom. I didn't want her to have to make dinner for so many people. My mom did enough.

"Hola, mijo, is everything okay?"

"Si, Mami. Are Sammie's kids there?"

"Si. ¿Por qué?"

"I'm gonna take everyone out to dinner at Hi Grill tonight, so please don't stress over dinner."

"Are you sure?"

"Si, I'll see you around five."

"Gracias, mijo."

Perfect. I got back to work. The radio crackled with an incoming call from dispatch about a break-in at one of the rental properties. I looked up and saw Lucian bolt from his chair. Not wanting to stare at a computer screen for another four hours, I followed him to the call.

I parked on the street and followed Lucian into the house.

"I'm tired of these break-ins, Chief." Lucian handed me a pair of gloves.

"Yeah," I sighed, and we gloved up. "Do you think it was kids again?"

"If I were a betting man, I'd bet you some money." Lucian grinned. "Let's go see if I would win."

I shook my head and followed Lucian. The door frame was splintered, and tiny fragments of wood littered the ground. Lucian pointed to it. The break-ins all shared the same pattern, just like this one.

"Crowbar?" Lucian quirked an eyebrow.

"Or something like that."

The air was thick with the stale scent of smoke as we stepped inside and saw the cigarette butts and empty beer cans littering the floor. Two of my officers, were walking throughout the house.

"Hudson, Charlotte, did you see any of them?" I squatted and nudged a beer can, smelling the stale, yeasty aroma of the discarded brew. "Where's forensics?" I called out.

"Pulling in now, Chief," Lucian mentioned as he walked around.

"I chased one out the back door, but he jumped on a bike and took off." Hudson stood panting with his hands on his hips. "I chased on foot. But he got away. He was wearing a black hoodie, black shorts, and white sneakers. He was on a gray bike."

"Hudson, radio that in so everyone can be on the lookout for this kid." I stood. "If we can get one to talk, we can figure out the brains behind this operation. Charlotte, did you see anyone when you got here?"

"I saw Hudson give chase, but I didn't see any kids."

"Did you follow Hudson?"

"No, sir. I stayed here and checked out the rest of the house."

"Okay." I nodded. "I can't wait for school to start. These kids have too much time on their hands in the summer." I walked toward Kyle on my forensics team.

"Kyle, do you need any help bagging and tagging?"

"No, Chief, we've got this. Jamie will photograph the evidence while I dust for prints. When she's done, we'll collect all the cigarette butts and cans. Looks like Hudson interrupted quite the party."

"Yeah, if one person drank all this, Hudson would've caught him cause he'd be drunker than a skunk."

"I'm gonna patrol the area, Chief, see if I can spot him." Hudson left.

"I'll help." Charlotte followed him out.

"I'll help you bag." Lucian interjected while he scanned the room.

"I'm gonna head home. Lucian—" I slapped his back, "—keep me updated."

"Will do, Chief."

Chapter 13

Dinner Out

Alejandro

"**K**ids, I'm home!" I hollered as soon as I entered the front door. "Who's hungry?"

"We are!" came their voices from the living room.

Smiling, I stepped into the room and gave my son a hug. "Let me change and we'll go to Hi Grill for dinner."

"Yay!" The kids were jumping up and down.

"You don't have to take us." Mami hugged me. "I can make your father something at home."

"Nonsense, you've had a full day watching four kids, let me do this for you." I kissed her cheek.

"Okay." She patted my cheeks. "We're ready whenever you are."

I hurried to my bedroom and changed out of my uniform. I was just as hungry as the kids, but shot off a text to Sammie in case she closed up early.

> Alex: Taking the kids to Hi Grill. Meet us if you finish early.

> Sammie: k

We packed into my SUV and headed to the restaurant. Papi sat in the front with me while Mami sat in the middle with the girls. Holden and Cody always sat together in the back.

Judy, Cassie's mom, greeted us when we entered. I saw Cassie delivering some plates.

"Hi, Judy," I smiled.

"Hi, Chief. Seven tonight?"

"No, eight if Sammie can get off work early. Can we sit in Cassie's section?"

"Of course."

Judy led us to a round table with seating for eight. Judy gave us menus and left. Cassie worked at Hi Cafe and Hi Grill. Her parents owned both places. She and her sister Katie took turns at Hi Grill, but both worked at the café in the mornings.

"Hi guys," Cassie came over quickly. "You're missing one. Where's Sammie?"

"She's still at work." While the kids were occupied with the menu, I gestured to Cassie with a curled finger, signaling for her to lean down.

"What's going on?" she mumbled.

I lifted the menu to cover my face. "I think Sammie could use a friend. Can you call her?"

"Okay," Cassie frowned. "What's wrong?"

"Ex back in town."

Cassie covered her mouth with her hand. "Oh shit. Yeah, I'll call her."

"Thanks." I lowered my menu. "Can I get a glass of water?"

"Yep, let me get everyone's drink order first and then I'll come back for the food."

"Hi, Cassie, can I get a sweetened iced tea?" Mami smiled.

"I'll have an unsweetened tea." Papi went next.

Cody and Holden glanced at me and both said, "water please."

The girls asked for Sprite, but before I could correct them because I knew Sammie wouldn't want them drinking soda, Cassie said. "Okay, water for you girls as well." And winked at them.

"Yes, ma'am," they grumbled, and Cassie winked at me.

Gotta love Cassie. She knew not to let the girls pull one over on them. The boys knew better, but they also spent more time with me than the girls.

"Is Sammie joining us?" Papi asked while he stared at his menu.

There was no reason for him to stare at the menu so hard. We ate here at least three times a week, and the menu hadn't changed in years. He just didn't want to make eye contact. *Had my mom talked to him?*

"I don't know Sammie's schedule." I stared at my menu. If he wanted to play this game, I could play it too.

"Here are your drinks." Cassie placed them in front of each of us. Then, she took out her pad and went to my mother for her order. "Ladies first." She smiled at Mami.

"I'll have the chef salad with balsamic vinaigrette, please."

Papi went next. "I'll get the burger, medium well, with fries, please."

"I'll have the same as Dad, thanks, Cassie."

Holden and Cody ordered the burgers like me and dad.

"Chicken nuggets and Mac and Cheese," Hallie ordered.

"Same as Hallie," Hollie said.

"Sounds good." Cassie collected the menus and tucked the pad in her apron pocket. "I'll bring out your food as soon as it's ready."

"So, Sammie can't meet us here?" Papi leaned over to ask me.

Didn't he already ask me that question? I thought I'd avoided it, but he was like a dog with a bone.

"Uh, I don't think so. She's closing the store at eight tonight, but I let her know we were here just in case." I took a sip of water and watched the kids interact with each other.

"Are you gonna see her this weekend?" Papi continued.

"Why the sudden interest in Sammie?" I glanced at him.

"Your mom told me she spoke to you about moving on, and I think Sammie is an amazing young woman." Papi took a drink of his tea.

"Really, Mami?" I glared at her, but she smirked and shrugged.

"I'm not ready to date yet, Papi."

"Well, I think you should be is all I'm saying."

"Dad." Cody tapped my shoulder. "Can we go for ice cream tomorrow?"

"I'm not sure. I need to talk to Miss Sammie. It might have to wait until Sunday."

"Aw, man." Cody and Holden grumbled.

"If you finish your meal, you can ask Miss Cassie about their desserts."

"Thanks, Dad," Cody beamed at him.

"Thank you, Chief Reyes," Holden, Hallie, and Hollie all responded.

"Your dad is so cool." Holden elbowed Cody.

I enjoyed being the cool dad. Even if Sammie got mad at me for letting her kids eat dessert before they went to bed. Then again, she might never find out. I considered texting her, but I didn't want to disappoint the kids if she refused. *Nah. I'd prefer to say sorry later than deny them dessert.*

The food was delivered, and silence settled over the table as everyone dug in. The kids ate all their food and ordered dessert when I heard Sammie's kids scream out Mommy. They were grinning from ear to ear as they stared behind me. I turned and saw Sammie wave to them while she talked to Cassie.

"I guess you don't know her schedule, because Sammie's here. Looking beautiful as ever." Papi nudged my shoulder and winked at Mami.

Figures. I glared at him but looked up at Sammie when I felt her hand on my shoulder.

"Hi, Milagro, Roberto, so good to see you. I hope they haven't been too much trouble?" Sammie said while she leaned on my shoulder.

Her touch and flowery perfume sent tingles down my spine.

"No trouble at all, dear." Mami smiled at her. "We loved watching them. They are all so well behaved."

"They better be." Sammie squeezed my shoulder and looked at me. "Thank you for bringing them. Now that I'm here, I'll pay for their meal."

I smirked at her. "You are not paying for their meal. This was my idea. Are you hungry?"

Sammie looked around. "You guys are done. I'll just make a sandwich when I get home."

"Nonsense," Papi interjected. "Sit, have dinner. The kids are waiting for dessert. You have plenty of time."

"Dessert, huh?" Sammie squeezed my shoulder again.

"Sorry," I winced. "They asked, and I gave in."

"Of course you did, you old softie."

Sammie laughed and rubbed my shoulder. A feeling of warmth shot throughout my body. Her touch had never affected me this way before. *Was it because everyone was trying to hook us up? Shit, my lower body hardened. I was not standing up anytime soon.*

"It's fine." I cleared my throat. "I'm just teasing you. Last night was rough, and tomorrow is Saturday. May as well let them enjoy the last few weeks of summer."

Sammie removed her hand and went to her kids. Her absence left me empty, aching for the warmth of her touch. She'd only been gone seconds, and I already missed her. *What was happening to me? How could my body forget my love for Annie? Granted, I loved sex, and I'd been celibate for seven years, but Sammie, Annie's best friend. Really?*

I watched Sammie give each of her kids a hug and a kiss on the top of their heads. Then she sat in the empty chair between Mami and Hallie.

"Here you go, kids." Cassie brought her tray loaded with four ice cream sundaes.

The kids' eyes widened when they saw the sundae placed in front of them. Besides their favorite ice cream flavor, it also had hot fudge dripping down the sides, a mountain of whipped cream, and a bright red cherry on top. *Damn, they looked good. I should've ordered one.*

"Cassie." I lifted my hand up to get her attention before she walked away. "Sammie would like to order dinner. Put her food on my tab."

"Of course." Cassie turned to Sammie, forcing Sammie to stop glaring at me. "You want your usual?"

"Yeah, that sounds great, thanks, Cassie."

Shit, Sammie had a usual? I couldn't wait to see what that was.

"Yummy," Hollie was the first one to take a huge spoonful into her mouth and holler what sounded like, "thanks, Chief Reyes."

"Don't talk with your mouth full." Sammie corrected her before she scowled at me.

Yeah, I was going to pay for that treat big time.

"You're welcome, sweetheart." I grinned at Hollie.

"Excuse me while I use the restroom." I told Mami and Papi because Sammie was busy tasting spoonfuls of her kids' sundaes.

Imagine my shock when I bumped into Sammie on my way back to the table. I wasn't expecting her to be standing outside the men's room door.

"Is everything okay?" I grabbed her arms to stop her from falling backwards.

"I told you I could pay for our meals."

"You did." I eased my grip on her arms. "And I told you it was my idea."

"You've already done so much." She looked down and fidgeted with her hands.

"Hey." I cupped her face and stooped to her level. "It's been a rough couple of days, I don't mind helping you. Hell, you practically took care of Annie single-handedly when she was sick because my job was so demanding during that time. I'm returning the favor."

"You've returned my favor for years." Sammie became rigid.

"I know, but I can't seem to stop looking out for you." I slid my hands down her arms until our hands intertwined.

"Neither can I," Sammie whispered and bit her lip.

"Sammie, I..." I wasn't sure what I was going to say. I caught myself leaning towards her lips and stopped. *What was I doing?* My eyes widened, and I released her hands with a jolt, as though I had touched something dangerous.

Sammie cleared her throat and erased any expression from her face. "I...I need to use the restroom." Sammie nodded and darted into the ladies' restroom.

What just happened? Did I try to kiss Sammie? What the hell was I thinking?

Chapter 14

Bad Day Gone Worse

Sammie

S tepping into the bathroom, I locked the door and stared at myself in the mirror. *What the hell was wrong with me? Why did I keep falling for unattainable men?* First my triplets' baby daddy and now Alex. To be fair, I'd fallen for Alex before Annie met him, but since Annie was my best friend and told me about her crush, I didn't have the heart to tell her I liked him first. I caved and ended up with Lincoln Rogers, the rich, rebellious guy who pursued me until we got together and moved to the mainland. I jumped at the chance to grab my happily ever after, like my best friend, except it blew up in my face. Lincoln was not Alex.

My life wasn't even close to a happily ever after. I was still in love with Alex, and he was still in love with Annie. *Fantastic. How was I supposed to compete with the memory of his deceased wife?*

My phone buzzed.

Lincoln: My kids better be at the park at 2.

Dammit! Why was he being such a jerk? Why Now? I dabbed a wet paper towel on my face and left the bathroom.

I walked straight to my seat. Across the table, I saw Alex's furrowed brow as he frowned at me. The kids had finished eating their sundaes, and I was tired of moving my food around my plate. I spied Cassie across the room and waved her over.

"What's up?" Cassie smiled.

"Can I have a box? I'll finish this at home. I'm exhausted."

"Sure, I'll take it and box it for you. Be right back."

I made the mistake of glancing at Alex. He tilted his head and squinted his eyes. *Perfect, just perfect. That look of concern was a silent plea for an explanation.* I was too chickenshit to tell him I was in love with him. I hated rejection, and that was all I was going to get from him. I'd be better off once I realized Alex's kindness to me was a favor to Annie, not because he was in love with me.

Cassie placed the box in front of me. "Here you go." Cassie rubbed my back. "Get some sleep and call me tomorrow."

"Thanks." I stood and grabbed my to-go box. "Come on, kids. It's time to go."

We said our goodbyes to Alex and his parents. I heard Alex behind me tell his parents that he would be right back. *What was he doing?* Then I felt a hand on my lower back guiding me out to my car.

"You don't have to escort us out." I said when we exited the restaurant.

"I'll feel better once I know you guys are safe in the car."

"Okay." *Suck it up, Sammie. You've been around him for years and been able to control your hormones. Stop looking at him like a hottie and look at him like your friend.*

We walked in silence, and I popped the lock on the doors. Once the kids were in the car, seat-belted, I closed the back door and reached for the driver's door.

"What did I do?" Alex placed his hand over the door, leaving it mostly closed so we had some privacy from my kids.

"Nothing."

"Why are you mad at me?"

"I'm not. Can you please let go of the door? I'm tired."

Alex pulled his hand back. I opened the door, sat, and pulled it shut. Starting the car, I glanced his way. He stood where I'd left him, with one hand in his pocket and the other up in a wave. One corner of his mouth lifted in a crooked smile, as if he didn't quite believe me.

I waved back and pulled out. The kids all screamed goodbye and waved.

"Kids, tomorrow we're going to the park to meet your dad."

"Yay!" Hollie screamed.

"I don't want to." Hallie grumbled.

"Neither do I," Holden said.

"I understand how you feel, but he is your father, and if he wants to get to know you, we have to give him a chance."

I glanced in the rearview mirror, and my heart broke. Hollie smiled with such high hopes, a stark contrast to the other two's scowling faces and crossed arms. *Dear God, please let Lincoln act like a loving father tomorrow.*

As soon as we got home, the kids ran out of the car and banged on the front door.

"Hey." My mom answered. "How was dinner?"

"Great!" Hollie shouted and gave her a hug before running inside.

"Holden, Hallie, are you okay?"

"No," Hallie said before stomping through the door.

"Holden, it's going to be okay." I said when I reached my mom.

"Whatever," he grumbled and followed Hallie.

My mom was looking between all of us with a shocked look on her face. "What happened?"

"We get to meet Daddy tomorrow!" Hollie jumped up and down before she ran to their room.

"Ah." Mom nodded. "I take it Hallie and Holden don't want to go."

"Yep." I walked past my mom and said hi to my dad in the living room on my way to the kitchen so I could refrigerate my leftovers.

My mom followed me. "Do you want me to go?"

"No," I sighed and sat at the kitchen table. "I asked Lindsey if she would take my afternoon shift so I could supervise their visit. I'll open and work until noon, come home to eat lunch with the kids, and then head over to the park. But thanks."

"You want some coffee?"

"No, I'm gonna check on the kids and go to bed."

***

I awakened from my dream to see my father's pained gaze as he stood over me. His hand was shaking my shoulder.

"Sammie, wake up."

"Why? What's wrong?" I jolted upright. "Is it Mom?" He shook his head. "The kids?"

"No, they're all fine. There's been a break-in at the boutique. The alarm company just called."

"What?" I jumped out of bed, brushing my hair away from my face. Had my father said we'd got robbed?

"Get dressed. We need to go. Your mom will stay with the kids."

"I'll meet you outside." I grabbed a pair of jeans and a t-shirt and ran into the bathroom to change. We'd never had a break-in. *What the hell was going on? Was it a false alarm?*

My dad already had his car running in the driveway. I jumped in, and we drove off.

"Who was it?" I grabbed the seatbelt.

"I don't know. I forgot to install the cameras."

"Dad," I whined. "We talked about this."

"I know. I know." He berated himself and slammed his hand on the steering wheel. "I kept putting it off to enjoy my days off with your mom and the kids. I was going to do it as soon as school started."

"It's okay, Dad." I placed my hand on his shoulder. He released his right hand from the steering wheel and gripped it. "I get it." I sighed. "I enjoy our summers too." I couldn't fault him for wanting to spend time with his grandkids.

"At the very least, I should've put the sign up that came with the system announcing that we had one. That might've been enough of a deterrent. With the alarms going off, it's going to be a shitshow. I'm sure the police will be there by the time we arrive."

I checked the clock in the car. "Since it's five o'clock in the morning and there's no traffic, I'd bet money they're already there."

Why would anyone steal from us? Had Lindsey accidentally left the back door unlocked, and someone opened it, setting off the alarm? No, that wasn't like her. A false alarm would be better than someone targeting our shop. My leg bounced as I stared out the window, my eyes scanning for anyone looking suspicious.

My dad pulled up in front of the boutique, and my heart dropped. The police parked their cars with flashing lights at different angles in front of the boutique, their headlights directed at my shattered front door. I spotted Alex speaking with Detective Lucian while the other officers were scanning the debris.

I raced out of the car, headed to the front of the store and froze. Officers were talking all around me, but I couldn't hear them. The only part left of my glass front door was the frame with several small shards poking out. The remaining glass lay on the floor inside the boutique. *Who did this? Oh shit, had they gotten into my register?*

Blowing out a series of quick breaths to gain control, I stepped over the bottom frame of the door. My eyes scanned the entire store before finally settling on the back counter, where I hoped to see the register.

Alex appeared in front of me, blocking my entrance.

"Whoa, there." Alex grabbed my shoulders. "Sammie. Stop. You can't go in there."

"Why not?" I glared at him. "I need to see what's missing."

"Sammie–" Alex's brow wrinkled and his words slowed like when a person is trying to calm a wild animal. *Why was he doing that?* He should do his job, not stand here with me. "–Your feet are bleeding."

"What?" I shook my head and looked down.

"You're barefoot, and you stepped on glass."

The sharp pain hit as soon as his words registered, and I saw blood running out of my feet. "Aaaaaah!" I shrieked.

"Call an ambulance!" Alex hollered and swooped me up into his arms. I gripped his uniform and cried into his neck as my feet throbbed. He sat me on the back counter near the register.

Alex cupped my face and pulled it off his chest. "I'm sorry." He stared into my eyes. "This might hurt, but I need to take the glass out." Then he looked over his shoulder and shouted. "Someone get me a towel, shirt, pants,...shit, anything to stop the bleeding!"

"Oh my God, Sammie!" My dad ran over to me.

"I'm okay, Dad." I hiccuped. "Where were you?"

A shirt landed on my lap before Alex grabbed it.

"I came in the back, but now I see I should've stayed with you. I could've stopped you."

I nodded because if I opened my mouth, I would scream again. I glanced at my feet and saw Alex pull out a large shard covered in my blood. *Oh, Shit!* I covered my mouth, closed my eyes, and gagged.

"Get me a trash can!" Alex hollered. "Don't beat yourself up, William," Alex spoke up. "I tried to stop her, but she wasn't listening to me."

I opened my eyes to glare at Alex, but all I saw was a trash can shoved in my face. *Was I so worried about the register that I didn't hear Alex or remember all the glass on the floor? What an idiot.*

"Sammie! Sammie!" I heard Cassie's cries and waved my hand above my head. "Oh, my God! What happened?"

Cassie jumped onto the counter, sliding in beside me. She gathered me into her arms while Alex continued to pull out more shards and dabbed my feet with the shirt.

"I...I...didn't realize...I...was...barefoot." I shivered in her arms.

"Ambulance is here!" one officer bellowed.

"I think I got them all." Alex turned my foot at different angles. "But you might need stitches." He tore the t-shirt in half and wrapped both of my feet. Standing, he pointed his finger at me. "Do not move. Cassie, make sure she stays put." Then he left us.

"Got it." Cassie declared. "Shh, it's going to be okay, Sammie." Cassie rocked me as best as she could from atop the counter.

I nestled my head on her chest. My feet throbbed with each frantic heartbeat. A medical bag and black rubber-soled shoes appeared in my line of sight.

"Ma'am, Sammie? I'm Chris." The paramedic knelt before me. "I need to put you on this gurney so I can clean your wound, wrap up your feet and take you to Hi Med. They can decide if you need stitches."

I nodded and braced myself to slide down off the counter.

"No!" Alex thundered before he snatched me off the counter and placed me on the gurney. "Damn it, woman, you can't walk on your feet. I just cleaned you up."

"Is this your wife, Chief?" Chris frowned.

"No, a friend." Alex stepped back and scurried away.

"Oh...kay." The paramedic snickered.

"My feet hurt really bad," I winced when I moved them. "Is there something you can give me?"

"Are you allergic to any medications?"

"No."

"Okay, let me check your vitals, and then I'll give you something for the pain."

Chris took my blood pressure, checked my heart rate and pulse before giving me a shot for the pain. I didn't say a word as I watched the paramedic gently remove the shirt from my left foot. He grabbed a bottle of water and cleansed my foot, looking for more glass. He used a towel to wipe my foot and then wrapped it in gauze. Then he repeated the same actions on my right foot.

"It's not as bad as it seems, but your right foot might need stitches. We're gonna take you to Hi Med." The paramedic nodded to his partner before he looked at Cassie. "Cassie, do you want to ride with her?"

"Of course you would know his name," I smiled at Cassie.

"Hey, I can't help it if everyone loves my coffee." Cassie shrugged and grasped my hand. "I wish I could go with you, but Katie texted me that all these hotties are causing quite the commotion next door. It seems the whole town needs coffee today at five-thirty in the morning." Cassie winked at Chris, who blushed and looked at the floor.

"I'll go." Alex appeared next to me. *Where had he come from? I swear he was like the mole in that whac-a-mole game, popping in and out of my life.*

"I'm her father. I'll go."

"William." Alex turned to face my dad. "My officers need you to stay here and report what's missing. I promise I'll watch over Sammie and call you with any updates."

"Okay." My dad came over and kissed my forehead. "I'll see you soon. I love you."

"Love you too, Daddy." I smiled. I'm drifting, weightless, as if my body and mind have let go of each other. *Damn, those drugs were good.*

"Wheels up, let's go." Alex lifted his arm and circled his finger like the blades of a helicopter. I guess I am his mission now.

Chapter 15

You are Not the Boss of Me

Sammie

I was at the hospital with Alex until lunchtime. The doctor used dissolvable stitches on my right foot, wrapped it up, sat me in a wheelchair, and sent me home with crutches. I had to stay off my feet for a few days.

"I'll get the car." Alex said as soon as the doctor left.

"What car? We came in an ambulance." I grinned at him. My head was less foggy now, but I still wanted to get home and take painkillers to stop the pain before it started.

"I called Lucian and asked him to drop off a car for us."

"And you have the keys?"

"He left them at a secret location." He smiled, proud of his answer.

"Really? Where?"

"Figure it out." He chuckled as we entered the elevator with the young man who was pushing my wheelchair.

I loved an intriguing puzzle. "Will you tell me if I guess correctly?"

"Yep," Alex winked at me.

"Under the seat. On top of a tire. Between the visor and the ceiling of the car." I bit my thumbnail. "Ooh, no, wait." I raised my hand as if I were in school and had the correct answer. "Under the car behind the driver's wheel." I smiled at him, proud of myself.

"Uh, no." Alex laughed. "But now I know the places you would look if I left you the keys to a car." Alex broke off when we approached the hospital check-in desk. "I'll be right back."

He walked to the desk and spoke with the officer next to the hospital worker. The officer handed him a set of keys. Alex smiled all the way to me.

"The officer at the front desk? Really?" I smirked. "Not very creative."

"Didn't say it was." Alex continued past me and unlocked the police car waiting by the curb.

As soon as I settled in, I dropped the bomb that I knew would piss Alex off.

"I want to go to the boutique." *One, Two, Three...BOOM!*

"No fucking way!" He exploded.

"I need to check things. My dad hasn't been at the shop as often as I have because he's been spending more time with my kids. I know how much money was in the register. He doesn't." This was my parents' livelihood and now mine. We couldn't afford to lose it.

"Ugh! You can be such a pain in my ass." He grumbled. "Wouldn't you rather go home and lie down like a damsel in distress?"

"Yeah, right!" I sneered. "Wrong girl, Alex."

"Obviously," he murmured.

Annie, his wife, would go home and lie down, not me. I preferred to face my problems head-on. If I could raise triplets without a father, I could do anything. I am woman, hear me roar, and all that shit.

Alex drove past the front of the boutique. I saw two police cars parked next to my dad's car before Alex parked in the back.

"Let's go in the back door in case there's still glass on the floor," Alex said before he came around the car to help me out.

Putting the crutches under my arms, I placed some weight on my left foot. That one didn't hurt as much. Planting the crutches and swinging my legs was going to take some practice. I sucked at it. Alex gripped my arm to help with my balance.

"I hate these damn things." I grumbled.

"I can carry you."

"No. I can do this." I focused on the rhythm. Plant the crutches, swing the feet, put some weight on the left foot, repeat.

"If I had taken you home, you wouldn't be on those damn things." Alex mumbled.

I ignored him and whipped the door open. But it banged on my crutch and slammed shut. "Oh...My...God...Really?" I shouted to the heavens.

"Come on, Gimpy." Alex chuckled. "I'll help you."

"That's not nice." I would've stomped my foot, but that would've hurt, so I glared at him instead before limping through the door with my crutches.

My place looked better than this morning. Officer Sean, Cassie's husband, was sweeping. Officer Ryker was cleaning the front door, his movements slow and deliberate, while K-9 Judge stood guard outside the shop. I spotted my dad with Detective Lucian at the register, so I beelined it toward them.

"Chief?" Detective Lucian addressed Alex when he saw us approaching.

"Did they take it all?" I asked.

"Sammie?" My dad spun around. "What are you doing here? Go home."

"That's what I told her, but your daughter—" Alex glared at me and crossed his arms, braced for another go-round. "—wouldn't listen."

"Sammie, are you okay?" Ryker ran to me and hugged me, crutches and all. Ryker was the guy friend in our girl tribe in high school. Cassie, Josie, Silver, Annie, and I always appreciated his input on the guys we liked in high school. None of us ever dated; he was the brother none of us had.

"I'm fine. Will everyone stop treating me like a fucking china doll?" I huffed and pointed at Alex. "And I'm not going home." I turned to my dad. "I know I put two thousand dollars in there. Did they take it all?"

"Every last fucking penny," Detective Lucian answered from behind the register. "It looks like they hit it first with that metal pole—" he pointed to the pole lying in front of the changing room, "—from that broken clothes rack. When that didn't work, they pried it open and broke the lock." With his gloved hand, he grabbed the inner drawer and held it up. "They took out the drawer, took the money and threw this away."

"I'm gonna look around." Alex looked around the store. "I don't see forensics. Did they finish with their photos and prints?"

"Yep. They left a few minutes ago." Lucian nodded toward the door. "I asked Ryker to bring Judge to see if he recognized any smells similar to the other robberies and break-ins."

"Did Judge find anything?"

"Nope."

Alex headed toward the changing rooms.

"Sammie!" I turned my head and saw Josie, one of my other friends, running toward me. "I just finished showing a house and was going to Cassie's for coffee when I saw all the cops. What happened?"

"Stop running, Hale!" Detective Lucian hollered. "You're gonna upset Judge."

"Hey, Josie." I said into her chest as she crushed me with her hug. I'd hug her back, but my hands were busy keeping the crutches under me. "I got robbed."

"Oh, shut up, Detective." She said the word detective with such bitterness in her voice. "Judge knows me."

Detective Lucian's lips flattened as his jaw tightened. He took several breaths before he looked at me, his eyes softening. "Does the $2,000 include the change?" Lucian set the drawer down to write in his pad. *What the hell was going on with these two? Since when did Detective Lucian call Josie by her last name?*

"No." I stepped up to the counter, removed my crutches, and leaned on it. "I'm sorry."

"Sit on this and take a load off." Alex shoved a stool under my ass. "Hi, Josie."

"Chief," Josie mumbled while she stared daggers at Detective Lucian. "I hope your detective is going to figure out all these robberies before we die of old age."

"Really?" Detective Lucian's jaw twitched before he and Josie screamed insults at each other with my father between them.

"Why are you being such a jerk?" I mumbled to Alex, under my breath.

"Why are you being so stubborn?"

"Ugh!" I threw my hands up, and he walked away.

"Honey?" My dad's eyes widened, and he hurried away from Lucian and Josie. "Those two have some serious issues. Are you okay?"

"No, Dad. I'm not." I dropped my head onto my hands.

Between the robbery, Lincoln, and Alex, I was at my wit's end. *Oh no! Lincoln!* I was supposed to get the kids to the park to meet him. I checked my watch. *Shit!*

I lifted my head and screeched. "Dad! Can you drive me to Milagro's house to get the kids? I'm supposed to have them at the park at two, and I'm late."

"Why the hell are you going to the park now?" Alex growled behind me. *He'd just walked away,* so where *the hell did he come from?*

"Because Lincoln wanted to meet the kids there today at two, and it's a quarter past!" I scooted off the stool, landed on my right foot, and howled as pain shot up my leg the minute I put weight on it. I would've crumbled to the ground had Alex not caught me.

"Fucking shit!" Alex picked me up and sat me on the counter. "Stay put. I have an idea."

Alex pulled out his phone and made a call. "Mom, can you put Dad on the phone? No, everything's fine, but I need to talk to him. Yes, now, please."

"What are you doing?" I glared at Alex.

"Shh."

"Don't you shh me!" I gawked.

"Dad, I need a favor. Can you take Sammie's kids to the park? Sammie promised Lincoln he could meet the kids today, and she's in no shape to chaperone them. Yeah, she's on crutches. Yes, Cody can go. Okay, thanks." Alex hung up and squinted at me. "For the record, I think the kids meeting Lincoln is a big mistake."

"For the record, I don't care what you think. They're my kids." *Who the hell did he think he was?* "I should go. I don't feel right asking your dad to do that for me."

"You didn't ask him...I did."

"Funny."

"I'm not trying to be funny. I'm trying to solve the problem. My dad's an ex-Marine. He can take care of himself and the kids if Lincoln tries anything."

"Fine. But let him know this was your crazy-ass idea."

"Fine," Alex repeated before he stormed off.

"Girrrl, I can feel the sexual tension rolling off of both of you." Josie winked.

"Is that like the sexual tension between you and our fine detective?" I cocked my eyebrow.

"He wishes." Josie huffed. "Don't be a hater. I think Alex has feelings for you."

"Don't even go there. You know he's still in love with Annie." I whispered.

"Not to sound insensitive, but Annie's gone. We all miss her, but he needs to move on." Josie said, not realizing Lucian was standing right behind her.

"I've already told him that," Lucian mumbled with his head next to Josie.

Josie spun around and pushed him back. "This is girl stuff. Stay out of it."

"Just trying to help." Lucian shrugged his shoulders.

"I'm sure if the chief needs tips on fucking everything in sight, he'll come to you—the expert." Josie spat out.

I watched Lucian's gaze harden before he gave Josie his sarcastic smile. "At least I'm getting my dick wet instead of growing cobwebs."

Oh no, he didn't. My mouth dropped open. My gaze bounced between them, waiting to see who was going to attack first because those were fighting words.

"Yeah, well, at least my cobwebs won't be infested with venereal diseases." Then her eyes watered, and her voice cracked. "You can be such a dick."

Lucian's demeanor changed with those six words from Josie. His shoulders dropped, and his face paled. "Josie." He reached out to her.

"Leave me alone and do what we pay you to do." Josie turned and ran into the back room.

"Good job, Detective," I snarled at him before I slid off the counter, grabbed my crutches, and followed Josie.

Chapter 16

The Park was a Bust

Lincoln

Where the fuck were they? I'd been waiting at this fucking park for almost an hour. I should never have trusted her. I got up from a park bench to go to my car when I saw my kids with another boy and an older man approaching me. I stopped frozen to the spot. I'd gotten a glimpse of my girls the other night at Sammie's, but not my son. He was so handsome, just like his old man. They looked just like their photos from social media.

"Who the fuck are you?" I asked the man walking over to me with the four kids.

"Clean up your mouth in front of the kids." The man did not look welcoming. "I'm the man supervising your visit." The tall, in-shape older man with an accent said.

"Where's Sammie?"

"She had to work, so she called me. I'm Roberto."

"Mother of the Year working on a Saturday instead of spending time with her kids."

"Look Lincoln. May I call you Lincoln?"

I nodded.

"If you bash Sammie, you and I—" Roberto pointed between us "—are going to have a problem. Let's start over for their sake. This is your son Holden with my grandson Cody. I believe you've met Hallie and Hollie." Roberto pointed to each of them as he said their names.

I squatted. "Hi guys. I'm your father."

"In name only," Holden grumbled. "Come on, Cody. Let's go play."

The girl named Hallie followed them while she pulled on Hollie's hand.

"No, Hallie, I want to talk to Daddy." Hallie shrugged and let go of Hollie's hand before she followed the boys.

"Hi, Hollie. You're so pretty. Can Daddy have a hug?" I spread my arms out, and she ran into them. She smelled of roses.

"Let's all have a seat so we can talk." Roberto motioned toward a nearby picnic table.

"You don't need to stick around." I held Hollie's hand as we walked to the table.

"I think I do."

Hollie and I sat on the bench side by side. "So, how old are you now?"

"Daddy, you don't know?" Hollie tilted her head.

"Uh," I tapped my temple. "My memory isn't very good."

"Oh," Hollie covered her mouth and giggled. "We're nine, almost ten. We're starting fourth grade in a few weeks."

"That's exciting. So, is your mom married?"

"Hollie, why don't you go play with your brother and sister so I can talk to your dad for a minute?" Roberto chimed in.

"Okay, see you later, Daddy."

I watched Hollie run away. This old man was ruining all my plans. *What the hell was his problem, anyway? Who was he to Sammie?*

"What was that for?" I turned to face Roberto.

"You were fishing for information about Sammie. Not cool. You're here to meet your kids, and get to know them, not find out about her."

"Why do you care? Are you her sugar daddy?" I scoffed.

"I'm a friend who loves her like a daughter, and I don't need you messing with her. Talk to your kids and get to know them, but leave questions about Sammie out of it, or else you will have to deal with me. And I promise...you won't like that."

"Whatever." I got up and headed toward Holden and the other boy, who were walking across the rope net. The asshole followed me like a fucking shadow.

"Hey, son." I stood next to the net. "You're incredibly steady on that rope net. You've got exceptional balance."

Holden glanced at me and mumbled, "Whatever." The other boy didn't say a word.

"So, Cody—" I pointed to the boy. He seemed less aggressive toward me. "How long have you guys been friends?"

"None ya," Holden said and smirked.

"Nunya?" *That wasn't a year.*

"Yeah." Holden turned to me and laughed. "None of ya business."

While he was still laughing, he pulled his friend along to the back of the jungle gym, where the only way I could reach him was to climb the damn thing. My son was a sarcastic fucking comedian. *Wonder where he got that from?* As I pondered that, Shadow chuckled behind me. *Asshole.*

Hoping to have better luck with the girls, I pivoted and saw Hollie and Hallie on the swings. I smiled and got behind them, ready to give them a push. Hallie jumped off mid-swing. If I weren't so pissed she didn't want to talk to me, I would have given her a ten for her perfect dismount.

"Thanks for staying, Hollie. Do you mind if I push you?"

"No, Daddy, I like to be pushed."

I smiled. "When does school start for you guys?"

"We start in two weeks. As a special treat, Mommy's taking us to the mountains on our last weekend. I'm so excited, we've never stayed in a cabin before. Are you coming too?"

"No, but I would love to go to the mountains with you guys."

"I could ask Mommy?" Hollie kicked her legs out as I gave her a push.

"Watch it." Shadow mumbled when Hollie was out of earshot.

"Maybe next time." I said when she was ready for another push.

"Mr. Reyes, can we go home now?" Hallie pulled on Shadow's hand. "My tummy hurts."

"Don't you want to stay a little longer? I can take you guys to Yummy's for ice cream?" I didn't want them to leave before I got to know them.

"Please, Mr. Reyes?" Hallie ignored my comment and pulled on Shadow's hand.

"Of course." Shadow stooped to pick her up.

Damn, I couldn't wait for my father to hold his granddaughter like that. Daddy Warbucks would love that as much as I would love the money he rained down on me.

"Thank you, Mr. Reyes." Hallie wrapped her arms around his neck, laying her head on his shoulder.

"Hollie, let's go get your brother and Cody," Shadow said as he rubbed Hallie's back.

I stopped pushing Hollie. She dragged feet across the sand to slow her swinging.

"Thanks for the push, Daddy," Hollie said before she placed her hand in Shadow's hand. *What the fuck?* She should hold my hand.

I hated this asshole. Mr. Roberto Reyes, or as I liked to call him, Shadow, because he was stuck to me like glue. *How was I supposed to get to know my kids with him following my every move?* Shadow gave a shrill whistle, and the boys came running. *Was I in a twilight zone? My kids listened to him* as *if he* were *part of the family. He wasn't Sammie's sugar daddy, but who the hell was he besides my son's best friend's grandpa?*

"Time to go, boys. Your sister doesn't feel well. You can set up another time with your dad." Shadow turned to me. "Well, looks like your time is up. Nice to meet you. Come on, kids."

"I'll see you guys soon," I roared as they walked away. The only one who waved at me was Hollie as she skipped away.

I put my hands inside my pockets. This was going to be harder than I thought because two out of three didn't want to have anything to do with me. *Fuck!*

Chapter 17

Crossing a Line

Sammie

Josie calmed down, but we preferred to sit in the back stockroom, avoiding Lucian and Alex like the plague. Whenever one or the other would come to talk to me, I answered in monosyllables and glared at them. Eventually, Alex and Lucian got a clue and only sent Sean or Ryker in with questions.

"Sammie." Alex came into the stockroom. "I'm gonna go with your dad to get some wood to cover the front door. Are you gonna be okay?"

"What do you mean, cover the front door? Can't we open as soon as you guys are done?"

"Uh, no. You don't have a safe entry into your boutique? Do you not remember what your storefront looks like?"

"Condescending asshole," I muttered.

"Put your damn claws away." Alex strolled in and stood in front of me. "I'm trying to help you. I talked to your dad. He said you were closed, and since he still owns the place, you're closed." He pointed his finger in my face. "Discussion over."

I grabbed the counter and stood, pointing my finger in his face. He made me so fucking angry with his macho bullshit. "You are being such a dick."

Alex braced his hands on his hips. "I'm trying to keep you safe."

"You are not my husband and can't tell me what to do." I lifted onto my tiptoes and screamed in his face. "You weren't this bossy with Annie! Maybe if you'd taken charge of her illness, she would've lived longer!" Josie gasped.

His face dropped and turned white as a ghost. *Oh Shit! Why did I say that?*

"Alex." I reached out to him, but he took a step back. "I'm so sorry. I didn't mean that. I don't even know where that came from."

Alex blinked and tightened his jaw. "I'm a Haven Island police officer who protects and serves his community. As such, I'm telling you to stay closed, Miss Rogers. This isn't personal." His words, sharp as steel, cut through me. "Ladies." He nodded and turned to leave.

I reached out for his arm. "Alex, wait," but he shrugged out of my grip and continued out the doorway into the boutique.

"Oh, shit," Josie mumbled. "I know you're mad, but you didn't have to bring Annie into it. I mean, shit, Sammie, she had cancer. There wasn't anything he could do to save her."

"I know." I dropped my head into my cupped hands. "That was a mean thing for me to say." I looked at Josie. "I'm so fucking frustrated right now. The break-in, Lincoln, and my confusing feelings for him all combined, and I lashed out, saying things I didn't mean. I just wanted to piss him off since he's being such a jerk."

"Well, it worked." Josie quipped. "What feelings?"

"I still love him," I mumbled.

"Oh, shit." Josie's eyes bugged out.

"I gotta apologize." I grabbed my crutches and hobbled out of the back room. The boutique was deathly silent.

"Hey guys." I approached Sean, Ryker, and Lucian, who were huddled by the front door. "Where's Alex?"

"He stormed out of here with your dad." Ryker pointed outside.

"I didn't catch what you said, but he was fuming; I could see it in his clenched fists." Sean grumbled.

Their glares pierced through me, and I felt the palpable tension of their anger.

"I said something mean that I shouldn't have said. I wanted to apologize."

"I think it might take more than words." Lucian rubbed the back of his neck. "I haven't seen Alex that mad in a long-ass time. You might have to do some grovelling."

"Yeah," I sighed and stared out the window. "I think you're right."

"Sammie, get off your feet. I think we got all the glass, but Chief will kick our asses if he comes back and your foot is bleeding through that gauze. Josie, grab her crutches." Lucian picked me up and sat me back on the counter. "Or, God forbid, your foot finds a runaway shard."

"I don't think he would care." I sighed.

"You might be surprised," he mumbled before he walked away.

"I'll help them." Josie picked up Lucian's broom from the floor. "I don't have another showing today, and I'm not working at the hotel tonight."

Lucian grabbed the broom and tossed it aside. "Go up there with Sammie. I don't want you getting hurt either."

"I'm fine. I have shoes on."

"Dammit, Josie." Lucian scooped Josie up in a fireman's carry and plopped her down next to me. "Ladies, stay there, please."

I swung my legs around the counter and faced the dented register.

"Josie, can you look behind the counter and get me the tape?"

"Yep." Josie swung around also and jumped down.

"Really?" Lucian yelled at us.

"There's no glass here." Josie shouted back. "I checked."

Lucian growled, "Stubborn-ass women."

Josie handed me the tape. I taped the drawer closed, attempting to secure it, but it didn't hold. *Shit*! I would have to buy a new one. I also needed to buy a new rolling rack. When they took it apart to beat my register with it, they bent the metal.

"Sammie, we're done." Sean said as he dipped the dustpan into the trash can. "Lucian and I have to get back to the station, but Ryker and Judge are staying by the front door so no one comes inside until Chief arrives with a door." Sean pulled the trash bag out and closed it. "I'll take this out to the dump on my way out."

I looked around. My boutique looked good as new, sans the front door and broken register.

"Sammie," Josie placed her hand on my shoulder. "Do you want me to drive you home?"

"No, I'll wait for Alex and my dad."

"Okay, but call me if you need anything."

"I'll walk you out." Lucian placed his hand low on Josie's back.

"You guys were awesome. Thank you so much."

"Sammie, we're back!" My dad hollered from the back door.

Lucian stared at me. "Play nice."

"I will." I nodded.

Alex carried the large slab of wood around the outside of the boutique and set it down against the door frame.

"Chief, you need help?" Lucian yelled.

"No, Ryker can help me!" Alex screamed back.

Lucian, Josie, and Sean greeted my dad on their way out.

"Dad," I swung my legs around facing him. "I thought you were buying a door?"

"They didn't have a glass one in stock. They have to order it," he said, on his way to the front to help Alex.

Thank goodness the door frame was wood. Otherwise, I didn't know what they would have attached that slab of wood to. Way to go, Dad, for redesigning the door frame when he bought the boutique, making it easier to board up in case of a hurricane. As soon as they finished, Ryker, Judge, and Alex left.

Dad walked up to me and gave me a hug. "I'm gonna go home. I gotta tell your mom we need to stay closed until the new door comes in. She's not gonna be happy. I'll see you at home." Dad kissed my forehead and turned to leave.

"Wait." I grabbed my crutches. "I'll come with you."

"Sammie, stop!" Alex ran toward me before I could jump off the counter.

"I thought you went home?" I stared at him.

"No," Alex grabbed my crutches and set them aside. "I was putting away my tools."

"Alex will drive you home since your kids are at his house." My dad shook Alex's hand. "Thank you for all your help today."

"No problem, sir."

I waited until my dad left before I prepared myself to grovel.

"Alex, about what I said earlier—" Alex lifted his hand to stop me.

"Let's go." He helped me off the counter, handed me the crutches, and accompanied me to the back door.

Lucian wasn't wrong when he said I had to grovel. The last time I saw Alex this non-responsive and cold was the day Annie died. *Did I kill our friendship?*

He pointed to the alarm system. "Wait outside. I'll set the alarm." Alex's voice sounded like a robot. No emotions whatsoever. "Your dad gave me the code and his keys to lock up since you're on crutches."

I stepped outside, and he closed the door. I heard the beeping right before he came out and locked the door. Turning the knob to double-check the lock.

Shit! I didn't want Alex to hate me. *I was in love with Alejandro Reyes—again.* But the man I loved was still in love with his deceased wife, who was also my deceased best friend. *Welcome to heartbreak hell—I'm an idiot.*

Chapter 18

Questions and Doubts

Alex

S ammie's words were on repeat in my head. *"You are not my husband and can't tell me what to do. You weren't this bossy with Annie! Maybe if you'd taken charge of her illness, she would've lived longer!"*

Fuck! Had I ignored Annie so much with my new job that I didn't do everything I could to help her? Had there been a miracle cure out there that I didn't research because my head wasn't in the game? Sammie didn't say things she didn't mean. Deep down, she must blame me for Annie's death.

Sammie was Annie's best friend. She must've seen something that I missed. *Was I too stubborn to have heard any of her suggestions? Had I killed my wife? Could I have saved Annie so she might've had several more years with Cody?*

All these questions and doubts ran through my head as I shopped with William for a piece of plywood large enough to cover the previous door. While William spoke to the salesperson, my phone buzzed. I whipped it out of my back pocket. *Please don't let it be Sammie with more trouble at the boutique.* It was Papi.

> Papi: Met the loser. We're back. Kids didn't want to stay.

> Alex: I hope you didn't call him a loser in front of the kids.

> Papi: Nope, but I did warn him off messing with Sammie.

> Alex: Can't wait to hear all about it. Are you home?

> Papi: Yep, my house. Take your time. I'm grilling hamburgers and hotdogs for dinner.

> Alex: Do you need anything from the store?

> Papi: Nope.

> Alex: See you soon.

Fuck! I had totally forgotten about the fucking park playdate with Lincoln.

"Alex?" William tapped my shoulder. "Are you okay?"

"Yeah, sorry." I shook my head. "Which piece of wood do you want? I'll get it for you."

"No need. The salesperson is going to take it up to the register for us. Bring your SUV around so we can load it."

"Got it." I left and pulled my car up. The salesman loaded it up, and we drove to the boutique.

"You look pissed." William said, breaking the silence in the car.

"My dad just got back from the park. He didn't like Lincoln."

"No one likes Lincoln. No surprise there." William sighed. "Are the kids okay?"

"Yeah, although he didn't give me any details."

I pulled into the parking lot and got Ryker to help me carry the slab of wood. Sammie sat on the counter watching us the entire time. Her words still sliced up my heart. *How could she think I wouldn't save Annie if I could?*

After I locked up, I helped her into the car. Sammie was quiet on the drive home. I didn't mind the silence. Words didn't need to be spoken just to fill up space, but I hated this uncomfortable silence. Sammie stared out the window. I didn't know what to say, so I referred to my officer side.

"Officer Hudson and Officer Charlotte will do regular drive-bys during the day to check on your store. I also notified the night patrol officers to drive by as well."

"Thank you."

"My dad texted me while I was at the store with your dad. He and the kids are at his house waiting for us. Papi said he would grill some hamburgers and hotdogs for dinner."

"Did he say what happened with Lincoln at the park?" Sammie spun toward me.

"No, he only said Lincoln is a loser," Alex snickered.

"I already know that." Sammie rolled her eyes. "I don't want to inconvenience your dad. If you can get my kids and drop us off at home? That would be great."

"It's not an inconvenience. Papi already bought all the food, and Mami is already prepping it. It would be worse if you guys don't stay and Cody and I have to eat it all. Trust me."

"Okay," Sammie sighed. "He didn't give you any details?"

"No. You can ask him when we get there."

"Alex," I glanced at her. "Please don't be mad at me."

"Forget it."

"I can't because I didn't mean it, and I feel horrible. The stress of what happened at the store and my kids being with Lincoln got to me. I just feel so damn helpless, and I took it out on you. Please, forgive me?" Sammie placed her hand on my thigh.

"Sure." I pulled into my parents' driveway, shut off the car, and got out.

I didn't want to talk about this. Her apology still didn't shake me out of my misery of not helping my wife or spending more time with her. We'd made so many plans. So many places we wanted to take Cody so he could experience the world before we had more kids. We never planned to stop at one. We wanted Cody to have siblings, lots of them.

I felt Sammie's hand on my elbow and turned to face her.

"Please don't be mad at me. I don't know what I'd do if you hated me."

"I don't hate you." I grimaced. "Just trying to face some hard truths about my relationship with Annie when she needed me the most."

"No." Sammie grunted and pulled me toward her. "You listen to me, Alejandro Reyes. You were the best husband any woman could want. You did everything you could to make her happy until her last breath. I was stupid in what I said. It wasn't true." I cupped his face and brought him down to my level. "Do you hear me?"

I nodded and closed my eyes. Sammie wrapped her arms around me.

"You are such a wonderful man. Please don't internalize what I said. Annie loved you so much. She always raved about how attentive you were. She felt your love until her last breath."

I shuddered. "Thank you."

"Oye, Mijo!"

Papi stood in the doorway staring at us. "Are you guys going to stand out there all night? I'm getting ready to grill, and I could use your help."

I released Sammie. "Sorry, Papi—I cleared my throat—we're coming." Then motioned for Sammie to go ahead of me.

"Sammie, I invited your parents," Papi announced after he hugged her. "I figured they could use a break. They should be here soon."

"Thank you, Roberto. I want to see my kids, and then I'd like to talk to you about the park playdate."

"Let's talk after dinner. Mijo, get Sammie a glass of wine so she can relax." Roberto closed the front door.

"Yes, sir. Sammie, white or red?"

"Can I have a beer?"

"Girl after my heart," Roberto chuckled. "Your mom's in the kitchen getting everything ready."

I gave my mom a big hug. "Gracias, Mami."

"Anytime." She smiled and hugged Sammie.

"Thank you, Milagro." Sammie gave my mom a one-arm hug. "I really didn't want to have to go home and cook."

"I don't blame you. Especially while you're on crutches. Does it hurt? Do you need some ibuprofen?"

"It's not too bad."

I pulled out a chair for her. "Have a seat, Sammie."

"Thanks," Sammie gave my arm a squeeze and sat.

I grabbed a beer for her from the fridge, opened it, and placed it in front of her.

"I'm going to help Dad on the grill. Stay in here. I'll tell your kids you're here."

"Okay." Sammie nodded.

My mom took her crutches and leaned them against the wall. "How is the boutique?"

"We have to stay closed for a few days, which will affect our back-to-school sales event, but we'll make do."

"Alejandro!" Mom hollered, stopping me halfway out the door. "Take this to your dad." She handed me a tray of uncooked hamburger patties.

I left the ladies in the kitchen and headed toward the grill. The kids were playing four-way catch with a frisbee.

"These are from Mami. Let me say hi to Cody and I'll come back to grill."

I ran to the kids and grabbed the frisbee before Cody could catch it.

"Daadd!" Cody huffed.

"Sorry, it was too tempting." I handed him the frisbee and gave him a quick hug before turning to the triplets. "Guys, your mom is in the kitchen. I'm sure she'd love to see you."

"We'll be right back, Cody." The kids yelled before they ran inside.

"I'm gonna help your grandfather grill. Dinner should be ready in a few minutes."

"Okay," Cody grinned.

At the grill, I swiped the spatula from my dad and placed the patties on the grill.

"You can relax, Papi, I'll do this."

Chapter 19

Unattainable Love

Sammie

My parents arrived ten minutes after us. The men stayed outside while the ladies finished the sides for our dinner.

"How did it go with Lincoln?" Mom asked while I cut up tomatoes for the salad.

"I don't know." I answered. "Roberto hasn't talked to me about it. He said, we'd talk about it after dinner."

"Don't look at me." Milagro shrugged. "He never said a word. The minute he came home, he went outside and played with the kids."

"Well, I'm glad he took them. With the break-in, I wouldn't have been able to go and would've had to cancel. Then he would be pestering me." My phone buzzed. I wiped my hands on a dishtowel and took it out of my back pocket. "Speak of the devil."

> Lincoln: That guy was an asshole. I had them for only thirty minutes. I want to see them tomorrow.

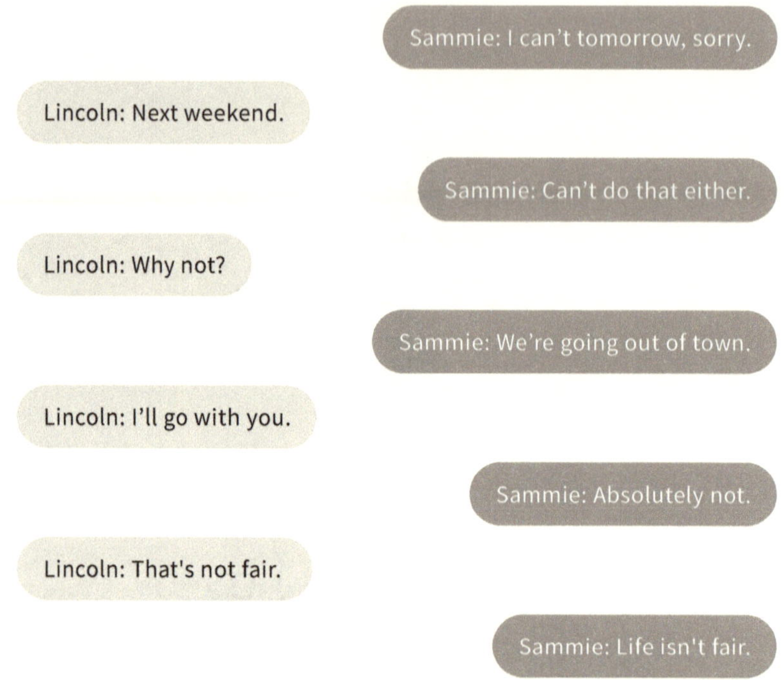

I turned off my phone. I was done with his commands.

"What did he say?" Mom grabbed the salad bowl.

"He wants to see them tomorrow. I said no. He asked about next weekend, and I told him no."

"You didn't tell him you were going out of town, did you?" My mom stared at me.

"I did. If he knows I'm out of town, then he can't pester me."

"What if he follows you?"

"Mom, he's not a stalker." I glared at her.

"Who's not a stalker?" Great, Alex just walked in at the wrong moment.

"Lincoln," Mom stated and turned to him. "Alex, tell Sammie she shouldn't have told him she was going out of town with the kids."

"Where are you going?" Alex placed the empty burger tray in the sink. "Mami, I need a clean tray for the cooked food."

"The mountains." I snatched the bag of buns.

"You are not going to the mountains alone." Alex gripped the new tray, blocked my path, and grabbed the buns. "You are not carrying anything while you're on crutches. Relax. I'll help carry stuff outside."

"Fine." I readjusted my hands on the crutches. "I won't be alone. I'll have the kids."

"You're not listening to me." He growled in my face. "You are not going to the mountains alone."

"I heard you the first time." I grabbed the salad bowl and walked around him. *What was his problem? He didn't want to talk to me, but he wanted to order me around?* I powered forward, the crutches snapping down with crisp precision as I spilled salad on my way to the table. *Maybe taking the salad bowl was a bad idea.*

"Give me that damn bowl." Alex tried to grab it, but I smacked his shin with my crutch. "Ow. What the fuck, Sammie? Cody and I are coming with you. End of discussion."

"Uh, no." I glared at him. I would've gone right up to him if it weren't for these damn crutches.

"It's only a two-bedroom log cabin. Cody can come cause he can share a bed with Holden or make a tent, but there's no room for you."

"I can sleep on a couch or the fucking floor, but you are not going out into the wild with just the kids, when your ex is hounding you."

"I'm not going into the wild." I rolled my eyes. "There are other cabins. It's not like I'll be in the middle of a forest with no one for miles. You're overreacting."

"Sammie, I'm not letting you go."

I slammed the salad bowl onto the table. Vegetables jumped in and out of the bowl before I whirled toward him and yelled. "You—" I leaned down on my crutches and jabbed his chest with my finger. "—can't tell me what to do."

"Okay, you two." My mom put her arm around my shoulder. "Let's talk about this later. We don't need to discuss this in front of the kids." She nodded to where they had stopped playing and were staring at us.

"You're right," I mumbled and glared at Alex.

"Sit down before you hurt yourself or toss our food all over the floor. I'm hungry." Alex growled.

"FU..." —Alex nodded to the kids— "Uh!" He was so fucking frustrating. "I got this." I stormed back into the house, pounding my crutches into the ground with every step.

Milagro had already put some chips in bowls. I grabbed a bowl with my left hand and steadied it against my crutch using the thumb, like I did for the salad bowl. Then, I did the same with my right hand. *So what if I dropped some chips?*

"Honey," Milagro followed me into the kitchen. "Don't be mad at Alejandro. He's just trying to look out for you. Can I help you with that?"

"No, I got it. I know he's trying to help me, but I wish he was nicer about it. I hate being talked down to like a four-year-old."

I didn't realize Alex had come up behind me until I felt his hand on my lower back.

"I'm sorry, I didn't mean for it to come out that way." Alex's voice was low near my ear.

"You both need to talk this out. I'll keep everyone busy out there." Milagro pulled the bowls out of my hands and left the kitchen.

"Please come with me so we can talk. I don't want to stay in here in case they need something from the kitchen." Alex applied pressure to my back and led me into his childhood bedroom downstairs on the other side of the house.

I'd been in this room before. It's where Cody and Holden slept when they had sleepovers here. Alex's high school sports trophies littered the top of the dresser along with several framed photos of his time in the Rangers. All the photos on the wall were Cody's school photos mixed in with family photos from vacations.

Alex closed the door and leaned against it. "We're not leaving until we settle this."

"We need to go back down. I don't want my kids wondering where I am." A weak excuse, but being in a room with a bed and Alex was already wreaking havoc on my nerves. I bit my thumbnail. My eyes bounced from one photo on the wall to the next. Until I saw the photos of Annie. I stopped in my tracks and looked away. I promised Annie to watch over Alex, not to have sex with him.

"They're fine. There's at least one grandparent for every child. Have a seat." Alex gestured to the bed.

I scanned the room for another place to sit. *Aha, the desk chair.* I took two steps toward it, but Alex blocked my path and grabbed my crutches, setting them against the wall.

I pointed at them. "I need those."

"Not right now." He pulled me down next to him on the bed.

Was it hot in here? I fanned myself. Needing distance, I shot up and hopped to the chair, grabbing the armrests for dear life, hoping it wouldn't roll away.

"I'm not gonna bite you." Alex grinned at me. "Well, unless you want me to."

My eyes widened. *Did he just flirt with me?* "This isn't such a good idea. I'd rather sit in the chair."

"What are you talking about? Why are you being so jumpy?" Alex frowned. *Was he that dense?*

He leaned toward the chair, grabbed the armrest, and wheeled me over to him. He grabbed my crutches and set them down on the floor. Clasping his hands over mine on my lap. "I didn't mean to go all caveman down there on you. You're my friend. I don't want you in a place where Lincoln could take advantage of you. He's done some shady shit. I don't trust him. Plus, we still don't know if the break-in at the boutique was one of several on the island or targeted specifically toward you."

"What kind of shady shit?"

I ignored his break-in comment because other places got robbed, just like I did and focused on the shady shit. After Lincoln left me and the kids, I served him the divorce papers through a lawyer and never looked back.

"The police arrested him for drugs, drunk driving, and public disturbance, but he never served time. I would hate myself if you were out there with the kids and something happened to you. Please, let me come with you."

"Do you really think he would try something?" Lincoln had never laid a hand on me even when he'd been drinking or high. *Could he want to take the kids from me after all these years? Or worse, hurt them?*

"I don't know." Alex scooted me closer to him. His thighs now on the outside of mine. He released one of his hands and cupped my face. "But I can only keep you safe if I'm there. Please let me come?"

Gazing into his pleading eyes, I knew I was going to give in. The thought of being with him sent my heart racing, making it impossible for me to refuse. My resolve faltered whenever he was near, and I was weak. I sighed. "Okay, you and Cody can come. But you're on the couch."

"Of Course. Whatever you say."

The butterflies in my stomach fluttered crazily when his sexy, gorgeous smile was aimed directly at me. I'd never known the feeling of butterflies in my stomach, though Annie spoke of having them when she met Alex. Did he know his smile caused the female population's stomachs to flutter? Is that why he smiled like that?

Oh shit, I was in trouble.

I looked away for a second and wondered if my already battered heart would survive this trip. He leaned forward to kiss my cheek, but I turned my face to let him know not to boss me around when his lips landed on mine.

They were soft at first. I stared at his face. His eyes gazed into mine like a deer caught in headlights. I could feel his breath on my lips. Smell the aftershave on his face. My body froze, waiting to see what he would do. Those seconds seemed like an eternity. He tilted his head and slid his hands to the back of my head, angling us for his mouth's assault. I closed my eyes and let his kiss wash over me. For so many years, I had dreamt of this moment.

His tongue took a slow and deliberate approach as it conquered every nook and cranny in my mouth, taking my breath away. His other hand slid under my ass and pulled me onto his lap. My knees bent around his waist. His arousal hard and unyielding between my legs. Every inch of my being craved him. I ground down on him, and we both let out a long, wistful moan.

That wicked hand that helped me sit on him was now massaging my breasts through my clothes. I hadn't been with anyone in the last eight years. I was needy and hungry for whatever he had to give.

"Annie," he groaned into my mouth.

Oh my God, he just called me by another woman's name. I shoved him so hard it broke our kiss. We both froze, staring at each other, struggling to control our breaths.

"I'm so sorry. I don't know why I said that." He gripped my shirt. No matter how much I squirmed to get off his lap, I couldn't get away. "You feel and taste different from Annie. Say something, please." His eyes pleaded.

"Let go of me." I whispered. I was on the verge of tears, but didn't want him to see me cry.

"Sammie, please. Talk to me." Alex cupped my face with both hands. "I'm so sorry."

My body trembled. I was seconds away from a breakdown. How could I have thought he had the same feelings for me I had for him? He was a guy; they just wanted someone to fuck. I was so stupid to fall under his sexy gaze. A sharp knock echoed through the room. Thank you, Lord.

"Sammie, Alejandro," Milagro said. "The kids are getting worried, and your food is getting cold."

Alex released my face but kept staring into my eyes. "We'll be right down," he hollered. "Sammie, say something."

I cleared my throat and got off his lap. "I...I need to go." I wiped at my eyes and limped to the door. Fuck the crutches. My left foot throbbed every time I landed on it, but I couldn't put weight on the one with the stitches. I didn't want to rip those fuckers open and gush blood all over the floor. Thank God, Milagro was gone. I needed to go to the bathroom and pull myself together.

"Sammie, stop. Your crutches. You're going to hurt yourself." Alex cried.

I didn't care how much pain I was in. I wasn't stopping until I reached the bathroom and locked myself in. Leaning against the counter, I stared at myself in the mirror and let the tears fall. *Yeah, we'd both fucked up.* I let him get to me when he was still in love with a ghost, and he used me to forget about said ghost. *How the hell were we going to survive staying in a cabin together for three days and two nights?*

Chapter 20

What Have I Done?

Alejandro

*F*uck *me!* I ran after Sammie, carrying her crutches, and knocked after she slammed the door in my face.

"Sammie, can I come in?"

"No." Sammie sniffled. "Please leave me alone. I'll be down in a minute."

Shit, she was crying. I hated myself for bringing her to tears. I shouldn't have kissed her.

"Okay. Your crutches are outside the door, leaning against the wall." I placed my palm on the door, wishing I could hold her. "I'll be downstairs."

How could I have fucked up so royally? I knew I was kissing Sammie. Her lips carried a hint of my favorite beer, her skin so responsive beneath my touch, her scent a heady, pungent perfume—none of those things were like Annie. They were like two sides of a coin, unless it came to being a mother. In that, they were both devoted to their kids.

I needed to get my head straight. I had been thinking of Sammie while my mouth and tongue explored the beauty of her mouth. Sammie was so much more responsive to me than Annie had ever been. I loved my wife, but in that moment, all I could think about was being with Sammie. She was the only woman who had sparked my interest since Annie died. I wanted to devour Sammie. To see if every part of her body tasted as good as her mouth. To sink into her body and feel her tighten around me, welcoming me home.

Sammie was everything. Moaning out Annie's name was an apology to Annie because I was ready to let Sammie in. Unfortunately, moaning Annie's name fucked everything up. The look of utter hurt and devastation in Sammie's eyes killed me. I panicked, but the damage was done. *How was I going to fix this if she wouldn't talk to me?* I rejoined everyone at the table and snatched a burger, placing it on the plate in front of me.

"Where's Mommy?" Hollie asked.

I looked around and noticed they were all eating my mom's homemade apple pie. We had been up there so long we missed eating the main course with them. The kids' gazes were curious, but my parents and her parents were not so nice in the way they stared at me.

I cleared my throat and smiled. "She's on her way down. She needed to use the little girls' room."

Pretending everything was okay was my best performance today because I'd sucked at everything else. I added chips to my plate. The burger was halfway to my mouth when Sammie stepped out, smiling at everyone. No watery eyes or tear stains on her face.

"Wow, that pie looks delicious."

"Mommy, what took you so long?" Hollie got up and ran to her for a hug.

I grabbed a burger and placed it on a plate for her. "You want a burger?"

Pushing Hollie's hair behind her ears, she didn't even look at me when she said, "No, I'm not hungry."

I wanted to yell at her to eat, but that would get me nowhere except further into the doghouse with her and our parents. Instead, I set the plate down on the table and continued to eat my burger. Glancing up, I noticed the disappointment in Mami's eyes. I gave her a crooked smile that fell off my face when I looked at Papi's clenched jaw. Guess I was having another conversation with them before I left. Might as well enjoy my burger before I get my ass handed to me by my parents.

"How about a slice of pie?" Mami cut a thin slice and handed it to her.

"Oh, you know you love Milagro's pie," Eleanor cut in.

"Sure," Sammie smiled at Mami.

Mami placed the slice of pie at the only empty seat, which was next to me, but Sammie lucked out when Hollie sat and said, "Mommy, sit next to me."

I grabbed the chair next to me and moved it to the far end of the table where the kids were sitting. Everyone scooted over so she would fit between Hollie and Hallie. I helped her with her crutches and brought the slice of pie to her before going back to my seat.

The conversation continued. I answered whenever someone spoke to me, but otherwise, I kept to myself. Which wasn't totally out of character at big gatherings. I always preferred to watch and listen to everyone's conversations.

When everyone finished with the pie, we all helped clean up. Years ago when I was young, Papi built me a fort in the trees of our backyard.

"Kids." Papi turned to face them. "Why don't you go play in the fort while the adults talk?"

"Are we in trouble?" Cody asked before glancing at Holden. "We didn't mean to sneak another piece of pie."

"No," Papi chuckled. "You can eat all the pie you want. You guys are not in trouble. Just adult stuff you don't need to worry about. Besides, your abuela loves it when everyone finishes her pies."

"Si." Mami patted her stomach. "Otherwise, I finish it. And I don't need the extra pounds."

Papi wrapped his arms around her and said, "You are perfect with more or less pie." Then kissed her.

I looked at Sammie, who was smiling at them.

"Eww, let's go, guys." Cody was the first one to run away.

"Someday, you'll understand," Papi yelled.

When they left, my dad's smile dropped. "Everyone to the living room. We need to talk."

Mami grabbed several plates and followed Papi. "Mi Amor, I need to get this food off the dishes."

"Not now. I'll help you with it later." Papi kissed her and put the dishes in the sink.

"Okay."

We all marched like obedient soldiers into the living room and sat. I sat at the end of the couch hoping Sammie would sit next to me, but she went straight for the loveseat with her mom. Mami sat with me, Papi in his favorite recliner and William in the accent chair.

Papi started. "I met Lincoln today. I didn't like him. He's up to something. I just can't put my finger on it, but I don't trust him. He tried to get info about Sammie from Hollie, but I shut him down and told him he was there to talk to his kids, not ask about Sammie."

Out of the corner of my eye, I saw Sammie's body stiffen. Eleanor grasped her hand, and I wished with a pang in my heart that it was my hand she was holding so tightly.

"Hollie was the only one who would speak to him. Hallie hung out with the boys when Hollie was talking to him. He approached Holden, but Holden snapped at him and stayed with Cody. If you guys are going to a cabin—" Papi turned to Sammie. "—I highly suggest you take Cody and Alejandro with you."

That was my Papi, direct and to the point.

"What did he want to know about Sammie?" I scooted forward and leaned my forearms on my thighs.

"If I was her sugar daddy? If she was married?"

"Asshole," I mumbled and glanced at Sammie. Her mouth fell open as her eyes clung to Papi, wide and unblinking.

"He asked when school started, and Hollie told him about the upcoming trip to the mountains. She asked him if he was coming. He said no, but that he loved the mountains. Hollie said she would ask if he could come."

"No, absolutely not." My body was vibrating with anger. "Does he know where you're going in the mountains? Is it somewhere you've been with him?"

"Alex, stop." Sammie closed her eyes for a second before she finally looked at me. "It is somewhere we've been before, but I'm not inviting him."

No fucking way she was going to that fucking cabin without me. "When are we leaving?" I pointed at her foot. "You can't drive with that foot."

"I was hoping my foot wouldn't still hurt by Wednesday."

"I don't think you should take any chances. Besides, imagine the look on the kids' faces when you tell them they're not going." *Yep, I was a scumbag playing the kid card to weaken her defenses.*

"Fine, you can come. I was going to leave early Thursday morning and come back Tuesday. I want to be back a few days before we meet their teacher for next year. It's approximately a seven-hour drive, and if I can drive while they are asleep, then it's fewer stops."

"How early?" I wondered, not that I cared, after being a Ranger and working as an officer, I required little sleep.

"4:00 am." She smirked.

"Done. I'll get you at four. Does this cabin have a kitchen? Do we need to bring any food?"

"Yes, and yes. I'll take care of it. I wasn't planning on eating out every meal."

"Text me the name of the place so I can check it out." I pulled out my phone.

"It's a nice place."

"I didn't say it wasn't, just like to get my bearings."

"Fine." She pulled out her phone and sent me the info.

"Okay, well, now that it's settled." William stood. "I'd like to get my wife home. It's been a long day. Thank you, Milagro and Roberto, always a pleasure."

"I'll go get the kids." Sammie left the room. I followed her like a lapdog. Which, had I been her lapdog, I would've gotten a hell of a lot more attention than she was giving me.

"Sammie, please let me know if you need anything before our trip." I stayed close behind her in case she was unsteady on the grass.

"I'll be fine." Quickening her steps, she reached the treehouse. "Kids, it's time to go."

"Why? Are you working tomorrow?" Holden peeked his head out.

"No, but I'm sure the Reyes would like to get some peace and quiet."

"Aw, Mom." Holden helped Hallie brace herself on the ladder before she came down.

"I can keep Holden overnight." I whispered in her ear so the kids wouldn't hear me. Her body shivered. "I don't work tomorrow, and when school starts, the boys won't be able to spend as much time together." *Again with the fucking kid card. I'm just batting a thousand.*

Sammie stayed quiet, keeping me on pins and needles until all the kids came down.

"Holden, do you want to stay overnight with Cody?"

"Yeah, that would be great."

"Can we stay too?" Hallie asked.

"No, it's just the boys doing boy things, right, Chief Reyes?" Holden looked to me for confirmation.

"Uh," I didn't know what to say, but Sammie saved me.

"No, Hallie, you and Hollie come with me. We'll do girl stuff."

"Like what?" Hallie whined.

"Mommy, can we do mani/pedi's?" Hollie smiled at Sammie.

"Sure," Sammie nodded. "Why not?"

"I'd rather go fishing." Hallie grumbled.

"Tell you what. Your mom gave me the name of the place we're going in the mountains. I'll look and see if there's a fishing hole, and I'll bring our poles." I placed my hand on Hallie's shoulder.

"We're going to?" Cody looked stunned.

"Yep," I answered while the boys fist-bumped each other and the girls jumped up and down clapping. Everyone was excited—except Sammie. She stared at me, her expression as cold as ice, as if she was plotting my murder.

"Okay, let's go home." Sammie grumbled.

I followed behind the boys. I considered myself lucky that I left my parents' house without Papi kicking my ass. Agreeing to protect Sammie in the mountains helped my case. We all said our goodbyes and left my parents' house.

Chapter 21

Spa/Movie Date

Sammie

*H*ow dare he tell my kids he was coming on our vacation. I wanted to tell them in private, when we were alone, not around others. *Why did I have to like him? Why not someone else?* He would break my heart, and I had no protection against him except for my anger, which usually dissolved like it had with the touch of his lips on mine. Or his breath on my face. Or his hot body near mine. *Stop dammit!* I was driving myself crazy.

I sat in the back with the girls while my dad drove us home.

"Mommy," Hollie said the minute we walked in the front door. "I'll go get the nail polish." Then she ran off.

"I don't want to paint my nails." Hallie huffed.

"Oh, come on, it will be fun." My mom side-hugged Hallie. "I'm gonna do it too. We'll do it in the kitchen and send your grandfather to the living room. Girls only. I'll even make us some homemade hot chocolate."

"I don't want hot chocolate." Hallie pulled away from my mom. "It's too hot. I like it only when it's cold outside."

"That's not true, Hallie." I draped my arm over her shoulder and guided her to the kitchen. You had hot chocolate the other night while you watched that superhero movie."

Hallie dropped her shoulders in a dramatic sigh. "Fine."

I wasn't looking forward to her teenage years. She had been a wonderful baby and toddler, but now, as puberty loomed, she was brimming with strong opinions. Damn, I wish I could stop time.

"How about I make some bite-sized chocolate chip cookies to go with our hot chocolate?"

Go mom. She was the best mom and grandmom ever, always trying to make me and the kids happy.

"Okay," Hallie grumbled, but I saw the tiny smile she tried to keep hidden before she turned away from us and plopped into a kitchen chair.

"I brought three colors." Hollie placed a light pink, sky blue, and red bottle on the table. "I want the sky blue. Which one do you want, Halls"

"Light pink."

"It is a pretty color. Maybe I'll do light pink." Hollie grimaced.

"Do the sky blue, Holls. It will look good on you." Hallie pushed the bottle in front of her.

"Okay, thanks, Halls."

Hollie had always looked up to Hallie, and I loved when Hallie complimented her instead of teasing her about being a follower and not a leader. They were close, had always been. When one cried, so did the other two. If one was being bullied, the other two stepped in. I prayed they would always look out for each other. Their unwavering bond was something to be treasured. The thought of that bond ever breaking would shatter my heart. Hollie wanting to spend time with her father when the others didn't, worried me. The last thing I wanted was for Lincoln to sever their bond.

"I'll do the red." I scooted that bottle in front of me.

"You always do the red," Hollie smiled at me.

"I like bright colors, so sue me." I joked with them.

"Okay, girls, I'm gonna work on the food and drinks while you all get started. That way your nails will dry, and you can do mine in light pink." My mom tapped the light-pink bottle and headed toward the cabinet to gather her ingredients.

I painted the girls' toenails before mine. Then, Hollie and I worked together to paint Hallie's nails. I knew we had to do hers first before she bolted from the kitchen.

"Here's your hot chocolate. I have more on the stove. I'll finish the cookies while you work on each other's nails." My mom ran her hand through Hollie's hair. "You did well, Hollie."

"Thanks, Grandma." Hollie beamed.

Hallie and I did Hollie's and then they did mine. The smell of the cookies sitting on the cooling rack was making my mouth water.

"Okay." My mom sat down. "Who's doing mine?"

"Me, me." Hollie raised her hand. "Can I have a cookie first?"

"Why don't each of you paint one of your grandmothers' hands and I'll get you each a cookie?" I stood and placed some cookies on a napkin, being careful not to ruin my manicure.

"Sure, I'll help you, Holls."

I looked at my mom and mouthed 'thank you'. She smiled and nodded. Once I had three bite-sized cookies on a napkin for each of us, I set them down at the table.

"We each get three. I'm gonna give some to Dad." I loaded up another napkin with five cookies and went into the living room.

My dad was watching sports.

"Here, Dad. I brought you some cookies. Do you want some hot chocolate, too?"

"If you have some left over, that would be great. If not, milk would be fine." He reached out to grab the cookies.

"We have enough. I'll be right back."

The girls were now working on my mom's pedicure. I scooped out some hot chocolate and brought it to my dad. "Here you go."

"Have a seat, Sammie." My dad took the cup and placed it on the end table near his recliner.

I sat on the edge of the couch facing him, wondering what he was going to say, but pretty sure it would have something to do with Alex and Lincoln.

"I know you don't want Alex to go with you to the cabin, but I'm glad he's going. I don't trust Lincoln, and I don't think it would be safe for you to be up there alone with the kids. Thank you for giving in."

I didn't know what to say. Should I say thank you? Did he realize I was in love with Alex? What if Alex and I became a thing? Would he accept our relationship or would he think I was a hussy for taking my best friend's husband? All these thoughts were running through my mind, but I wasn't ready to verbalize any of them, not to him. Maybe I would test the waters with my mom. She and I always talked about boys because talking to my dad seemed awkward.

"That's really all I wanted to say."

"Thanks, Dad." I stood. "To be honest, I will feel safer with Alex there."

"I know he will take care of you and the kids. Of that, I have no doubt. Besides, Holden gets to share his vacation with his best friend, and it seems Hallie has found a new love for fishing." My dad smirked.

"So, it would seem. Hallie is turning more into a tomboy every day. Not that I mind. I just find it funny how she and Hollie are becoming so different."

"It is nice to see them assert their own independence." Dad stood. "I'm going to bed if you girls want to come out here and watch something." Dad hugged me. "I love you."

"I love you too, Dad. Goodnight." I gathered his empty napkin and glass, taking them to the kitchen.

"Grandpa went to bed, so if you ladies want to watch something, we can turn this spa date into a movie date."

"Can we have popcorn?" Hallie loved popcorn and a movie.

"You just had hot chocolate and cookies," I frowned at her.

"Please, Mommy?" Hollie joined her sister's pouty face.

"Okay, you girls can share one bag."

"Okay," they both got up and ran to the living room.

"I wish I could move and eat like them." I grabbed a packet of popcorn and tossed it into the microwave. "I would love to have a fraction of their energy."

"Wouldn't we all." My mom got up. "I'm gonna go help them pick out a movie."

"Okay, I'll be there in a few minutes." I carefully took the popcorn out when the microwave dinged. If I messed up my nails, I would redo them after the girls went to bed. No one would be any the wiser.

Chapter 22

Pancakes and Bacon

Alejandro

> **Alex:** Morning, what time do you want to get ice cream?

> **Sammie:** 2? Unless you want me to get Holden before lunch.

> **Alex:** I can feed him. Meet you at Yummy at 2.

> **Sammie:** k

My phone flashed 9:00 am — too early for the boys to be awake. I could still hear echoes of their laughter from Cody's room, the sound that had lulled me to sleep hours ago.

I made myself a cup of coffee and strolled into my office to check the overnight police reports. Someone had broken into another rental property on the beach. Not good. Tourism was our main bread and butter. We had several mainland visitors who came to our beaches or shops, but the tourists who stayed on our island brought in more revenue.

We needed to catch those kids. None of the reports mentioned Lincoln's name or description. I logged into the Siren Boutique's incident report and saw that Lucian had added an update. The fingerprints were still being tested by the lab, but they'd found tire tracks by the front door.

I wanted to catch the motherfucker who had burglarized Sammie. For the children's well-being, I hoped with all my might that Lincoln was innocent. No child in the world would wish for a convicted felon to be their father. It would not only devastate the kids, but other kids might tease them at school. Even if I chose not to tell them, word spreads in a small town, and they'd find out soon enough.

I researched the cabin information Sammie sent me. The property housed six cabins, which looked to be the same size, nestled among the trees. I clicked on all the indoor photos first. Perfect. Every living room had a couch. *But were they long enough to fit my 6'3" frame?* The cabin had a fireplace. We didn't need it in this heat, but if the kids asked for a fire, by damn, I'd light one.

I scrolled through the local trails, comparing distances and difficulty levels. If Sammie couldn't stay on her crutches for long, I'd take the kids on the longer hikes myself. Still, I wanted her to have something too — something that let her soak in the mountains without pushing her limits. A few sightseeing tours and seasonal events caught my eye, the kind of things that promised laughter, new memories, and maybe a little magic. With so much waiting to be explored, I could already feel the pull of those mountains deep in my chest.

I'd been on the computer for well over two hours and still hadn't heard another sound in the house. Heading to my bedroom, I peeked into Cody's room. Both boys were dead asleep. Smiling, I continued to my closet and pulled down my Ranger-issued backpack, which had seen better days but could hold a lot of shit. I wanted to make sure I stocked it with enough water and snacks for the hiking trails I wanted to do with them. Cody and Holden always carried their own backpacks when we went hiking, but I'd never taken Sammie and the girls. *Did they have their own backpacks?*

Because Lincoln or other animals might be a problem and I wasn't on duty, I would take my personal revolver, hunting knife, and stun gun. I pulled those out of my safe, adding them to the compass already in my pack. In the bathroom, I pulled out sunscreen, mosquito repellent, and a first-aid kit.

We weren't leaving for a few days, so I would pack my clothes and hat then. I stashed my backpack back in my closet, setting it on top of my hiking boots. While I was thinking about it, I sent a text message to Sammie about what to bring for hiking.

> Alex: I'd like to do some hiking. I'll bring all the necessary stuff, but make sure the girls pack a hat, layers of clothes, socks, and comfortable hiking boots or shoes.

Of course, she'd been to these cabins before—with Asshole. God, I was an idiot. I went back to my computer, firing off links of things to do and silently hoping Sammie hadn't already done them all. When I checked the time, it was almost noon. *Shit.* The boys needed to wake up and get their asses moving.

I stepped into their room. They were whispering.

"Boys, time to get up and shower. Holden, you can borrow some of Cody's clothes. We're going for ice cream at two. Are you hungry now? I can make you pancakes and bacon."

"I'm starving, Chief Reyes," Holden rolled over and smiled.

"Thanks, Dad." Cody jumped out of bed. "We'll be ready in no time."

I chuckled. My pancakes and bacon always lit a fire under those boys.

"Okay, but make sure you wash all the important parts." I pointed at both of them before I stepped out of the room.

In the kitchen, I prepped the batter and began frying the bacon. I poured myself another cup of coffee while I cooked. I loved making pancakes and bacon as much as the boys enjoyed eating them. Did Sammie and the girls like breakfast? I would find out soon enough. While I was thinking about it, I pulled out a pad and wrote a list of grocery items to take to the cabin. I didn't want to ask Sammie because she would say she could handle it, but I wanted to help. Grocery shopping on crutches was no picnic.

Besides, I ate a hell of a lot more than they all did. I'd buy the stuff for pancakes, eggs, and some boxes of cereal. I would buy a variety of lunch meats, peanut butter, jelly, and bread in case we ate lunch at home. I stopped my list to flip the bacon. For dinner, I'd get hamburgers, hot dogs, steaks, and chicken with some sides of chips and veggies. No sodas, we were drinking water all the way. Oh, and I'd get the trimmings for s'mores. If they didn't have a fire pit outside, we could heat the marshmallows in the indoor fireplace.

I slid the extra-crispy bacon onto a plate and poured the batter onto the hot griddle. The kitchen smelled like Sunday mornings. The boys would be down soon. Four pancakes fit perfectly at a time, and by the time they wandered in, I'd already stacked eight high — golden, fluffy, and ready for syrup.

"We're here." Cody announced.

Holden sniffed the air. "Man, that bacon smells good."

I put a piece in my mouth. "It tastes good too. Cody, can you set the table, please?" I wanted them to be helpful, not to grow up expecting to be served. "Holden, come get the plate of bacon and the stack of pancakes."

The boys did an excellent job of setting the table. Everything we needed was at our fingertips. Pancakes, bacon, syrup, plates, silverware, napkins, and glasses filled with orange juice. "Dig in."

"Thanks, Chief Reyes. You make the best pancakes." Holden said as he made a four-stack on his plate with several slices of bacon.

"You're welcome." I waited until they had served themselves before I created my four-stack with bacon. "What time did you guys go to sleep?"

"We got to talking about our upcoming vacation and got to bed late." Cody replied through a mouthful of food.

"Oh, yeah." I cut a piece of the pancake. "What do you boys want to do?"

"Mom's been there before. She said there were lots of cool hiking trails. I want to do them all." Holden spoke first.

"I checked online and saw that. I'm looking forward to hiking. How long do you guys usually hike?" This was the perfect time to gather intel on Sammie and the girls.

"We usually don't go farther than three miles, because Hollie starts to complain. She's not a big outdoorsy girl." Holden smirked.

"Yeah, I kinda got that." I smiled.

"Hollie is definitely more girly girl than Hallie." Cody took a sip of juice.

"There's nothing wrong with that. I'm sure we can accommodate everyone on this trip." I nodded.

"Mom said she and my dad found a really cool waterfall the last time they were there. I want to find it, but I don't want to think about him when I'm there." Holden took another bite.

Agreed. I don't want to think about Lincoln either while we're there. "I can't wait to find it." I mumbled. "You know your mom—" I pointed my fork at Holden. "Might not be able to hike."

"Darn." Holden's shoulders drooped. "I forgot about her crutches."

"Don't worry," I grinned. "I'll figure something out."

"We're bringing our fishing poles, right, Dad?"

"Yup, especially since I promised Hallie I'd take her fishing with us." I said as I forked the last two pancakes.

"I bet Hallie will catch something." Holden finished his last bite. "She's so smart and good at just about everything she tries."

"You boys are both pretty darn smart and good too. But who knows, she might have beginner's luck."

"Thanks, Dad." Cody smiled at me and then grinned at Holden. "But Holden's right. Hallie is a natural at so many things."

Was that a crush I was sensing coming from my son? Aw, hell. I continued to listen to their conversation as they finished eating and we cleaned up the dishes.

"We still have about thirty minutes before we have to leave. I'll be in my office. Meet me at the front door. Oh, and figure out what board games you want to take to the cabin."

"Yes, sir," the boys saluted me, pretending to salute a soldier of higher rank.

"Smartypants, both of you!" I shouted at their backs as they ran laughing all the way back to Cody's room.

Chapter 23

We All Scream for Ice Cream

Sammie

My nerves were on edge. I wanted to see Alex, but I didn't want to see Alex. I loved him, but needed to keep my feelings to myself. Although he had kissed me yesterday, not the other way around.

The girls buckled in, and we headed to Yummy Scoops.

"It's so nice of Chief Reyes to buy us ice cream. Don't you think, Mommy?" Hollie asked.

"Yes, it is."

"He's so nice and cute, right, Mommy?" Hollie continued.

"Stop," Hallie whispered

I looked in the rearview mirror and caught Hallie elbowing Hollie. "Don't be so obvious."

Were they matchmaking? What the hell? I ignored them and pretended I hadn't heard them loud and clear. I cranked up the radio and glanced back at them as they giggled, conspiring against me in the back seat. *Crap.*

I sang along, hoping they'd sing with me instead of resuming their argument. We arrived after a few songs, and the boys were already outside the front door, eagerly awaiting our arrival.

"He's so dreamy." Hallie whispered.

I parked and swung my head around to my girls. "Chief Reyes?"

"Yes, isn't he cute?" Hollie bobbed her head.

"My friend," I pronounced the word slowly, "Chief Reyes?"

"Yep, Hollie thinks he's cute." Hallie smiled at Hollie.

"Well, you think Cody is cute." Hollie stuck her tongue out at Hallie.

"Hallie, that's who you thought was dreamy?" I grinned at her. *Not sure if a crush on Cody was better than a crush on Alex.*

"Holls, you said you wouldn't tell anyone." Hallie's eyes were as big as saucers.

"It's just Mom. She won't tell." Hollie unbuckled and scooted to the edge of her seat. "Right, Mommy."

Shit. This day was just fucking full of revelations. I ran my fingers along my lips like a zipper and threw away the key. "Your secret is safe with me."

Hallie wasn't buying it, but Hollie smiled and got out of the car.

"Okay, ladies, let's go."

"Hi, Chief Reyes," Hollie skipped to Alex.

"Hey, Hollie, are you ready for some ice cream?" He crouched down and hugged her.

"Yes, please."

I saw Hallie watching Cody as I got closer, but he was completely unaware, carefree and oblivious, like a young boy.

"Hey." Alex pointed at the crutches. "How's it going?"

"Hey, better but I'm ready to be rid of them." I smiled and followed the kids.

"I bet." Alex held the door open, and we all went to the ordering counter.

Hollie went first. "I want a strawberry sundae with strawberry sauce and whipped cream?"

My phone rang. Pulling it out of my back pocket, the caller ID flashed Lincoln.

"I gotta take this." I lifted the phone. "You guys order."

"What do you want?" Alex glanced at my phone, but I turned it around so he wouldn't notice it was Lincoln. I didn't need to start an argument in front of the kids.

"Uh...one scoop of Cookies and Cream in a cup." That would be easy enough to eat.

"Okay." He pointed to my ringing phone. "You gonna answer that? Have a seat and I'll bring it to you."

Shit. I swiped and said, "Hey, what's up."

"I want to see my kids today."

"Give me a minute." I told Lincoln.

"Where are you?"

I muted my phone. "Thanks, Alex. I'm gonna take this call outside." I pushed the door open and sat at the closest table.

"You just saw them yesterday. Today is not a good day."

"Tomorrow."

"Not this week. I need to keep the kids on a regulated schedule since school starts in a couple of weeks."

"Next weekend. Friday or Saturday are not school nights."

"I already told you we're going out of town."

"Did Hollie talk to you? I can meet you guys at the cabin. Spend some quality time with them."

"No, that's my time with them." He didn't need to know that Alex was also going.

"I'm trying, Sammie."

"I know." I closed my eyes and squeezed the bridge of my nose. "Give me a couple of weeks and we'll set something up." Alex sat my ice cream in front of me.

"Hey." Alex squatted next to me. "Are you okay?"

"Who the fuck is that? Dammit, Sammie. Don't be a bitch!" He screamed loud enough for Alex to hear.

With a swift movement, Alex snatched the phone with his right hand while his left held me back.

I reached for it, but he stood up, towering over me. The effort was pointless.

"Listen asshole. Don't talk to her like that."

"Who the fuck are you?"

"The man who's gonna clean up your mouth if you talk like that to her again."

"Alex, give me the phone, please." I looked around and was glad the kids were sitting inside instead of with us, where they could hear me.

"Alex, as in Alejandro, her best friend's husband. What, are you fucking her, cheating on your wife?"

"Listen, you little fucker, you leave my wife out of this. Sammie is my friend. She's trying to be nice to you, but if you keep this up, I'll file a restraining order for her."

"Alex, stop." I reached for the phone again.

"How the hell are you gonna do that?"

"I'm the fucking police chief on Haven Island, that's how." Alex growled into the phone.

"Shit, I bet the press would love to hear about the chief's extramarital affairs," Lincoln laughed.

Alex pulled the phone away from his ear and held it out to me while he pointed at it. "Stop talking to this fucker. He is not allowed to see you or the kids."

I grabbed the phone out of his hand and hit mute. "We've had this conversation before. You do not tell me what to do. Now, let me handle this. He's my kid's father, and they have the right to meet him whether I like it or not. Go inside." I growled at him and pointed behind me.

"No."

"Alex, I swear to God, do not let my kids and everyone here see me slap your caveman face." I was trembling with rage. I could feel my face heating with anger the more he defied me.

Placing his hands on his hips, he looked around and took several deep breaths. "Sammie."

"Don't Sammie, me. Please let me handle this." I glared at him.

"Fine." He threw his arms up in the air. "But if you need me, wave me over."

"Fine."

I waited until he went inside and the door shut before I hit unmute.

"I'm back."

"About damn time. I can't believe you're fucking around on your best friend."

"I'm not. Annie died six years ago, asshole. Something you would have known if you'd stuck around. And not that it's any of your business, but Alex and I are friends. I'll call you after school starts and set up a playdate. Stop calling me."

I removed the phone from my ear. Faintly, I could hear the whiny tone of his voice. Flexing my fingers into a fist, I released my index finger and slammed it against the hang-up button over and over again. *Ugh, he was such a jackass!* I placed my phone on silent. It could go to voicemail for all I cared.

For over nine years he neglected his kids, and now I had to jump through hoops to accommodate him. *Fuck no!* He could wait another few weeks.

To avoid ruining the outing, I faced the bustling street and took several deep breaths. I didn't want my kids to see the tears brimming in my eyes. I ate a couple of spoonfuls of my ice cream. The sweet, cold ice cream always soothed my troubles away. I motioned for Alex to come, not wanting to deal with the mess of ice cream dripping all over my crutches. The kids followed Alex to my table. My smile didn't reach my eyes, but I hoped it was enough not to ruin their outing.

Before Alex sat, he whispered, "Sorry" in my ear. I grunted.

"Mommy, your ice cream melted." Hallie pointed with her spoon. "Who was on the phone? You looked mad."

"Uh, it was a customer wanting to return something. They were upset the store was closed and were yelling at me." I stared at my ice cream and said, "I guess I should've gotten a milkshake, huh?"

"What happened at the store?" Holden frowned.

"I'm sure Chief Reyes will get one for you." Hollie winked at her. "Right, Chief."

"Of course." Alex cleared his throat and grabbed her cup. "Do you want one?"

"No." I pulled my cup out of his hand. "I'm good. This is fine."

"Mom." Holden waved his hand in front of my face. "What's wrong with the store?"

Shit, I had totally forgotten to tell them. "Someone broke the front entrance glass door. We had to board it up until the new door comes in. So we're closed until then."

"That's why you're off today?" Hallie inquired.

"Yes." I looked around, and everyone was done. Tilting my cup, I drank the rest of my ice cream. "Time to go. We have some cleaning to do."

"Awe, Mom," Holden whined. "Cleaning today?"

"Yep. We need to leave the house clean before we head out-of-town." Really, we still had Monday, Tuesday, and Wednesday, but I needed to get away from Alex and men in general. For my sanity.

"We should get going too, Cody." Alex stood. "I work Monday through Wednesday, so if there's anything we need for this trip, we need to go shopping today."

"Can we go shopping with Chief Reyes and Cody?" Hollie begged. "I love shopping, and you're on crutches, so it's hard for you to carry stuff. I'm sure Chief Reyes would carry your stuff." Hollie looked at Alex. "Right, Chief?"

"Of course." Alex grinned.

Oh, brother, now Alex knew Hollie was trying to put us together. Way to go, Holls.

"Not today." I shook my head. "Let's go."

We followed the kids to my car. Alex grabbed a fistful of the back of my shirt, tightening it close to my breasts, and pulled me to his chest.

I stumbled back. He wrapped his left arm around my waist. "What are you doing?" I mumbled.

"Apparently, making another bad decision."

"What?" My head turned to face him. My world narrowed to the intensity of his stare. My throat tightened. I looked down and saw my nipples respond to his gaze. Hardening, begging for his mouth. I cleared my throat. "Let go."

Alex immediately released my shirt. "I'm sorry about earlier, Sammie. I just hated him talking to you like that."

Thank God the kids weren't paying any attention to us. They were too busy talking about whatever kids their age talk about when they don't want their playdate to end.

"Let's just keep our distance until the trip. I seem to bring out the asshole in you."

"No, you don't. I don't need any help in bringing that guy out. I am an asshole."

I shook my head and unlocked the car. "Bye Cody, we'll see you Thursday morning, bright and early."

"Bye, Miss Sammie." Cody waved back.

"Please don't go shopping on crutches. Send me a list and I'll pick everything up."

"You don't have to. I can take my mom and the kids."

"Did you pay for the cabin already?"

"Yes," I frowned. "Why?"

"Then I'll pay for the food. Please?"

"Okay, fine."

Alex helped me get in the car and handed my crutches to Holden.

"Thanks," I grumbled.

"Help your mom when she gets home." Alex nodded to Holden.

"Yes, sir." Holden nodded back, and Alex shut the door

Alex and Cody stood in the same spot waving to us until we left the parking lot.

Chapter 24

Road Trip

Alejandro

I hadn't taken a real vacation with Cody since Annie died. We'd done a few short fishing trips, three days at most, but I never let myself stay away from work too long. The guys at the station were glad I was finally taking a full week off. Lucian promised they had everything under control — and that he'd keep me posted if anything came up.

Cody was still asleep when I picked him up from his bed and sat him in the back seat. He mumbled, "Dad, I could've walked." Then, he curled up with his pillow after I shut the door.

Fuck. Three-fucking-thirty. Too damn early for anyone to be up — except Sammie. She'd wanted to be on the road by four, and I wasn't about to let her down. Pulling into her driveway, I cut the lights the moment the tires crunched over gravel. No sense waking her parents — I didn't want my headlights blazing through their bedroom window.

"Are we there?" Cody mumbled.

"No, buddy. We're picking up the Rogers. I'll get them. You can keep sleeping." I locked the door behind me and texted Sammie.

Alex: We're here. Need help?

Sammie: We'll be out in a minute.

I stayed on the front porch but kept looking around. I didn't like leaving my child unattended in the car, even with the doors locked. I was a cop. I saw crazy shit happen every day. The front door opened, and Eleanor stood in her robe.

"Morning, Alejandro."

"Did I wake you?"

"No, honey. William and I got up early to help Sammie. We'll go back to bed after you guys leave, no worries."

"Can you watch Cody? He's in the car sleeping." I pointed behind me.

"Of course. I'll stay out here. Sammie's in the kitchen."

Sammie struggled to put the food on the counter in a cooler.

"Hey, Sammie." I grabbed the small bowl of fruit. "I bought all the food on the list. What's all this?" I asked.

"The kids' last-minute requests. Don't worry, Dad went to the store for me."

"Got it. I'll finish packing this stuff. You go get the kids."

"Okay, thanks."

"Mornin' Alex," William stepped inside with four water bottles. "You want some coffee."

"No, I brought some." I zipped up the cooler. "Are those the kids' water bottles?"

"Yeah, they keep them by their beds at night." William was unscrewing the tops.

"I can do that while you help Sammie put all the stuff they need by the front door. When I'm done, I'll carry it out to the car."

"Sounds good. Have you seen Ellie?"

"She's on the porch keeping an eye out for Cody, who's zonked out in the car."

"Gotcha," he smiled and left while I filled up the water bottles and carried them and the cooler to the front door.

Three suitcases, three backpacks, and several bags sat by the front door. I rearranged Cody and my stuff and started with their larger suitcases. Everything was in the trunk by the time Sammie came out with three sleepy children.

"Hey, Cody." I nudged him awake. "Move to the third row so the girls can sit here."

He grabbed his pillow and moved before Holden followed him to the back. The girls got comfortable in the middle row.

"Mom, Dad, thanks for your help this morning." Sammie pulled them each into a quick hug, gratitude softening her voice.

"Call or text us when you arrive. Drive safely." Mom stood next to Dad.

"And stay off that foot. You're not fully healed yet," Dad scolded.

"I will." Sammie sighed and opened her door.

I helped Sammie into the car. "I'll text you when we get there."

"Keep her off that leg, son." William slapped my back.

"I will, sir." I hugged Eleanor, then put Sammie's crutches in the back so she would have more leg room.

"Look—" I pointed to the clock on the dashboard. "4:00 am on the dot."

"Thanks for being here this early." Sammie belted herself in.

"No problem. I'm always up early." I backed out of the driveway. Sammie waved to her parents. "If you want to sleep, go ahead. I'm not tired, and I don't need you to talk to me to stay awake."

"Are you sure?"

"Yep."

"My hero." Sammie bunched up a sweater like a pillow, twisted her body in the seat, and leaned her head against the window. She was out like a light before I got off the island heading north.

I played some country-western music at a low volume. The longer everyone slept, the less I would hear, 'Are we there yet?' I'd never taken Annie or any other woman to a cabin in the woods. After sleeping on the ground in the military, I could sleep anywhere. When I asked Annie about a cabin or tent in the woods, she preferred cities, not the mountains. Clearly, Sammie was different in that respect if she had spent time here with her ex.

The thought of her ex bothered me more than I cared to admit, even though Sammie hadn't been with him in a long-ass time. Hell, I hadn't seen Sammie date anyone since she moved back home. The thought of becoming friends with benefits with Sammie crossed my mind, but I wanted more than a booty call. I could have scratched that itch anytime during the last six years of my celibacy, but no one had captivated me enough to break it—except Sammie.

Some nights, I'd taken the edge off on my own, but it never came close to imagining Sammie's hands gliding up and down my body. My gaze drifted to her hands resting in her lap, slender and still. The thought of what they could do sent a pulse through me I couldn't ignore.

My dick hardened, ready for action. *Fuck.* I adjusted myself and stopped looking at Sammie. The fantasy needed to stop. I still had six hours until we reached the cabin. And I still couldn't touch her like that with the kids around, for fuck's sake. I counted backwards from one hundred to get my libido under control, but every time she moaned in her sleep, I imagined her on her knees, flat on her back, or over me. I lost count and had to start back at one hundred.

Counting wasn't working. I changed from music to a sports podcast. The interview between the host and a popular football player was interesting enough to distract me. With the season starting soon, everyone was making all sorts of bets and sending prayers to their favorite teams to get to the playoffs several months away.

I was so engrossed in the stats discussion that I jumped when Sammie placed her hand on my thigh.

"Sorry," Sammie chuckled. "The kids need to use the restroom, and they're hungry."

The clock showed 9:05 am, the perfect time to stop and eat breakfast. We were only a couple of hours away.

"Kids, do you want a restaurant or fast food for breakfast?"

"Can we stop at a restaurant so we can stretch our legs?" Sammie yawned and gripped my thigh.

I would've told her to stop, but damn her hand felt good.

"Uh, yeah., I'll look at the next exit and see what they have." I moved into the middle lane and kept watching for signs. Sammie never moved her hand from my thigh until I shifted in my seat to accommodate my growing bulge.

"Sorry," she murmured and removed her hand.

"No problem." *I wanted to tell her to put it back. Hell, move it over a few more inches and relieve my pain. Fuck.*

Sammie pointed to the exit. "This exit has a restaurant that serves breakfast and lunch."

"And a cool gift shop!" Hollie hollered behind me. "I love to walk around and see all the stuff they have."

"This one it is." I took the exit and parked the car. I needed gas, but I would get it after we ate. We passed lots of gas stations before going north again.

The kids got out of the car and stretched. I got Sammie's crutches and brought them to her before we entered the restaurant. We lucked out and were seated immediately.

"Mommy, I need to use the restroom," Hollie said as soon as we sat.

"I'll take the girls." Sammie stood waiting for them.

"What do you ladies want to drink?" I asked before they left.

"Orange juice, please," Hallie answered.

"Apple juice, please," Hollie added.

"Coffee and water, for me." Sammie followed them.

"Can I take your drink orders, or do you want me to wait until your wife comes back?" The waitress asked.

The boys laughed and elbowed each other. I ignored them. "I have their drink orders. Boys, tell the lady what you want."

They both ordered orange juice.

"Make that three glasses of OJ, one of apple juice, two regular coffees and a glass of water for everyone."

"Sounds good. I'll be back with your drinks."

"Boys, when they come back, do you need to use the restroom?" I asked while they scanned the menu.

"I could go." Cody shrugged.

"Me too," Holden agreed.

"Okay."

A few minutes later, the waitress arrived with our drinks. Sammie and the girls waited until she placed them on the table before they sat.

"Are you guys ready to order?"

I looked at Sammie. I had already picked out my meal, but she and the girls had just gotten back.

"We're ready. We always get the same thing." Hallie pointed to the menu.

Everyone ordered after Hallie. When the waitress left, Holden spoke up.

"Mom, that waitress thinks you guys are married."

"What do you mean?" Sammie frowned.

"It was nothing." I stood before Sammie panicked. I already saw the red stain growing on her cheeks. "She just assumed we were married since there are two adults and four kids. Boys, let's go use the restroom and wash our hands."

Hallie and Hollie were giving each other the side-eye and smiling. My suspicions were correct. They were doing some matchmaking. *Go to it, girls! I needed all the help I could get. I'm rusty.*

The boys and I finished in the bathroom and returned to our table as our delicious food was being delivered. *Damn, they were quick today.* The conversation was light as we all talked about what we wanted to do as soon as we got to the cabin. Sammie had requested an early check-in so we could get lunch, drop off all our belongings and go explore.

Chapter 25

The Cabin

Sammie

Alex turned off the main road and drove under a metal awning with the name "Rustic Adventures." It looked like the type of awning you'd see at a wedding, except this one was wider than the one under which a couple would say their vows. The cabins nestled into the surrounding mountains. The wooden, log, and stone structure seemed to melt into the landscape seamlessly.

"Look for cabin number three." I told everyone. "The owner texted me and said it's ready."

"There it is!" Hallie shouted. "It's the one by the creek. Did you bring the fishing rods, Chief Reyes?"

My kids had been half asleep when they got in the car, so they did not know how much Alex stuffed into the overflowing trunk. I saw it only at a glance and wondered how the hell he got it all to fit.

"I sure did, Hallie." Alex chuckled.

Alex pulled up to Cabin 3 and parked on the gravel driveway leading up to the side of the cabin.

Wow, the cozy log cabin was even cuter than it looked online. Two weathered rocking chairs sat on the left side of the porch in front of the window, and a hammock hung to the right of the door. In the distance, I could see the other five cabins, each spaced far enough apart to give plenty of room — and privacy — to roam.

"This place is so cute, Mommy," Hollie screeched.

"Okay, let me put in the code, and then we are all helping Alex bring in our stuff." I didn't want Alex to have to lug all our supplies by himself. Although I didn't know how much help I would be.

"The kids can help me. You go in and check it all out. Oh, and text me the code to the front door, when you get a chance," Alex asked before he got out.

I texted him the code while he got my crutches.

"Thanks," he smiled as he stood by the door holding them for me.

"Thank you." I smiled back.

Alex beat me to the front door and opened it for all of us to enter. The kids were oohing and aahing at the rustic décor.

"Mummy, I love that it's a real log cabin!" Hallie's voice expressed the thrill of discovering something new.

"Let's go find our room." Holden tapped Cody.

"There should be two full beds for you guys to share." I hollered as the kids ran upstairs into the attic.

Alex took my crutches and leaned them against the couch.

"What are you doing? I need those."

"Not right now, you don't." Alex put his arm under my knees and picked me up. "Going up will be quicker this way."

"Alex, I weigh too much."

"Yeah, right," Alex snorted. "Put your arms around my neck and enjoy the ride."

As if I weighed nothing, he climbed the stairs two at a time, while I wrapped my arms around his neck. He wasn't even panting when we reached the top. The boys picked the bed to the right of the window, leaving the one on the left along the wall to the girls.

"Did you boys let the girls pick first?" Alex set me down, but held me against him.

"Yes, sir." Holden nodded.

"Of course, Dad." Cody rolled his eyes.

"Are you boys going to be okay sharing?" I asked, knowing that boys usually wanted their space more than girls.

"We'll be fine, Mom." Holden smiled.

"Yes, Miss Sammie. We already agreed to sleep with our heads on opposite sides of the bed, like this." The boys maneuvered their bodies so Holden's feet were at Cody's head.

"Okay, just don't kick each other in the middle of the night." I warned.

"Nah, we're good. We've slept like this before at Mr. Roberto's house."

Well, that was true. I distinctly remember the full bed in Alex's childhood bedroom where we necked like high school kids. I felt the heat burning my face and turned away. Right into Alex's chest.

"Sorry." I mumbled and leaned back.

"No problem." Alex squeezed my waist.

I glanced up and saw the heat in his eyes. He remembered the same thing.

Alex cleared his throat, breaking our trance, and grumbled. "Let's unpack the car."

"Good idea." Alex picked me up again, climbed down, and set me on the couch. "Stay put. We've got this."

"Don't worry, Mom," Holden said on his way out. "We'll help Chief Reyes."

I was of no help, but the five of them carried everything into the living room in less than ten minutes. They left it all there while they emptied the trunk.

"Girls," Alex said, pulling the front door closed. "I'll take your suitcases upstairs."

"I'll take their suitcases up, Dad," Cody blurted and grabbed Hallie's suitcase.

"And I'll help," Holden said, taking Hollie's suitcase.

"Girls," I suggested from the couch. "Take their backpacks up with yours since they carried your suitcases. Then come back down and help me empty the coolers."

"Okay," Hallie and Hollie both said.

"I'll help them after I put your stuff in the bedroom." Alex stated.

I hated these fucking crutches. I knew they were all trying to help, but their efforts made me feel utterly helpless. And I was not helpless. I grabbed the crutches while Alex was in the bedroom and hobbled to the cooler. With a crutch, I pushed the heavy cooler toward the kitchen an inch at a time.

"What the hell are you doing?"

I turned to see Alex standing outside the bedroom door with his arms crossed.

"What does it look like I'm doing?"

"Trying to hurt yourself."

"No, I'm trying to be useful."

Alex took a deep breath. "Okay, I get it. You want to help. I'll move the cooler." Alex picked it up and set it in front of the fridge. "You can sit on the stool and tell me where to put things."

"Oh, I'll tell you where you can put things." I snickered.

"Funny." Alex glared, but I could see his smile trying to break through.

"We can help too." Hollie and Hallie opened the cooler and began taking out the refrigerated items.

"We can help with the other groceries, Dad." Cody and Holden stood behind me.

"It's a little cramped in here. I'll put stuff in the cabinets, but can you check and see if the back porch has a roof? If it does, put all the fishing stuff out there."

"Got it." Holden followed Cody out the back.

The back must have a roof because the boys took all the rods and tackle boxes out back. Then Alex took the coolers outside and dumped the water and ice.

"Now that we're done, I think we should walk around outside and scope out our surroundings." Alex pointed toward the back deck. "Sammie, you can sit while we scope out the river for fish."

"As if," she scoffed.

"What?" Alex frowned at me.

"Nothing. Just talking to myself."

We stepped out and saw the creek running past our cabin.

"Dad," Cody spoke up. "This would be a great place to go fishing."

"I agree. Let's go down and see if there are any fish biting."

The uneven stone steps, topped with wooden planks, had a single railing. Alex stood at the bottom of the steps and helped the girls down. After all the kids were down, I hobbled to the steps wondering how the hell I was getting down. A ramp would've been nice, but at the time I rented the cabin, I didn't need a handicap ramp. Alex didn't even blink. He swooped me up and carried me to the river.

"Is this going to become a habit on this trip?" I grumbled.

"Yep."

The kids were already kneeling by the creek with their hands in the water.

"The water is colder than back home," Hallie said and pulled her hand back.

"Duh," Holden chuckled and lightly shoved her. "Don't fall in."

"Holden, stop." Cody reached out to Hallie.

"That's not nice," Hollie glared at her brother.

"Holden!" I screamed.

"Boys," Alex growled. "Come with me for a minute."

Alex set me down on the grass and walked with the boys in tow out of earshot. I couldn't hear what he was saying, but it was clear from the look on his face, he was setting up some ground rules. While I appreciated him speaking to them, I was Holden's mother, and that talk should've been mine.

"Girls, please step away from the creek. I need to speak to your brother." I said calmly, although my blood was boiling at Alex taking charge. *First, he hijacks my vacation, then he carries me everywhere like a damn caveman, and now he's taking charge of disciplining my child! Oh, hell no! He is not the man of my house—I am the woman of my house!* I limped and hopped over to them.

"Mom, stop!" Holden's eyes widened.

Alex spun around and ran to me. "What are you doing? You're gonna hurt yourself."

"I'm gonna hurt you in a minute." I growled at him.

"What the hell are you growling about?" Alex grunted.

"Boys, go inside with the girls. I need to speak with Chief Reyes for a minute."

The boys nodded before walking away with their heads down. Alex placed his hand against my lower back and picked me up again. Setting me down on the back bumper of his SUV.

"What's wrong?"

"Are you Holden's father?"

Alex blinked and put his hands in his pockets. "No."

"Then why did you feel the need to reprimand my son?"

"I was trying to help."

"Do not undermine my authority." I pointed at him and grunted each word slowly so he got a clue.

"I wasn't trying to." Alex stared at the ground, rocking back and forth on the balls of his feet.

"If my son"—I emphasized the words my son—"is misbehaving, it's my job to correct him, not yours."

Alex sighed and pulled one of his hands out to rub the back of his neck. "Okay. I'm sorry."

"Whatever," I huffed and stood. I hopped a couple of steps before being lifted into his arms again.

"I'm not trying to piss you off, Sammie. I won't do it again. Let's not let this ruin our vacation."

The minute his hand grazed the side of my breast adjusting his hold, my treacherous body forgave him. *Was he stroking the side of my breast on purpose or by accident with every step he took? Oh wow, whichever it was, I didn't want him to stop. He hadn't done this the last couple of times he carried me.* My body begged for him to stroke every inch of me. I wanted him. Every ounce of me was throbbing to release my sexual tension with him. *Was that why I was lashing out at him?* If my dad had been with us and he had pulled the boys aside, I would've thought nothing of it. His eyes scanned my face as I stared at him.

My breathing hitched, and his eyes went straight to my breasts. My nipples stood erect. He bit his lip and looked at me. The heat in his eyes melted me on the spot. We could not be doing this right now. The kids were within feet of us.

"Okay," I said breathlessly. "Let's go explore."

"I would love to explore the sights, sounds, smells, and tastes of new territory with you," he croaked.

Oh, crap. If my body hadn't been ready for him before, it definitely was now. He gave me that devilish smile, the kind that promised trouble, and adjusted his hold on me. The lightest brush of his hand as it grazed my nipple sent a shiver racing through me. A soft sound escaped my throat before I could stop it. That man was pure temptation, and I loved it.

Chapter 26

Exploring

Alejandro

I wanted to throw Sammie onto the bed and fuck her senseless. But our kids were here, and I had to act like a responsible adult. I needed a few minutes to let the bulge in my pants go down, so I set Sammie down on the porch and handed her the crutches. I followed her inside and then bent over to rummage through my hiking pack. Damn, Sammie was hot even when she was glaring at me. If she were mine, I would've put the kids up in their room and fucked her until she became the sweet Sammie everyone knew and loved.

But she wasn't mine, and that wasn't an option—yet. Instead, I would distract her from being angry at me with a short hike around the grounds. I would've carried her, but she insisted on using the crutches. We met some of the other renters. Some had kids around our kids' age, which was great, but others were there for the peacefulness of nature. After walking around all the cabins so I could get a lay of the land and the kids could explore, we headed back to our cabin.

"Mommy," Hollie tugged on Sammie's hand. "I'm hungry."

I checked my watch — almost four. The kids hadn't eaten lunch. They'd been so caught up exploring that it probably hadn't even occurred to them to stop for food.

"There's a grill on the back deck." I looked at Sammie. "How about I grill us some burgers and hot dogs?"

"That sounds yummy, thanks, Chief Reyes."

"No problem, Hollie. I'll get everything started."

"I'll help." Sammie looked at the kids. "Why don't you all start taking your showers?"

"You girls go first," Holden pointed at Hollie and Hallie. "Let us know when you're done."

"Yeah, we'll help you, Dad," Cody offered. "So Miss Sammie can relax."

"Thanks, Cody," Sammie hugged him.

Well shit. If he'd said that, he would've gotten glared at, but since it was Cody, he got a hug. Women.

The girls ran upstairs. I turned to Sammie. "Why don't you go shower and relax? The boys and I got this."

"Are you sure?" Sammie hesitated and looked at us.

"Yeah, Dad and I grill all the time." Cody smiled.

"And I'd rather hang out with them,"—Holden pointed at Cody and me—"than wait for the shower."

"Okay," Sammie nodded. "I'll be quick."

"Do you want a bath or need any help?" I grinned.

"I think I got it, but thanks." Sammie's face turned red before she spun away.

"Take your time. We've got this." I turned to the fridge and grabbed the ground beef and hot dogs. "Boys, find some plates for me."

I seasoned the patties while the boys found the plates and tongs. Cody was right. We hated washing pots and pans, so we grilled at least three to four times a week. *Dammit, I was so distracted by Sammie that I forgot to ask the girls what they wanted and how much of it.*

"Boys, I'll be right back. Set the table and find some sides."

If I hurried, I could reach Sammie before she took off her clothes and entered the shower. I knocked on the bedroom door, but she didn't answer. Slowly, I turned the knob, the metal cool beneath my fingers, certain she was in the bathroom with the door closed, since she hadn't heard my knock.

I didn't see her as I stepped inside and looked toward the bathroom door. It was wide open, like my mouth. *Fuck me!* My foot was smart enough to kick the bedroom door shut, but the rest of my body froze as I watched her disrobe in the bathroom.

She was beautiful. Full breasts, a thin waist, and sexy wide hips with a luscious ass. Holy hell. "Sammie," I whispered because I couldn't get my voice to work any louder. The only part of my body working as I scanned her body was the bulge tenting my shorts, ready to seek her fucking beautiful haven.

Sammie twisted around when the door shut. She tried to cover her front with her shirt, but it only caused her breasts to plump, baring a part of her pink areola. She was every man's wet dream standing before me.

My body craved her, an undeniable hunger pulling me towards her, and only she could satisfy it. I'd never felt such an intense connection with anyone, a feeling I hadn't even experienced with my late wife. I reached out and sat her on the counter. Gently, stroked her hair, I smelled her neck before I licked it.

"Yum, strawberries."

"It's my body wash." Sammie whispered.

"It's my new favorite fruit." I moaned into her neck. *Damn, was I too old to give a hickey?*

I ran my hand down the side of her cheek to her neck and felt her pulse racing out of control, like mine. My lips met hers slowly after I lifted her chin with my hand, silently telling her she could stop if she wanted. With my gaze fixed on her, I saw her eyes flutter shut, and her soft breath caressed my lips.

I licked her smooth, sexy lips before slipping my tongue inside. She opened wide, and our tongues danced, exploring each other's tastes. *Shit, this kiss alone was going to make me lose it.* She responded by kissing me back, but her hands remained gripping her clothes. I craved her touch. Her every wish was my command, and I would do anything to please her.

I'm not sure how much time passed, lost in the moment before Cody's voice shattered the silence, calling my name. I had forgotten the boys were helping me make dinner. As I withdrew, her eyes opened, and she blinked, adjusting to the light.

"Alex," she moaned.

"I...I came in to ask you how many hamburgers and hot dogs you wanted." I whispered before rubbing my lips against hers.

"One hamburger with cheese, please." She murmured against my lips.

I gave her another soft kiss and pulled away. "Done." I backed out of the bathroom, not wanting to miss a single moment of the beautiful vision she made standing before me. "Please lock the door. Because the next time I come in here, I will push you up against the shower wall and fuck you until neither one of us can stand."

Her body jolted, and she crossed her legs. *Fuck!* I gazed down at her thighs and saw her clench them. That was where I craved to be, not heading out to cook.

"Sammie, please," I muttered. "Lock the door."

Sammie moaned and shut the door. I waited until I heard the lock before I rearranged myself in my pants and left the bedroom.

"What took you so long?" Cody said.

He and Holden were in the kitchen. They had already set the table, and formed the burgers into patties ready to be grilled.

"Sorry, Miss Sammie was in the shower and couldn't hear me."

"I didn't hear you screaming?" Cody frowned.

"Did she tell you?" Holden walked out of the kitchen and stood before me. "Because I can be really loud and ask my mom."

"Uh, that's not necessary," I smiled. "She said she wanted a burger with cheese."

"Cool."

"Let me go ask the girls." I turned to head upstairs.

"No need, I went halfway up the stairs and screamed. Hallie wants a burger, and Hollie wants a hot dog."

How the hell did I not hear Holden screaming in this small-ass cabin? I know how. Sammie's beauty had taken my breath away, leaving me speechless and completely captivated. Her naked body so fucking beautiful, I knew I would never erase it from my memory.

"Dad?" Cody waved his hand in my face. "Are you okay?"

I snapped out of it. "Uh, yeah. So, do you boys want a burger?"

"We both want a cheeseburger and a hot dog."

"So, then three hot dogs and four cheeseburgers. Got it."

"Dad?" Cody quirked his eyebrow at me. "What are you going to eat?"

"A cheeseburger and a hot dog. Why?" I mumbled.

"Then, it's four hot dogs and four cheeseburgers, right?"

"Uh, yeah, that's what I said."

"No, you said three dogs and four burgers."

"Cody's right. That's what you said, Chief Reyes." Holden nodded.

"Oh, sorry. Thanks." I turned away and wrapped the extra burgers before putting them in the fridge. I could cook up the rest tomorrow.

The boys loaded up a plate with hot dogs and another with burgers, and we headed outside. The grill was a gas grill, so I turned it on, placed the food on the cooking surface, and shut the lid.

"Dad, don't you want to heat it up first, like we do at home?"

"You're right, sorry."

"Are you okay, Dad?"

"Yeah. Why?"

"Cause you're acting weird."

"Sorry," I smiled. "I'm good." *Damn, I needed a drink, and I'd forgotten to bring the hardcore stuff.*

I gave the boys a bottle of water when I grabbed a beer for myself as we sat on the back deck until the girls finished with their showers. No fucking way was I going to check on Sammie again. The girls came out first.

"We're done." Hollie opened the sliding glass door.

"Your turn." Hallie sat in the back deck chair and handed Hollie a bottle of water.

I went to the grill and flipped the burgers, rolling the hot dogs again. Cody and I liked our hot dogs to have grill marks on every side. Silly. But if I was grilling, then I wanted it our way.

Chapter 27

When Did His Feelings Change?

Sammie

I took a cold shower to calm my nerves. Alex was definitely flirting with me. I wasn't sure what had caused the sudden change, but I was on board. The girls were in the kitchen getting all the sides. I didn't see the boys and assumed they were showering.

"Let's leave the sides on the island. That table is way too small for all of us and the food." I told them.

"Okay, Mommy," Hallie smiled.

"Girls!" Alex hollered from outside. "Can you bring me two clean plates so I can get the food off the grill?"

"You girls are doing such a good job in here. I'll take the plates to Alex." I tucked the plates under one arm and limped on one crutch to Alex.

"Okay, Mommy," Hollie beamed.

"Here," I tapped Alex on the shoulder with the plates.

Alex's body jerked. I held the plates up, but he leaned down, his face almost to my head.

"Are you smelling my hair?" Sammie chuckled.

"No." He jolted upright. "You're a foot smaller than me. I was getting the plates." *Riiight. I clearly heard him sniff, but I'd let him off the hook.*

"Girls!" Alex hollered, and I jumped. "Sorry." He mumbled to me before Hallie ran outside.

"Yes, Chief Reyes?"

"Can you take this tray of hot dogs inside so your mom can sit?"

"Yes, sir." Hallie grabbed the tray and headed inside.

"What can I do?" Hollie pouted.

Alex plopped the burgers onto the other plate and gave it to her. "Can you add cheese to these?"

"Yes, sir." Hollie grabbed the plate and went inside.

"I'm gonna go in and help them." Sammie followed.

"Hallie," I leaned on a chair while I counted seats. "Go ask Chief Reyes for two more chairs from outside."

Alex set them down while Hollie moved chairs around. It was a snug fit, but it worked.

"Thanks for the chairs." Hollie pointed toward the kitchen. "We moved the food to the island because that table wasn't made for six."

Sammie grabbed the plate off the table. "Everyone needs to make their own plate before they sit."

"You know you can call me Alex in front of your kids, right?" He smirked at me. "We are on vacation."

"Okay."

"I got yours." Alex grabbed my plate. "Have a seat." The girls helped Alex load my plate.

"Hey, just in time!" Holden shouted, and the boys got their plates.

"What are we doing tomorrow, Mommy?" Hollie asked.

"Fishing?" Hallie looked at Alex, but he pointed at me. *Smart Man. Now he was getting it.*

"We can either go tour that historic house and visit the little towns for shopping–" the boys groaned while the girls clapped, "–or go hiking in the Pisgah National Forest." Now, all the kids were clapping. "We're gonna do both. It's just a matter of which one we do tomorrow and which one we do on Saturday.

"Can we please go hiking tomorrow?" Holden was the first to put in his request.

"Then fishing?" Hallie eyed Alex, and he chuckled.

"Sure, we'll hike tomorrow and shop on Saturday."

"Uh, can you go hiking?" Alex frowned and pointed at my crutches with his fork.

"There's a flat hike that leads to a waterfall. It's not too far."

"Okay," Alex grinned.

Why was he grinning like that? What was he up to?

"Yay!" all the kids shouted except for Hollie.

"Come on, Holls," Hallie nudged her shoulder. "It'll be fun. We'll go shopping on Saturday."

"Okay."

We talked about our hike during the meal. Everyone was eager to see the waterfall I'd found with Lincoln. That was a happier time in our lives. It was before I'd told him I was pregnant. That waterfall was amazing, and I wanted to make fresh memories with my kids.

"Alright, kids, help me clean up the dishes and then we can play a game. Hollie, you pick since they got their way for tomorrow." I stood and began gathering dishes.

"I want to play Jenga." Hollie grabbed her plate.

"Okay." I grabbed her plate. "You get the game ready and we'll finish up."

"Aw, Mom. Why doesn't she have to help with the cleanup?" Holden whined.

"I'm gonna give you all a night off while we're here. We're gonna do kid of the day, and today is her day."

"What's the kid of the day?" Alex frowned and grabbed the plates out of my hand. "Sammie, go sit on the couch and help Hollie. I'll help with the dishes."

"Ever since they were little, in order to stop fights, I started kid of the day. Whoever is kid of the day gets to pick out what we watch, where they sit in the car, and what we eat if we go through a fast-food restaurant. It's worked out great. All I have to say is 'kid of the day' and they all fall in line knowing their day is coming up." I smiled at him.

"Okay," Alex took the dishes to the sink. I limped to the kitchen. I was useful in the kitchen. Hollie didn't need my help to set up Jenga.

"So, who's the kid of the day tomorrow?" Alex inquired. "Why are you standing next to me?"

"I can lean against the counter and rinse them before you put them in the dishwasher." I smiled.

"Fine," Alex sighed. "Boys, put the dishes in the sink and then go help Hollie. Hallie, can you wipe the table, please?" Alex turned to me. "How do you decide who goes first in this kid of the day thing?"

"We go by birth order. So tomorrow will be Holden and then Hallie. I always get Sunday, and then we start all over again." I rinsed the plates and handed them to Alex as the boys brought them to me. "I could give Cody Monday, and you can have Tuesday."

"Cool!" Cody shouted and high-fived Holden.

"Won't that throw a monkey wrench into your rotation?" Alex squinted at me.

"It'll be fine. We'll figure it out."

Alex kept bumping and rubbing against me to grab the dishes. I couldn't tell if he meant to or not, but we were both getting turned on. Hallie might not know about the male anatomy, but the boys knew what was up, and I definitely felt it while I was washing dishes. Maybe I shouldn't have helped Alex with the dishes.

"Game's ready!" Hollie shouted from the living room.

"You kids go play. Alex and I will finish up." I waved them away.

"Do you want a beer?" Alex opened the fridge and grabbed one.

"Sure."

"I'll bring it to you." He said, still standing in front of the fridge. I grabbed one crutch. I set my left foot down, but kept my right one up. The right with the stitches was more tender than the left.

"Since I'm kid of the day, I go first." Hollie stated, and no one argued. *Damn, I loved 'Kid of the Day'.*

Funny enough, the kids were sitting on the floor in front of the coffee table in the correct kid of the day order. Cody, Holden, Hallie, and Hollie. I just sort of fell onto the couch, since I couldn't exactly be graceful on crutches. Alex chuckled, moved my crutch out of the way and handed me my beer. I took a refreshing drink and sighed.

Every time Alex leaned forward to pull a piece out of the tower, he leaned over me to set his beer down on the end table closest to me. His arm grazed my breasts, every single time. Then he repeated the action when he grabbed his beer. As the game progressed, he sat closer to me. I kept inching over until I was squished against the armrest and couldn't move any further. With his thigh pressed up against mine, his arm grazing my breasts, and my body drenched with desire, I was about to beg him to take me right there on the couch and forget all about the kids.

Dammit, I needed water to cool down. Game night had never made me so hot and needy until I played it with Alex. Lucky for me, the game ended a half an hour later when Holden took out the piece that tumbled the entire tower. I needed to get away from Alex and get to bed.

"Okay, bedtime." I announced. "If we're going hiking, we need to get up early."

"How early?" Holden asked while they picked up the pieces.

"How about we leave here around nine?" I looked at Alex, and he nodded.

Holden grumbled, and Hollie boasted. "See if we were going shopping, we wouldn't have to get up that early. Right, Mommy?"

"You're right. The stores don't open until later. But then we'd have to get up that early the next day, so it's all good."

Chapter 28

Temptation

Sammie

"Girls, go put on your pajamas and let us know when you're done so the boys can do the same. Boys, brush your teeth while they're changing in the room. Damn, I sound like a drill sergeant." I murmured after the kids left the room.

"Uh, clearly you've never heard a drill sergeant." Alex chuckled. "If you did, you would've thrown in some cuss words along with how lazy they are."

"I guess you would know, huh?"

"Oh, yeah." Alex smiled and pointed to my beer. "You want another?"

"No. I'm good, thanks. I don't think my kids would appreciate their mom slurring her words as she read Harry Potter to them."

Alex nodded and threw the bottles in the trash. "I don't know. It could be quite entertaining, especially if you dressed like Hermione. You know a schoolgirl outfit with knee-highs and a short skirt." Alex wiggled his eyebrows.

"Perv." I rolled my eyes and Alex laughed so hard his body shook.

"Seriously though, I'm glad you chose Harry Potter. Cody loves that series. My dad and I read them to him every night. You'd think he'd be tired of them by now." Alex grabbed the game and put it away. "I'm gonna go shower, but when

I'm done, do you mind if I come up and listen? I'll even read if you want to take a break."

"Nope, come on up. Let me get my book before you go into the shower."

Alex grabbed his duffel bag and stepped into the bedroom.

"Why don't you leave that in here?" I pointed to the bag. "So you don't have to keep carrying it in and out."

"Thanks." Alex smiled. "Do you need me to help you upstairs before I shower?"

I grabbed my romance novel and ran smack into him as he headed to the bathroom. If I'd watched where I was going, I would've seen him. He reached out and grabbed me around my waist, pressing me against him. His body stiffened, and I knew he was having the same reaction to me as I was having to him.

"Sorry," I mumbled and looked up.

"No problem," he mumbled back.

We were just about to kiss when I heard Hollie's bloodcurdling scream. "Mommy!"

"What the hell!" Alex picked me up and took the stairs two at a time. He set me down on the bed and scanned the room. "What happened?" He ran to Hollie and took a knee. His hands roaming her hands and legs. "Are you okay? Are you hurt?"

"Spider! Spider!" Hollie hollered and pointed behind Alex's shoulder to the wall on the other side of Cody and Holden's bed. "Cody won't let me kill it."

Alex spun around and sighed. "I got this." He stood and watched the spider take a few steps. Then he cupped it in his hands and went downstairs.

"I'm sorry, Miss Sammie." Cody stared at the floor. "It wasn't poisonous, so I wanted to set it free."

"It's okay, Cody." I hobbled over and hugged him. "But I have to be honest, if your dad wasn't here, I would've killed it because there's no way I could have touched it."

"I understand."

Holden came running out of the bathroom with his toothbrush in his mouth. In a garbled voice, he said something that sounded like what happened.

"There was a spider this big in the room." Hollie spread her arms out as wide as a medium-sized dog.

"Don't be so dramatic, Holls." Hallie rolled her eyes. "It wasn't that big."

"It was huge!" Hollie cried and ran to me, wrapping her arms around my waist in a death grip.

"Okay, girls. Let's settle down. It's gone now." I rubbed Hollie's back.

"The spider has gone back to the wild." Alex said from the top of the stairs. "Any other critters?"

"No," Hallie stared at Hollie. "Thank you, Chief Reyes."

Hollie garbled what sounded like a thank you into my stomach.

"My pleasure, ladies." Alex pointed over his shoulder. "I'm going in the shower if you guys are good."

"We're good." I smiled at Alex. I still had my other arm draped over Cody's shoulder, so I rubbed his back as well. "Cody, your turn to brush your teeth."

Cody followed Holden into the bathroom and shut the door.

"Hollie, change before your brother comes out."

Hollie dried her eyes and grabbed her pajamas. Hallie had already finished changing and held her hygiene bag. I waited until the boys finished in the bathroom. When the girls went in, I left. I sat my bottom on the top step and booty-scooted down to the bottom so the boys could change in privacy. *No judging. It was effective, I could do it myself, and it didn't hurt my foot.*

I'd dropped my book when Alex scooped me up. *Crap.* I wasn't going in there now. I limped around to the front of the couch and saw my book sitting on the couch. Alex must have seen it and left it for me.

I lay back on the cushions on the couch and opened it, taking out my bookmark. It was the part where the guy opened the steamy shower door, naked and dripping, and invited the girl in. I heard the shower stop, so I glanced up. The bedroom door was open. Alex must have forgotten to shut it after the spider incident. *Why was I staring into the bedroom? Was I waiting for him to come out dripping wet like the guy in my book?* Ready to look away, the bathroom door swung open, and there he stood, dripping wet with a towel wrapped around his waist.

Wow, talk about abs. I followed a drop of water as it rushed down into the towel. Counting four abs on my way down and four on my way back up. Eight perfectly chiseled abs on display. He was beautiful. I'd only seen such beauty in movies or on the naked men on romance novel covers, but none of them compared to Alex. I'd known him for years, but always saw him with a shirt on. Granted, the shirt was always tight, and I could imagine how perfect he was, but shirtless, wow.

Without warning, I craved water, my throat dry. I licked my dry lips, and then I swallowed to moisten my mouth. Alex remained motionless. With every breath, I watched his abs move in a rhythmic pattern, and I couldn't tear my eyes away. I pleaded with the knot to come undone. And the knot listened as the towel expanded from his massive growing tent. His hand shot out, and his fingers grabbed the knot before the towel fell. The sheer size of the tented towel was astonishing. *Would he fit?*

Alex cleared his throat, and I glanced at his face. *Oops. Caught red-handed.* Alex smiled and whipped the towel off. My eyes bulged out of their sockets, and I raised the book to the level of the doorway, but not quickly enough to miss his beautiful anatomy standing up ready to greet me. I could feel the heat rising on my face and heard him chuckle.

That man was impossible. I tried to focus on my book, but all I saw my Alex in all his glory.

"You can look now. I'm dressed." Alex said from the bedroom doorway.

Thank goodness. I lowered my book and noticed he had on pajama pants, but no shirt.

"Can you put a shirt on?"

"You're lucky I put pants on. I usually sleep naked."

Of course, he did. "There are young ladies in the cabin, so please put on a t-shirt."

"Me thinks thou dost protest too much." Alex chuckled and slipped on the shirt he was holding.

I was so busy staring at his chest, I never noticed he was holding a shirt. *Crap. Was it hot in here?*

"Mommy!" Hollie screamed at her normal decibel. "We're ready!"

"Do you think Harry Potter is the right book to read? Isn't there a spider in that book?"

"Nah, Aragog is in the second book. The first one has 'He who should not be named' sharing that professor's body." Alex shrugged. "Not scary at all."

"Aw, crap."

"Haven't you read it before?" Alex asked me.

"We all have, but I always forget which scary scene is in which book." I sighed.

"Don't worry, the beginning isn't too scary. I'll protect you guys." Alex draped his arm around my waist and hauled me up into his arms.

"Aren't you tired of picking me up?" I grumbled.

"Never," Alex took the stairs two at a time again. *How did he do that? It must be those beautiful abs.*

"You can always read them the other book you were reading."

"What?"

"I said you can read them your book." He nodded behind him. "The one you left on the couch."

"Are you crazy? I can't read a steamy romance to them." I scoffed.

"If I lay down in the bed, will you read it to me?" Alex wiggled his eyebrows.

"Uh...no." I huffed, but was intrigued. My mind was still on reading Alex a smutty bedtime story when I noticed I was upright, the kids were in their beds, and they were all staring at me.

Alex and I sat on the floor with our backs to their beds, and I began. "Mr. and Mrs. Dursley...,"

*** Alex ***

I sat back and listened to Sammie's melodic voice. She used different voices for the men and the women. I'd read this book to Cody so many times this past year, but I can honestly say, she was doing a better job.

Sammie got to the end of the chapter, and all the kids were yawning. It had been a long day. I was ready to go to bed although I was pretty sure their beds were a hell of a lot more comfortable than mine. But I forced myself into this vacation, I was not complaining. After sitting on it earlier tonight, I was pretty damn sure that couch/futon/bed was not long enough for me.

"Okay," Sammie yawned and closed the book. "Enough for tonight."

I got up before Sammie and held out my hand to help her up. We both kissed each kid on the forehead before I picked her up and headed downstairs.

"Chief Reyes!" Holden shouted.

"Yeah, buddy?" Alex stopped and turned to face him.

"Thanks for helping Mom down so she doesn't have to scoot on her butt again."

Holden and Cody laughed. The girls giggled.

"What is he talking about?" I frowned at Sammie.

"Put me down and I'll show you," she smiled mischievously at me.

I set her down near the steps and crossed my arms, waiting to see what she was going to do. I had an idea, but wasn't positive.

"It's booty-scooting time!" Sammie yelled.

She braced her arms and scooted her butt down to the next step. Her ass was going to hurt if she did this anymore today.

"Sammie, stop," Alex cried between guffaws. "I'll help you. I don't want you to hurt yourself."

"Nonsense. I'm fine. See you in the morning, kids."

I let her enjoy her moment of glory, but I'd be damned if she was doing that every day we're here. I lowered the back of the futon couch to turn it into a bed.

"I saw an extra pillow and blanket in the closet." Sammie mentioned from the doorway.

"Thanks, I'll get it." I brushed past her.

"Are you sure you don't want the bed?" Sammie asked when I stepped out of the closet.

"Nope. I've slept in worse places." *Not for a long-ass time, old man.* "I'll be fine."

"Oh, okay."

"Get in bed. I'll check the doors and be back to turn off your light." I checked all the doors and windows before I put my hand on the light switch in her bedroom. "Are you good?"

"Yeah, I'm good."

She lay under the covers, her book propped open, the soft light catching in her hair. I watched her for a moment, longer than I should have. She looked so at peace, tucked into warmth I could only imagine. For a heartbeat, I wished I could trade places with that blanket — just to feel her against me, steady and close — but I pushed the thought away before it got the better of me.

"Night, Sammie."

"Alex...," she mumbled.

"I'm fine. See you in the morning."

I wasn't fine. I felt like a fucking pretzel, all twisted up inside, but I didn't want to tell her that. After an hour of tossing and turning, I grabbed the futon mattress and dropped it on the floor. Now I could lengthen my legs even if they draped over the futon. Hell, I'd slept on worse as a Ranger. I just needed to suck it up.

Chapter 29

Hi Ho, It's Up the Hill We Go

Sammie

O h, my God. *Whose idea was it to hike this fucking mountain? We were supposed to go to the fucking waterfall, but noooo, Alex convinced them this mountain trail wasn't steep.* I was in decent shape, but not on crutches.

"Alex!" I screamed for the third time." I'm slipping."

"Well, if you let me carry you?"

"Just go slower." I glared at him. I could do it. I just needed them to slow down. I refused to give in. He looked as angry with me as I was with him.

The kids went ahead, marveling at the towering trees, and fresh smells surrounding them. I couldn't enjoy it because I stared at the ground, finding the safe spots for my feet. I should've stayed at the bottom like Alex suggested, but my stubborn-ass said I was fine. *Stupid, stupid, stupid.* Alex stayed between us to make sure I wasn't dying on the mountain and the kids were safe. The rocks and grass were slick and glistened with the morning dew. I put my foot in the wrong place and slid.

"Ahh," I screamed. My free arm wind-milling to grab something while my crutch flew out of my hand.

Alex pivoted and ran toward me, but not before I planted my ass on the ground. Well, at least it wasn't my face. I could feel the cold seeping through my jeans.

"Dammit, Sammie. Will you listen to me now and let me carry you?" He pulled me up into his arms.

"Fine." I gritted my teeth and swiped the leaves off my butt. *How humiliating.*

"Mommy, are you okay?" Hollie ran toward me.

"Your mom is going to be okay. According to the map, we're almost at the top. I'll carry her."

"Thanks, Chief Reyes."

"How far to the top?" I mumbled.

"Half a mile." Alex grunted.

"Just set me down and get me on the way back, like you did with my crutch."

"Absolutely not."

"Alex. This will not work when we go back downhill. Too much weight in the front."

"I'm not going to carry you like this on the way down. You're gonna go piggyback." Alex stopped. "Look, it's beautiful out there."

I turned my face and saw the majestic mountains surrounding us. "That is beautiful.

"Mom, isn't this great." Holden waved behind him.

"Yes, but stay away from the edge. Alex, put me down so I can take a photo of them with the mountains behind them."

"I'll take it." Alex whipped out his phone. "Guys, face me. I'm gonna take a photo."

When the photos were done, Alex picked me up again, and Hollie snapped a photo with my phone. "I thought I was going piggyback?"

"You are, but I wanted you to get leverage with that rock." Alex strolled to the rock and set me down. "Put your left foot on the rock and jump onto my back." Alex took a knee. "Holden, help your mom."

I did as Alex said and dove toward his back. Wrapping my arms around his neck.

"Not so tight around my neck." He grunted, stood, and wrapped his arms under my legs. "If you choke me, we both fall."

"Sorry." I mumbled into his neck. "Can we go down and not up again today?"

"Deal." Alex chuckled.

Holden grabbed my crutch from where we had left it, and we made our way down the mountain.

"I'm hungry. Can we go to lunch?" Holden turned around after he stood in front of the car.

"Sure." I smiled. "Let's find a local restaurant and get something. Holden, what do you want to eat?"

"Barbeque."

"Why don't you look it up while I drive?" Alex started the car.

We had driven from the bottom of the mountain to the midpoint. Then, hiked to the top. I wish we could've driven to the top. I was exhausted, and I didn't walk half as much as they did. Alex wasn't even huffing and puffing. *Damn, I needed to do his exercise routine.* I found a restaurant at the bottom of the mountain as I scrolled through local options.

"When you get to the bottom, make a right." I directed Alex. "There's a barbecue restaurant there."

"Sounds good."

Alex followed my directions, and there it was — the Smoky Mountain Pig Restaurant, its porch glowing beneath an inviting OPEN sign. The place looked like a big log-cabin home, warm and welcoming. The moment I stepped out of the car, the air wrapped around me, thick with the scent of barbecue. Smoke drifted lazily from the fire pit, carrying the sweet, earthy smell of burning wood. Nothing beats local barbecue.

"Yum," Holden said as soon as he stepped out of the car. "I bet this is gonna be good."

"It smells great." Cody walked beside him up the steps.

I was ready for the usual delay. Whenever I brought my parents along, our party of six seemed to overwhelm the "family of four" setups. More often than not, we'd stand around waiting for a table to free up. But the lunch crowd was slow, and within minutes we were led to a round table tucked neatly into the corner.

The waitress handed out the menus and took our water order.

"Girls, what looks good?" I asked Hollie and Hallie.

"I want chicken nuggets." Hollie blurted and shut her menu.

"You don't want to try their barbecue chicken or turkey?" I wanted Hollie to break out of her chicken nugget phase.

"Nope."

"Hallie?"

"I'm gonna have the barbecue turkey with corn on the cob."

"That sounds good. Holden, how about you?"

Holden and Cody were discussing their options.

"What are you getting?" Alex tapped his menu with mine.

"The turkey with sweet potato. You?"

"I'm torn between the baby backs and a pulled pork sandwich."

"Mom, Cody and I are getting the pulled pork sandwich," Holden announced.

"Ah, kids after my heart," Alex mumbled.

The waitress came back and took our orders. Alex settled on the pulled pork sandwich too.

"Do you guys want to go back and find another hiking trail?" I took a sip of water and watched the kids' reactions, praying they'd say no.

"Can we go fishing instead?" Hallie gave Alex her best puppy-dog eyes. And he was a goner.

"Sure, if it's okay with your mom and Holden since it's his day." Ten points for Alex.

"I'm good with going fishing." Holden nodded.

"Okay, fishing it is. Are you gonna do it behind the cabin?" I eyed Alex.

"We can try it there first. If we don't see any fish, I'll find us a spot."

"Yay! Thank you, Chief Reyes." Hallie was jumping in her seat.

"You're welcome, honey."

Our food arrived, and we all dug in. When we finished, Alex grabbed the bill and paid while I glared at him. He ignored me. The kids ran ahead of us to the car.

"Thanks for paying. But I could've paid for me and my kids." I whispered.

"No worries. When we get to the cabin, if you don't want to go fishing, I'll take the kids. You can stay in and read your smutty book." Alex smirked.

"I might take you up on that. I'm not big on fishing. I was on a fishing boat once. Between the smell of the bait and the rocking of the ocean, I hurled over the side."

"We won't be on a boat."

"I went another time with my dad and got a hook stuck in my forehead, so no, I don't particularly care to go fishing."

"Ouch." Alex winced.

I sat in the car and belted in while Alex shut my door. We reached the cabin, and the boys grabbed all the fishing gear and rods. Alex had even brought a lightweight rod for Hallie. They stepped out onto the back deck, and Alex baited Hallie's hook. The minute I smelled the live bait, I gagged.

"I'm going in." I announced.

"I'm going in with you too, Mommy." Hollie pinched her nose and followed me inside.

"Hollie, you can lie on the couch to read. I can sit in the rocking chair."

"Okay, Mommy."

Hollie ran up, grabbed her book, and came back down.

"I'm gonna make myself a cup of coffee. Do you want anything to drink?" I asked Hollie.

"No, I'm good. But when it's done. I'll carry it for you."

"Thank you, Holls."

We both settled down to read. Every once in a while I heard them hooting and hollering on the deck. It looked like Hallie was having a fun time, which made me thrilled since she had been dying to go fishing with Alex and the boys. Alex was so good with her. He was patient and spent most of his time helping her than with his fishing rod. Hallie's eyes would light up with awe whenever she looked at him. Like mother, like daughter. Alex was the perfect man.

I still remember the first time I saw him at the hotel bar. We went there to celebrate Josie's job as a guest services agent for the hotel. I got up, ready to approach him, but Annie put her hand over mine and whispered. "He is so hot. Sammie, I want to meet him." Unbeknownst to her, she pushed a dagger into my heart, and from that moment on, Alex was Annie's and off the market.

Was it my turn now? Or was I a horrible person for still loving him? It had been years since Annie had died, but it felt like yesterday that we were talking about weddings and raising our kids together. Annie would've loved to see Cody. He was a mini-me of Alex. He was serious, smart, kind, and overall a great kid. She would be so proud.

Hallie's screeching voice jarred me from my thoughts. She was jumping up and down while Alex unhooked a rather large fish from her fishing line. Hallie swung the door open.

"Mommy, look what I caught!"

Alex handed her the big fish, and she pushed it through the open sliding glass door.

"Wow, that's huge."

"I know." Hallie looked back at Alex. "Chief Reyes helped me."

"Are we cooking it?" I frowned and prayed Alex would say no. I had never been fishing, let alone had to prep it for dinner.

"Don't worry, Mom," Alex chuckled. "We're throwing it back after we take a picture."

I took an enormous sigh of relief. "Okay."

"Mommy, I think my bookmark fell out in the car." Hollie was flipping the pages of her book. "Can I go look?"

"Sure, the keys are on the kitchen island. Leave the front door open so I can watch you."

I saw Hollie walk to the car. Through the living room windows, I saw her open the back door and crawl inside. I glanced down to read a couple of sentences and heard a male voice. *Was that Lincoln?* Bolting off the couch,

I grabbed my crutch and headed to the front door just as Hollie stood there holding Lincoln's hand.

"Mommy, look." Hollie was swinging Lincoln's hand. "Daddy's here. I thought you didn't invite him?" She frowned.

"Uh, Hollie," I grimaced. "Could you please go out back with your brother and sister while I speak to your dad?"

"Sure. I'll let them know Daddy's here."

Hollie skipped past me. I grabbed the door and partially closed it as I stood in the doorway. I didn't want him coming inside.

"What are you doing here? I didn't invite you." I snarled at him.

"I missed you, and I wanted to see my kids." Lincoln slurred.

"You'll see them after we get back, not today." I put my hand out so he wouldn't come any further. His eyes were bloodshot, and he swayed as he stood in front of me.

"You can't turn me away now." Lincoln's eyebrows rose almost to his hairline. "I drove all the way here." He grabbed my hand and looked behind me. "Besides, I see a couch."

The door slid out of my hand, and Alex's arm wrapped around my waist as his hard body pressed up against me.

"Yeah, that's my bed, and there's no more room at this inn unless you want to do something stupid and spend the night at the Haven Island PD's Blue Roof Inn. I can always make room for you there."

"Mommy? We have a Blue Roof Inn? Is that a new hotel on the island?" Hollie said from behind me.

"Hollie, shhh." Hallie said from behind us.

I turned around and placed my hands on Alex's chest. "Can you please stay inside with the kids while I speak to Lincoln?"

"Yeah, cop. You don't have any jurisdiction here." Lincoln laughed.

Alex stepped forward and pointed at Lincoln. "Don't fuck with me." He growled.

"Alex?"

"Fine." Alex stepped back and crossed his arms. "But I'm watching you." Alex glared at Lincoln.

I pulled the door shut and leaned against it.

Chapter 30

Men

Sammie

“Y ou know your guard dog is still watching us from the front window, right?” Lincoln muttered.

“I’m sure. Are you drunk or high?” I crossed my arms. I didn’t need to turn around to see Alex. I could feel his stare boring into my back. I appreciated his protection, but while both men were measuring each other’s dicks, I could hold my own. “Never mind, just go.”

"What the hell happened to your foot?"

"I stepped on glass. I'm fine."

“Don’t be like this, baby,” Lincoln whined and reached for my arms.

Alex pounded on the window, and Lincoln immediately released me and took a step back.

“You need to leave now before I let my guard dog, as you call him, loose.”

“No, let me go on a hike with them tomorrow.” Lincoln pointed to my foot. "You can't go."

“Not a chance. I don’t trust you.”

“Why not? You can come too.” Lincoln threw his arms up in the air.

“Why are you doing this now? You didn’t care when we left you nine years ago. Why now?” I couldn’t figure him out, but I knew he had an endgame.

"I...I miss you and them."

"I find that hard to believe."

"So let me prove it to you."

"We're not hiking tomorrow," I blurted, hoping he would not spend two-nights God knows where waiting to hike with the kids. "We're going shopping."

"Just a quick walk around these cabins then. Come on, Sammie, please?"

I hated Lincoln, but he was their father.

"Fine, how about a short walk tomorrow around three in the afternoon? But only for an hour, then you need to leave. We are not housing or feeding you."

"I'll take it. Can I say goodbye?"

"No, cause you're drunk or high. I'm not sure which. They shouldn't see you like that. When you come tomorrow, you better make sure you are sober and clean or the short walk is off."

"Fine."

I turned to go back inside just as Alex opened the door and glared at Lincoln. He reached out with a hand and pulled me toward him.

"Bitch," I heard Lincoln murmur.

"I'm gonna show him some fucking respect," Alex growled and tried to go around me, but I wrapped my arms around his waist.

"Alex, no. Just let him go. I don't want the kids to see you fighting. He's leaving. Let's go inside."

"Mommy, why is Daddy leaving?" Hollie was staring out the window. "And why is he walking crooked?"

"Cause he's drunk," Holden sighed. "Or high off his rocker.

"Come on, Holls, let's go upstairs." Hallie took Hollie's hand.

I stepped inside, and Alex shut the door. "Girls, go shower before dinner."

"We'll go clean up the fishing stuff, Dad." Cody and Holden went out back.

"Are you okay?" Alex held my shoulders and stooped to my level.

"Yeah, but he's going to come over tomorrow for a short hike around the cabins."

"No." Alex shook his head.

"What do you mean, no?" I could feel the anger coming on. First Lincoln tries to trap me in a corner, and now Alex. Alex closed his eyes and stood to his full height, pulling me in for a hug.

"Sorry, I didn't mean it like that. I just don't like him getting a lay of the land and being around the kids."

"I don't either, but if I fight him and he gets mad, he can take me to court and sue me for custody?" That was my worst fear. My kids were my life. I wouldn't be able to survive a day without them. For all these years it had been them and me against the world.

"He's an alcoholic, a drug addict, and a loser." Alex rubbed my back. "He would never win."

"You don't know that." I mumbled into his chest.

"How about you take a nice long shower and I get dinner ready?" Alex whispered.

One of his hands was rubbing my back, while the other was massaging the back of my head. I moaned because it felt amazing.

"Please don't moan like that when I have my hands on your body and the boys are on the back porch," Alex croaked.

"Sorry." I pulled back and looked up at him.

Our eyes met, and we gazed at each other, lost in our own silent thoughts. His head stooped toward mine, just a breath away when we heard the sliding glass door open.

"Dad, we're done."

Alex stopped. "Go shower," he whispered so close to my lips, I could feel his quick breath intake on my face.

I nodded and left the room. In my mind, I kept playing our almost-kiss on replay. After our last kiss in the bathroom, I craved another one. Since he was on kid duty, I took a nice long shower until the water turned cold. I rubbed lotion all over my body before choosing comfy pajamas. Feeling like a new woman, I left the bedroom.

The kids were all setting the table while Alex placed all the grilled food on the kitchen island. It was nice not to have to plan out a meal and cook it. Alex had given me an enjoyable break.

"Wow." I stepped up to the island. "This looks wonderful."

Alex pulled out a chair. "Come, have a seat. We almost have everything set. Do you want a beer?"

"Just water tonight, but thanks." After hiking today, I felt dehydrated.

"Here, Mommy," Hallie put a full glass of icy cold water next to my plate.

"Thanks, Halls." I gave her a side hug.

"Here's your plate." Alex served me one grilled barbecue chicken breast with corn on the cob, and lots of grilled zucchini and squash. "Is that enough?"

"More than enough." I smiled up at him. "Thank you." I loved the crunchy texture of grilled corn on the cob.

"Thanks, guys. It all smells delicious."

I relaxed while we discussed our hike today and shopping tomorrow. Holden chose Apples to Apples as our evening game. Everything was fine, until Hollie asked about seeing Daddy tomorrow.

"No." Alex shook his head at the exact same time I said, "Yes."

He turned his head and glared at me. "I thought I heard you say no."

"I changed my mind and told him he could come for an hour and walk around the cabin with the kids." As I looked around the table, I realized I had no allies except Hollie.

"Why?" Alex raised his eyebrow.

"Because he wants to get to know the kids. Don't you guys want to get to know your father?" Again I looked around.

"I don't." Hallie murmured and pushed her food around her plate.

"I do." Hollie smiled and took a bite of corn.

"I don't want to talk to him if he's drunk or high." Holden shook his head.

The only one who didn't say a word was Cody. He continued to eat as if nothing was going on. Smart kid. I wish his father had taken a cue from him.

"Kids, can you clean up, please? I'd like to talk to Sammie." Alex wiped his mouth and stood.

"Yes, Dad." Cody nodded.

"I'm not done." I put a spoonful of veggies in my mouth that I didn't want. Unfortunately, Alex still pulled out my chair. He must've been paying attention to the fact that I'd stopped eating a while ago.

"Please, Sammie." That was all he said before I gave in and used him as my crutch. We went outside to the side of the porch where the kids couldn't see us. Smart move. I didn't want the kids to hear or see my body language.

"Alex, he's their father."

"I know. But why can't he see them after we return?"

"He drove a long way. It's the least I can do."

"You are such a sucker for him." Alex paced. "He fucking leaves you–" he points his finger at my face, "–pregnant with triplets." Paced some more. "Never gives you a fucking dime, and–" he stopped in front of me, bracing his hands on his hips. "–you're still giving him chances."

"Back up." I raise my palm to his face. "Did you just call me a sucker?"

"Yes," he growls. "If the shoe fits."

I gasp. "Wow, how quickly you forget–" I poke him in the chest, "–how many times I had to ask my parents to watch the triplets and drop everything to come help you with Cody during and after Annie's sickness. Who was I a sucker for then?"

"Annie was your best friend." Alex raised his hand and pointed behind him. "He's an asshole who hung you out to dry."

"We had some good times?" I crossed my arms and wondered why the hell I was defending Lincoln, when deep down I totally agreed with Alex. *But Alex had pissed me off, and I was not backing down, dammit.*

"Before or after the drugs and alcohol?" Alex huffed. "He cared about you so much, he didn't glove up."

"Who told you that?"

"Annie!" He threw his arms up. "She told me you were on antibiotics and asked him to wear a condom. Fuck, even I know that medicine can interfere with birth control pills. But that fucking idiot was too stupid to man up."

My jaw dropped. I figured Annie told Alex everything, but I hoped that little tidbit of information had been between us. Because now I felt like an idiot too. Guess not. Annie never liked Lincoln. I wondered what else Annie had told him. Alex knowing about my sex life with Lincoln was humiliating.

"I don't want to talk to you about this." My voice dropped a few octaves and sounded cold even to my ears. "I'm going in, and you're going to drop this. Lincoln will see his kids tomorrow, and if you don't like it, you can go away while he's here." I shoved past him.

"Sammie, wait." Alex grabbed my elbow, but I pulled away and limped into the cabin. My foot was throbbing, but I didn't give a shit. I just needed to get away from Alex.

The kids had cleared all the dishes and were finishing up loading the dishwasher.

"Would you guys mind playing Apples to Apples upstairs? I'm really tired and want to get some rest."

"Okay, Mommy," Hollie gave me a hug. "I love you."

"I love you, too." I hugged each of my kids and Cody. "I'll come up in about an hour and tuck you guys in and read the next chapter."

"I can read the next chapter so you can go to bed," Alex said from the living room.

"I'll clean the table, Mommy." Hallie grabbed a paper towel. "You can go into the bedroom."

"Thanks, Halls." I kissed the top of her head and headed straight for the bedroom.

I shut the door and leaned against it. That man was driving me crazy. I shouldn't have let him come on this vacation. Then again, he drove and cooked for me. I jolted at the knock on the door.

"Yeah?" I opened it and stood in the doorway.

"Can I come in?" Alex stood with his hands in his pockets.

"Sure." I opened the door all the way and stepped back.

"I'm sorry. I didn't mean to insult you. I don't think you are a sucker." Stepping closer to me, he cupped my face and raised it to his. "I think you are a beautiful woman with the kindest heart I've ever seen."

I sighed and gazed into his brown bedroom eyes, watching as he slowly lowered his lips and gave me a soft kiss.

"I'm gonna go play with the kids upstairs and read them a chapter. I'll text you when they are ready if you want to come up and tuck them in." Alex released my face and tenderly brushed a strand of hair behind my ear. "Okay?"

"Okay."

Alex smiled, grabbed the doorknob and stepped out of the bedroom.

"Alex?" I called out, and he turned to face me.

"Do you want the bed tonight? I can sleep on the couch."

"Nah," he grinned. "I'm fine. I've figured it out." He winked at me. "You take the bed. I'll be fine."

I nodded and shut the door.

Chapter 31

Bitch

Lincoln

T hat fucking, stuck-up, Bitch! I wasn't fucking drunk. So what if I had a few beers and smoked several joints on my drive here? What I did in my spare time was none of her fucking business. I could still function. Coming here was a last-minute decision, so I never booked a room, not that I could afford one. I also never planned on another man being with my kids, fucking my wife—well, ex-wife. At least I got her to let me see them tomorrow.

I'd sleep in my car, no problem. I parked down the road from the cabins because I was going to spy on Sammie and the kids, but then Hollie came out, and I wanted to chat with her. She was the only one who would even acknowledge me. Winning her over might also mean that Hallie and Holden would finally accept me.

And what the hell. *Why had Sammie named them with such fucking similar names? Was she drunk when she named them or high on epidural?* When I reached my car, I got in the backseat for the night.

My phone buzzed again, and I pulled it out of my back pocket. *Fuck!* It was Ava again. She had been blowing up my phone all day. Not wanting to read all her fucking texts or listen to her voicemails, I called her.

"Where have you been? I've been worried sick about you all day!" Ava screeched into the phone so loud I had to pull it away from my ear.

"Hey, baby, I miss you too."

"Don't fucking 'hey baby' me, asshole. Where are you?"

"I drove up to the mountains to spend time with my kids."

"You fucking two-timing, cock sucking, asshole. Are you sleeping with her? She seemed so nice when I met her. Does she know who I am? Was it all an act?"

"No, so calm the fuck down." Ava was a jealous little thing. She had reason to be since I stepped out on her all the time. Not that she was aware of my other side pieces. But Sammie wasn't one of them.

"Then why are you there with her and the kids and I wasn't invited, huh?"

"I'm sleeping in my car on a side road. I'm not sleeping with her."

"Why don't you get a hotel?"

"Because we don't have the money. Hence, that's why you got that job starting next week." I growled. She wasn't that dense.

"I thought you got some money from your parents?"

"Not enough to waste on another fucking hotel. That money was for the apartment rental on Haven Island so you wouldn't have to drive back and forth from your new job, remember?"

"When are you coming back?"

"Uh, Sunday morning."

"No, you are not sleeping in a car for two nights in a row and then driving several hours home."

Damn, she was clingy on top of jealous. I'd hoped to go to a bar after my time with the kids tomorrow and hook up. Sleep at the booty calls house and drive home the next morning.

"Fine. I'll drive home tomorrow after I see the kids."

"Okay." She was quiet but still on the line. "Babe, I can talk to my parents about giving us another loan."

I've been extorting money from them for years on my fake-ass Ponzi scheme that supported my drug, alcohol, and gambling debt. I know I have a problem, but I just need more money to make it right.

If I can get in my parent's good graces with the triplets, they will give me another loan and I can hold off on asking Grace's parents for a few months. Besides, my parents will go apeshit when they find out they have triplet grandkids. I need to ensure I tell my parents at the right time, or I risk being disinherited.

"No, I have it under control. With your temporary job, we will get by, and I'll set up a new plan for my investors."

"Okay. I love you."

"I love you, too. See you tomorrow."

I didn't tell Ava that I broke into Sammie's boutique and stole some money. I was mad that night because I wasn't sure Sammie was going to let me see my kids. When I walked by her shop that night, I noticed a brick on the side. I grabbed it and hauled it through her front door. The glass shattered immediately, but I didn't hear the alarm, so I ran to the back, broke the coat rack, and banged the hell out of the register. When it didn't open, I grabbed my pocket knife and pried it open. I heard the police sirens and knew I had tripped a silent alarm. I grabbed the cash and ran out the back door.

I ran down the block and across the street and watched from behind a tree. I saw when she stepped on the fucking glass at the boutique and Alex, that same asshole, picked her up and carried her to the back. It pissed me off that I only got $2,000 and some change out of the fucking register. She owed me, and I would collect more than that soon.

Chapter 32

Hot Damn

Alejandro

After I took care of the kids last night, Sammie came in to tuck them in before she disappeared into the bedroom. I didn't see her again until this morning at breakfast. I made pancakes, but it wasn't until the smell of bacon permeated throughout the cabin that everyone came into the kitchen to eat. *Shocker.*

"Dad, are you making bacon?" Cody smiled.

"Yep. And there's enough for everyone. Grab your pancakes and have a seat. The bacon will be ready in a minute." I noticed the other kids behind Cody and Sammie holding up the rear. I had two pans of bacon going. The first was ready, and I dumped it onto a plate for them to grab.

When the second pan was ready, I took it to the table and served them the rest, setting aside three strips of bacon for me.

"Mommy, since I'm kid of the day today, can we hike for a little bit and then go fishing? I don't want to go shopping." Hallie begged Sammie.

"Sure." Sammie nodded. "We'll go shopping tomorrow on my day."

"Thanks, Mommy," Hallie was all smiles.

"Why don't we hike to the waterfall?" I suggested. "I looked at the map and saw a small creek where we can go fishing on the way back." I looked around the table before I stopped at Sammie. "It's not too far, and I can carry all the gear."

"Ooh, yes, Mommy, please?" Hallie clasped her hands together in prayer.

"Okay." Sammie smiled.

"Do I have to go?" Hollie frowned.

"We're all going." Sammie cut her pancakes. "Bring your book, Holls. We can take a blanket and read while they fish."

"Okay," Hollie grinned and shoved a spoonful of pancake in her mouth.

"Dad, I can help you carry some of the gear." Cody took a sip of water.

"I can help you too, Chief Reyes." Holden nodded.

"That's great, boys. Thanks." We continued to eat while the kids asked me questions about fishing.

After breakfast, Sammie and the girls took care of the dishes, leaving the boys and me to sort out our gear for the day's hike and fishing trip. Hallie proudly carried her own rod, while Holden grabbed the rest and Cody took charge of the tackle box. My rucksack was loaded with snacks, water, and a first-aid kit — everything we'd need for a fantastic day out.

We set off at a slow pace around the cabins and hiked for about a mile until we reached a waterfall.

"Can we go in?" Hollie was already taking off her shoes.

"Do you think it's safe?" Sammie asked me. "I didn't go in it last time."

"I looked it up, and it said it was safe. But I'll go in first." I stripped out of my gear, shirt, socks, and shoes. Heading toward the edge, I carefully stepped in, my feet landing on rocks. I walked until I reached the waterfall. The water was cool, but it felt good. I stepped into the waterfall and submerged my body up to my neck. Running my hands over my head, slicking back my hair, I stood letting the water fall onto my back. Oh yeah, the kids would love this.

I stepped out from behind the waterfall and headed toward them. Sammie froze, eyes huge, mouth hanging open in shock — or maybe awe. *Was that drool coming out of the side of her mouth?* If I didn't know better, I'd say she forgot to breathe for a second. Her breasts were perky as hell, inflating my ego and letting me know she liked what she saw.

"Can we get in?" the kids were shouting.

"Yep, come on in. It feels exquisite." I motioned for them to join me.

The kids dove in fully clothed, laughing as the cold water splashed around us. None of us had thought to bring swimsuits — it didn't matter. Their laughter echoed through the clearing, but I barely heard it. My focus was on Sammie, and the way her gaze lingered on me, hungry and unguarded. *Damn.*

"Are you coming?" I gave her a devilish grin. She could take that comment however she wanted.

"Uh, sure." Sammie said before she slipped off her shoes and pulled off her socks.

She scooted close to the edge and put one foot in before she screamed and pulled her foot back.

"What's wrong?" I stepped toward her. *Did she hit her bad foot on a rock?*

"It's cold!"

"No, mom it's refreshing!" Holden hollered.

"It feels fantastic, Miss Sammie," Cody said.

"Not to me." Sammie backed up as I came out of the water. "What are you doing?"

I grabbed her arm and pulled her into a fireman's carry. "Helping you in."

"Alex, don't you dare!" Sammie screamed, but I wasn't listening.

I eased into the water and pulled her into my arms. She tried to scramble out of my embrace, but I held her tight.

"Alex, it's freezing." Sammie wrapped her arms around my neck trying to stay out of the water, but I dipped down and walked her under the waterfall.

"Alex," she sputtered. "I'm gonna kill you."

The kids and I helped get her entire body wet. Then I wrapped her legs around my waist and held her close to me while we squatted so only our heads were above the water.

"See, Mommy, isn't it better once you go under?" Hollie said as she swam around us.

"Sure."

Sammie's body was trembling, so I pulled her closer to mine. I always radiated a lot of body heat. "Come closer. I'll keep you warm." I tucked her chin onto my shoulder and kept her as close to me as I could.

"Thanks," Sammie whispered into my neck. "You might want to tell your buddy down south to settle down."

"Hard to do when your sweet body is pressed against mine." I grumbled.

"Mmm."

"No moaning." I growled as I watched the kids playing.

"Alex," Sammie moaned into my neck and pushed her pelvis into mine. Her scent wrapped around me, her body pressed close, every movement pulling me tighter to the edge. I forced a breath, reminding myself the kids were only a few feet away.

"Fuck, Sammie, stop." I lowered my hands and grasped her hips, holding them in place.

"I can't."

"Shit." I walked us to the edge and helped her out. She couldn't stay in the water if she was freezing. I had to let her go, or I would want to fuck her here and now. "Fuck," I growled.

"What?" Sammie looked down at her chest and her eyes bulged. "Oh, no."

"I love your white t-shirt contest look, but not in front of our kids." I grabbed the blanket she brought to sit on and wrapped it around her while I turned my back to the kids.

"Mommy, do we have to get out?" Hallie inquired.

"No, just me. I'm gonna dry off."

"I gotta go back in." I rubbed her arms through the blanket. "I need some distance from your hot body and cold water to calm me down."

I glanced over my shoulder at the kids playing in the water. When they were looking away from us, I went back in and submerged to my neck. We played in the water until Sammie told us to come out and eat our sandwiches. I brought an extra blanket, which I laid out for the kids.

"Can we go fishing after we eat, Chief Reyes?" Hallie begged.

"Yep, we'll pack up and head back to the cabins." I nodded.

"Then we can read, right, Mommy?" Hollie took a bite of her PB&J.

"Absolutely."

Sammie was giving me several heated glances, which I was trying not to dwell on. As soon as my chest dried, I pulled on my shirt. Not that it stopped her from checking me out. Her looks were driving me crazy. If the kids weren't around, I would've already had her pinned under me in the bed, couch, floor, wall, anywhere I could get my hands on her.

Chapter 33

Fishing

Sammie

While Hallie, Holden, Cody, and Alex fished, Hollie and I were curled up, reading our books on a blanket draped over the side of a rock. Holden and Cody were laughing as they compared their catches, snapped photos, and tossed the fish back, while Alex remained by Hallie's side. Each time I glanced over, Alex was occupied, helping Hallie instead of fishing. His fishing rod remained on the ground, unused. It seemed to be a recurring theme.

I wish he'd been my kids' father instead of Lincoln. My life would've been so much better. I always envied how he and Annie got along. Unfortunately, they had little time together. But for the days that Annie was with us, I know she was a happy wife and mom. Enough about that, I looked down at my book and got back to my vampire love story. I was so engrossed in the sex scene in my book that I didn't hear Lincoln walking up to us.

"Hey guys." Lincoln stopped in front of Hollie and I.

Shit, I checked my watch and realized it was after three. He must've come looking for us.

"Daddy!" Hollie shouted and jumped up to give him a hug.

I glanced at the fishing troop and saw the kids look over their shoulder and look away, but Alex turned and braced his hands on his hips watching Lincoln.

Alex didn't say a word, and I was glad that Lincoln seemed sober. I didn't want to have to play referee between the two of them again.

"Honey, you didn't want to fish?" Lincoln squatted down and asked Hollie.

Hollie scrunched up her nose. "I don't like fishing. It's smelly." Then she plugged her nose.

Lincoln and I chuckled. "Yeah, it can be." Lincoln shrugged. "Let me go see how they're doing." He straightened and headed for Hallie and Holden.

I set my book down and got up, hobbling toward Alex. And the pissing contest began when I reached Alex and he draped his arm around my waist, pulling me into him, sending goose bumps all over my body. Even though he smelled like fish, I appreciated his warmth and support.

"Lincoln." He nodded. "What are you doing here?"

"Sammie said I could see the kids. When I didn't see you guys at the cabin, I went for a walk.I recognized my kids' voices, so I followed the sound and here they are." Lincoln draped his arm around Hallie's shoulder. "Have you caught anything?"

Hallie stepped out of his embrace and mumbled, "Some."

"Where are they?" Lincoln looked around.

"We throw them back." Hallie grunted.

"Why? I could cook them for dinner for you guys."

"I'd rather not." Hallie dropped her rod and scurried over to my side. I put my arm around her.

Lincoln got the hint and stepped over to Holden, who had been ignoring him the entire time.

"Son." Lincoln pointed to the water. "How are you doing?"

"Great."

"Who's your friend?" Lincoln squeezed Cody's shoulder and continued to make conversation with Holden.

"Cody's my best friend. You met him at the park." Holden then pointed to Alex. "That's his dad. Police Chief Reyes."

Lincoln's body stiffened, but he never turned to look at Alex. "I see. What kind of bait are you using?"

"Chief Reyes brought some lures and some live bait. We're alternating." Holden answered all his father's questions without making eye contact.

"Cody, how is your fishing going?" Lincoln stepped behind both of them.

"Good, sir." Cody nodded but kept his vision on his rod in the water.

"So proper. You can call me Lincoln." Lincoln tapped his shoulder, and I thought Alex was going to punch him in the face.

I immediately tightened my hold around Alex's waist, keeping him next to me. There was no reason to fight Lincoln. He hadn't done anything wrong—yet.

"I mean, if you're Holden's best friend, then we are going to see a lot of each other. Right, Holden?" Lincoln now tapped Holden's shoulder.

Cody kept his mouth shut. I'm sure the poor kid didn't know what to do.

"Come on, Hallie." Alex removed his arm from around me and held his hand out to Hallie. "Let's see if we can get some more fish."

"Oh." Lincoln spun around and walked toward Hallie. "I can help her."

"No, I want Chief Reyes." Hallie grabbed Alex's hand in what looked to be a death grip and followed him back to her fishing rod.

"I'm her father, not him." Lincoln grumbled close to me.

"They don't know you. You need to give them time." I crossed my arms. "Surprising them is not the answer."

"I think they need time alone with me without you and your guard dog."

Alex must have excellent hearing because he looked over his shoulder and smirked at Lincoln when he heard the words guard dog.

"Daddy, you can sit with me on the blanket." Hollie grabbed his hand and pulled him down to sit next to him.

"What are you reading?"

"I'm reading Amelia Bedelia. I'm on book two."

"Wow, tell me what it's about." Hollie told him about the series while I went back to reading my book.

I read page fifty several times because I kept watching Lincoln and Alex. They both seemed so calm, but I wasn't buying it. There was a storm brewing, and I wasn't sure who would bring the thunder and lightning, but going by the angry looks, I was betting on Alex.

Lincoln was behaving. He even let her read to him. Several times he scooted closer to me and even extended his legs out and leaned on his hands behind him. One hand coming close to my shin.

I saw Alex tense and moved my leg further away. Not that it deterred Lincoln, he sat criss-cross applesauce and reached over to my leg, rubbing it. *What the hell was he doing?* I moved my legs and used the rock to help me stand. Alex was heading my way. His face was boiling mad. Had he been a cartoon character, I would have seen steam blowing out of his ears.

I grabbed my crutch, hobbled over to him, and put my hands on his chest. Each rise of his chest seemed measured, each fall laced with the threat of an explosion as he glared over my shoulder at Lincoln.

"Hey," I whispered. "Stop. He's not doing anything wrong."

"He was rubbing your leg," he growled.

"It was nothing. Forget it." I pushed him back, but it was like moving a steel wall. He didn't budge.

"Alex, look at me."

Alex glanced down and steadied his breathing.

"It's fine. We'll get rid of him when we go in for dinner."

Alex gave a sharp nod. "Fine."

I grabbed his hand and pulled him along with me to Hallie. "How's it going, honey?"

"It's good, Mommy. Alex gave me some tips. This is fun." Hallie smiled at me.

"I'm glad you're having a good time. We're going to be leaving in about thirty minutes, okay?"

"Okay, but can we go fishing again tomorrow?" Hallie threw her line in.

"We'll see."

"If we can't," Alex interrupted. "I'll take you fishing when we get home. The boys love to go, so you can come along with us."

"Thanks, Chief Reyes." Hallie pulled out her line and threw it in again.

I pulled Alex a few steps over to Holden. "Boys, you have another thirty minutes, okay?"

"Sure, Mom." Holden nodded toward Lincoln. "Why is he still here?"

"You know why." I sighed.

"He's not eating dinner with us, right?" Holden frowned.

"No." I squeezed Alex's hand. "I'm sure he'll leave when we finish fishing and go home."

"Good." Holden murmured.

"Cody, are you doing okay?" I needed to check on him too, since Lincoln had tried to drag him into his drama.

"I'm good, Miss Sammie." Cody smiled at me. Holden was blessed to have such a good best friend.

"Can you help me back to my rock?" I asked Alex.

"Of course."

Alex scooped me up and dropped onto the rock, planting me in his lap like I was his trophy. He grinned, smug and unapologetic. Men — they lived for this nonsense, puffing their chests and poking each other's egos. Whatever. They could play alpha all day, just not in front of the kids. Lincoln could've thanked me for stepping in, but it didn't matter. Alex had already checkmated him.

*** Lincoln ***

I sat and listened to Hollie go on and on reading her book when what I really wanted was to bond with Holden and mess with Sammie. Unfortunately, while the guard dog and his kid were around, I would not get that chance.

"Kids, it's time to head in for dinner." Sammie announced and packed up all their shit.

"What are we having for dinner?" I asked, fully aware I wasn't invited, but loving every minute of seeing the guard dog get pissed.

"Uh, not sure." Sammie looked at me, at Alex, then back to me. "But you need to get on the road. It's a long drive, and it'll be dark soon."

"Nah, I can leave later." Lincoln smirked at me.

"Can Daddy stay for dinner?" Hollie bolted from the blanket and grabbed Sammie's hand.

Well, well, well, getting Hollie on my side was looking to be a better idea than Holden.

"Holls," Holden came over holding his fishing rod. "Mom said Lincoln has to leave."

Thanks a lot for the assist, son. *What's with not calling me Dad?*

"Maybe another night." Sammie scooped down and grabbed the blanket. "Right, Lincoln?"

"Sure, another night." I grabbed the other end to help Sammie fold it, but was quickly pushed aside by her guard dog. *Man, did he ever take a break from protecting her? Were they a thing, or was he just that into his job as* police chief? *Duh, idiot.* Of course, they were a thing. He was here with his kid, and they were sharing a cabin.

I held Hollie's hand and followed them to the cabin. She was the only one who gave me the time of day. I tried to talk to Holden and Hallie again, but they ignored me and slowed down to walk with Alex.

That asshole had what I wanted. Sammie looked hot as hell. The years had been good to her. But I had to keep my eye on the prize. Ava Grace had an inheritance, status, and loaded parents. Sammie's parents owned a boutique—not much money there.

When we reached the cabin. I gave Hollie a hug. "I love you, honey." And kissed her cheek. "I'll see you when you get back in town. Thanks for reading to me."

"You're welcome, Daddy." Hollie beamed at me. "I love you, too." Then she followed Sammie into the cabin.

I was not surprised that the guard dog stayed on the porch watching me. I tried to hug Hallie, but she walked around me. Holden let me hug him, but he didn't hug me back. Then again, he was carrying several fishing rods and a tackle box. I preferred to think that if his hands were empty, he would've returned my hug. Wishful thinking on my part, but I wanted to believe it.

Sammie came back out after the kids entered the cabin and stood next to Alex.

"I'll call about seeing them once you guys are home." I called out.

"Not this week. They start school on Friday." Sammie crossed her arms. "Give them a couple of weeks to settle down into a routine and we'll set something up."

"Okay." I nodded and waved as I got into my car.

Sammie went in, but the guard dog waited until my car left her driveway. Asshole. If I had wanted to stay, I know I could've used Hollie to persuade Sammie, and there was nothing he could've done. Hell, I could take him. He was probably all bark and no bite. That's okay, I had something else in the works to get me time with my kids. I just had to be patient.

Chapter 34

Calm After the Storm

Sammie

I breathed easier after Lincoln left and didn't return that night. For once, he listened to me and left us alone. We had dinner and then played several card games. Hallie always loved her nights, and she often chose card games like Go Fish, Old Maid, War, and Uno.

"Since it's Hallie's night, why don't you boys go shower and get ready for bed first so the girls can finish their War game?" I'd brought two decks of cards, and the girls were still at half a deck each. The great thing about this game was that you could count your cards and declare a winner if you didn't get to the full deck.

"Uh, Mom," Holden whined. "We're almost done."

"It's okay, Miss Sammie." Cody collected Holden's cards. "We can play again another time."

"Thanks, Cody."

I had been reading on the couch, and Alex was checking emails.

"Have you talked to your dad?" Alex looked up from the phone.

"I talked to him when we got here, but not lately. Why?"

"You know he installed the new door to your shop, right?"

"Yep, he texted me. Said it looks perfect, and we reopened yesterday." I set the book down on my lap.

"My boys are still doing drive-bys checking Main Street, but no one else has had any burglaries. Lucian said it's been a quiet couple of days."

"Well, that's good." If it had been so quiet, why was he frowning?

"Yeah, I guess." Alex murmured.

I wanted to ask more questions, but I wanted to wait until the girls left the room, so I went back to my book.

"We're done!" Holden shouted from upstairs thirty minutes later.

I closed my book. "Girls, your turn. Let us know when you're ready for us to come to read the next chapter."

"Okay, Mommy." Hollie got up while Hallie put the cards away.

Once the girls left, I looked at Alex. "Why are you frowning over there? Aren't you happy things are calm at home?"

"Things are usually not this quiet at home."

"What do you mean? It's not like we live in the city."

I never heard about any problems on the island, as my life consisted of my children, family, and my shop, plus the occasional get-together with friends.

"It's not like the city, but after your break-in, I'm surprised there hasn't been some disturbance at the hotel, another shop, or the marina."

"Do you want us to have more issues on the island? Are you bored?" Back when Alex was with Annie, I knew he liked to be busy, a habit that kept him away from home often.

"No," Alex looked up at me and shook his head. "That's not what I'm saying. I like it being quiet, especially after Cassie's kidnapping. It's just weird."

"That was crazy, right?" My kids had been sick when all that went down, and I wasn't able to help Cassie. "I'm just glad you guys found the guy before he married her. Was it true the father was buried where they were doing the ceremony?"

"Yeah." Alex sat forward, bracing his hands on his knees. "Crazy, right?"

"Nothing like that has ever happened on the island, right?"

"No," Alex sighed. "I mean, we've had crazy, drunk, or high people, but that was significantly worse than anything we've experienced. I'm just glad that the mainland police assisted us."

"Me too."

"Mommy, we're done!" Hollie shouted.

"Well, Mommy, let's go." Alex stood and held out his hand to me.

I grabbed his hand to stand up, but he whisked me up into his arms. We sat in our usual spots on the floor against the beds, and this time I read the chapter. We kissed each child goodnight and headed back down.

"I'm gonna shower." Alex followed me into the bedroom.

"Sure."

I watched him grab his clothes and step into the bathroom. He closed the door, but I didn't hear the lock. I had showered earlier while Alex cooked, so I was already in my pajamas. Pulling the covers aside, I got into bed and leaned against the headboard to read.

I heard the shower turn off, and a few minutes later, Alex emerged with wet hair, low-slung pajama bottoms, and no shirt. Damn, I would love to run my tongue over his sexy chest. He cleared his throat, and I looked up. My face heated when I realized he'd been staring at me.

"I'll get out of your way."

"I really wish you would switch with me. That couch is too short for you." Every night I tried to get him to switch sleeping arrangements with me, but he never did.

"I'm good, but thanks." He tossed his clothes into his duffel bag and headed out the bedroom door.

"Alex?" I called out before he grabbed the door.

"Yeah?"

"We could share a bed." I motioned to the king-size bed. "There's plenty of room, and I don't move around."

"What about the kids?"

"We always get up before them." I shrugged. "Please, I know you don't fit on the couch and you've been sleeping on the floor."

"How do you know that?"

"I saw you when I went to the bathroom last night." I never shut the bedroom door in case the kids need me.

"Are you sure?"

"Positive." I nodded.

"Okay." Alex stepped away from the door. "Do you want the light off?"

"Yes, please." I closed my book and scooted down under the covers. "There's a night-light in the bathroom."

Alex nodded and walked around the bed.

His size and weight dipped the bed as he slid between the sheets. I stayed on my back to stop myself from rolling into him, wondering if my body would roll into him anyway in the middle of the night. *What would he do?*

"I promise I'll stay on my side," Alex murmured into the night.

"Okay. Me too." I would try, but no promises.

I closed my eyes and tried to relax, but it was impossible knowing that man — that impossibly sexy man — was lying just inches away. I could hear his steady breathing, each exhale tugging at the edges of my calm. After a few minutes, he shifted, rolling onto his side with his back to me. Perfect. I did the same, matching his movements, pretending sleep came easily. I'd never been good at sleeping on my back, anyway.

Soon enough, listening to his even breathing lulled me to sleep.

Chapter 35

Foggy State of Mind

Alejandro

Her body felt so soft in my arms. Feeling the weight of her exposed thigh against my groin was fueling a powerful urge to be inside her. I could feel her rapid breaths against my neck as my fingers slid up and down her thigh. Her low moan encouraged my fingers to sneak around between her thighs. My index finger eased her panties aside so my middle finger could slide into her wet mound. *Fuck, she was drenched.*

I turned toward her. My other hand slid up the curve of her back and slipped beneath her hair to rest at her neck. Our mouths met, and the world narrowed to that single breath between us. I hadn't kissed anyone since Annie died, and I'd forgotten what it felt like — that rush of warmth, the jolt of being alive again. Her warmth pressed tight against me, every curve sparking against my skin, the rush of flesh gliding with desperate friction. The faint trace of strawberries on her body pulled me deeper into the moment.

I raised her thigh higher on my waist. My entire hand was now ready to bring her the orgasm her body craved. Adding a couple more fingers inside her wet pussy, I used my thumb to play with her clit. I could feel her hard nipples boring into my chest. The delicious peaks I craved were inches from my lips, but the sound of her voice pulled me out of my dream.

"Alex," Sammie moaned. "I..."

Was this a dream? My head was foggy, but my pulse pounded, every nerve alive with the need for Sammie. I kept my eyes shut, drowning in the heat of her mouth, swallowing every sound she tried to make. If she told me to stop,

I would — but dammit, until then I'd wring every gasp, every shiver from her body with my hands and my lips.

She grabbed my biceps with her hands and pulled me tight against her body, trapping my hand between our bodies and against my cock. *Fuck me, her body was so damn responsive to my touch.* Her body trembled and tightened around my fingers, and she opened her mouth to scream out her climax. I dove towards her luscious mouth and swallowed her scream. The last thing I wanted was for the kids to hear us.

I eased my hand away and held her close, letting our kiss taper into gentle pecks on her lips before tucking her face against my neck, my chest tight with the fear she might be upset with me. From the feel of her body, I didn't sense any anger.

After her breathing returned to normal, I took a deep breath, cupped her face, and tilted it up to mine.

"Are you mad at me?" I mumbled. "I swear, at first I thought I was dreaming, but when you called my name, I knew it was real." If my eyes hadn't been scanning her face, I would've missed the slight frown.

"Were you dreaming of Annie?" Sammie's eyes closed.

"No! Sammie, look at me." When she gazed at me, I could see the hurt in her eyes. "I wasn't thinking of Annie. I'm not sure if that makes me a horrible widower, but I was dreaming of you. I wanted you."

Sammie cracked a smile. "If you are a horrible widower, then I'm a horrible best friend. I don't think Annie would mind if we got on with our lives. She loved us."

"True."

"And it has been six years since she left us," Sammie whispered. "I miss her every day."

I pulled her into my arms and kissed her temple. "I miss her too. Cody wishes his mom was alive, and he had gotten the chance to get to know her, but I also know he loves you and thinks of you as his adoptive mom."

Sammie pulled back. "Really?"

"Yep." I cupped her face to make sure I had her undivided attention when I said what I needed to say to her. "I haven't been with another woman since Annie. Never felt the need, except now with you. Will you give us a chance? We'll go slow and stop whenever either of us freaks out."

"I haven't been with anyone since my pregnancy." Sammie smiled. "I would love to have a relationship with you."

"Oh, baby. Those words are music to my ears." I kissed her like my life depended on it and would've kissed her some more if I hadn't heard lots of footsteps on the stairs heading to us.

"Shit, I'll get breakfast going while you relax." I leapt out of bed, but I couldn't resist one more kiss before I left the bedroom and shut the door.

"Hey, Dad." Cody followed Holden into the kitchen. "Where's breakfast?"

"Uh, isn't it a little early?" I grabbed a pan and set it on the stove to make pancakes.

"You're funny, Chief Reyes." Hollie laughed. "This is the same time we always come down for breakfast."

I looked at the clock and realized she was absolutely right. The softness of the bed and the feel of Sammie beside me had caused me to linger. But hell, I wouldn't have missed that special moment with her for anything in the world.

"Were you sleeping in the bedroom with my mom?" Hallie questioned.

"Uh, um..." Think of something, asshole. "No, I got up early and was putting all the bedding back in the bedroom. Shh, your mom was still asleep when I snuck out."

"I don't think she's still asleep after you slammed the door on your way out," Holden grumbled.

Darn smart kids. "Sorry," I mumbled and got all the ingredients in the bowl for the pancakes. "Why don't you guys play a game while I get breakfast going?"

"Okay," Hollie skipped to where all the games were stashed.

I didn't care what game they played as long as it stopped the questions. I finished the pancakes and bacon and put everything on the table.

"Breakfast is ready. Cody, can you get the drinks? I'm gonna go check on Sammie."

"Sure, Dad."

"I'll help." Hallie got up with Cody.

Interesting to see Hallie's crush on Cody developing. The way she watched him during fishing and hiking. *Cute. I think.*

I knocked twice before I opened the bedroom door and peeked inside. The bed was empty, but I could hear the blow-dryer going from the cracked bathroom door. I shut the bedroom door behind me and stepped into the bathroom.

Sammie had a towel wrapped around her body, tucked between her breasts while she dried her hair. I stepped up behind her and stooped to kiss her shoulder while I placed my hands under the towel on her hips.

"I love this body wash. I'm gonna buy it for you by the gallon," I moaned. Pushing her hair away from her neck, I licked and nipped from her shoulder to her neck.

The dryer banged against the counter. *Ah, I found a sweet spot on her neck. I couldn't wait to find more.* I pulled the dryer out of her hands and turned it off. She pressed her body against mine.

"Mm, Alex, we need to stop. You are not helping me get ready."

I ran my hands up the front of her body and massaged her breasts before pushing the towel open. It dropped to the floor, and I met her gaze in the mirror. Her breasts were perfect, with her hard as fuck nipples begging for my attention.

"You're beautiful." I glanced down her body before meeting her eyes.

"You're blind." Sammie covered her abdomen. "I have a C-section scar and stretch marks."

"I don't see that." I reached for her wrists and pulled her arms apart. "I see a beautiful woman who gave birth to a wonderful set of triplets and is an amazing mother."

"Aren't you a smooth talker?" Sammie smirked.

"I mean what I said." I whirled her around and put her hand on my dick. "Here's your proof of my words."

Sammie stroked me through my pajamas, and I got harder than I was, if that was even possible. I groaned and kissed her. My hands grabbed her ass and pulled her into me.

"Mommy?"

"Hey, Dad?"

"Tag, you're it." I moaned into her mouth. "Breakfast is on the table, and I need a cold shower."

Sammie giggled and left the bathroom.

"I'll be out in a minute!" She hollered.

Awww fuck. I needed an icy cold shower and my hand if the temperature didn't calm me down.

Chapter 36

Shopping Day

Sammie

After breakfast, we all got into the car and drove to Main Street for some shopping.

"We'll walk to the end and back so you can see all the shops. Will that work?" Alex glanced at me.

"Yep, sounds good to me."

"Are we going to shop all day?" Hallie huffed.

"I love shopping!" Hollie interjected.

"Not all day." I unbuckled my seat belt. "But maybe we can find a first day of school outfit or something cool for your first day of 4th grade."

"Do you think they sell fishing rods?" Hallie stepped out of the car.

"They might if they have an outdoor shop." Alex stood beside my door holding my crutches.

Hollie held my hand the minute she got out of the car. The first store we came to was an ice cream shop.

"Can we get ice cream?" Holden looked between Alex and me.

"You just ate." I frowned.

"They are growing boys," Alex chuckled.

"How about we get ice cream before we leave?" By then we would be hot and tired, and the ice cream would be a refreshing treat.

"Okay." Holden shrugged and walked next to Cody.

I usually held up the rear, but Alex seemed to prefer to walk behind all of us.

"Let's go in here." I pointed to the clothing store.

"I'll take the boys to the men's side while you girls do your thing." Alex pulled the door open for us.

"Thanks," I winked at him. "Okay, girls, let's see if they have anything you want to wear for the first day of school."

"Why?" Hallie sighed. "Can't you get us something from our store?"

"I could, but something from here will be unique." I shrugged. "Let's just look around."

"Oohh, Mommy, look at this cute skirt." Hollie, my little fashionista, ran to a rack displaying a hot pink shirt with a hot pink and plaid pleated skirt.

Hallie liked clothes, but lately she seemed to be on a fishing kick. *Maybe because of Cody?* Hollie grabbed several outfits, and even Hallie joined in the fun after she saw a t-shirt with a fish on it she had to have. I led the girls to the men's side to see how the boys were doing.

"Hey, how's it going over here?" I asked Alex.

He was walking around with his hands in his pockets. The boys each had a t-shirt and jeans draped over their forearms.

"They saw a fishing t-shirt they couldn't live without." Alex snickered.

"Is it like mine?" Hallie showed them hers.

"Yeah, it's the same." Cody smiled. "We can all wear it the first day."

"Hollie, will you get one too?" Hallie looked at her.

Hollie scrunched up her nose. "I'd rather wear this outfit." She lifted her arms.

"Okay, let's find some fitting rooms so you guys can try them on." I glanced around and saw the fitting room sign at the back of the store.

"Back there," Alex pointed.

The kids ran ahead of us.

"Did you see anything you liked?" I nudged his shoulder.

"Yep," Alex smiled at me and draped his arm around my waist.

It was hard to move away from him on my crutches, so I bumped him with my hip and glared. "Don't do that. The kids don't know we agreed to date."

"You're being silly. I've been carrying you around for the past three days. Having my hand around your waist to help you would be a blip on their radar." Alex put up his hands. "But I'll keep my hands to myself if that's what you want."

The kids strolled into the fitting room area. I stopped in front of Alex and got on my tiptoes for a quick kiss. "It's not what I want, but I want to discuss our relationship with them first. Okay?" I spun around and sashayed my hips as I followed the kids.

"You're killing me, you know that, right?" Alex said loud enough for me to hear.

I glanced over my shoulder and winked at him.

We ended up buying the clothes the kids chose, and Hollie bought the fish shirt, but swore she wasn't wearing it the first day of school. Alex took our bags to the car so we could continue to walk down Main Street unencumbered.

We went into a small tourist shop and got small gifts for all the grandparents. After crossing the street, we bought some books at a local bookstore. I never complained about spending money on books. Alex carried all our bags like a loaded-down Santa Claus.

"Do you want to get a massage?" Alex whispered as we walked by a spa.

"No, I don't like people massaging me."

"I bet you'd like my massage." Alex drawled.

"I bet I would." I whispered.

"Ooh, Mommy!" Hollie spun around. "Can we get our nails painted?"

"You used to get pedicures with Annie." Alex pointed to my foot. "You can't do that, but maybe a manicure?"

On weekends, Annie and I would sneak away. Our feet yearned for a pedicure while the kids stayed with their grandparents. We enjoyed the pampering, which made the stress melt away, if only for an hour.

"Yes, a manicure, please?" Hollie placed her hands in prayer form and gave me her best puppy dog eyes.

"Come on, Mommy." Alex nudged my shoulder. "I'll take the kids for ice cream while you get a manicure."

"Wouldn't you rather get ice cream?" I asked Hollie.

Hollie's face fell.

"Okay, how about Hallie, Holden, Cody and I go to the arcade?" Alex pointed ahead with the bags.

"What arcade?"

I peered down our side of the block as far as my eyes could see. We hadn't passed an arcade on our walk down Main Street.

"I saw one a block before I parked. We can walk there. Unless you want to go to the arcade, too, Hollie?"

"No," Hollie shook her head. "I can skip the arcade for a manicure."

"Are you sure?" I didn't want to take time away from my kids. Once school started, I wouldn't see them as often, but I knew they loved arcade games.

"Positive. Besides, it's only for about an hour. Trust me, I got this."

Hollie smiled and faced Alex. " Perfect...Chief Reyes, you guys can play in the arcade for about an hour and then meet us at the ice cream place."

"Nice," Holden blurted and high-fived Hollie.

I shook my head and laughed. Hollie had Alex wrapped around her little finger.

"Hallie, do you want to come with us?" I held Hollie's hand.

"I'm gonna go with Cody—" Hallie stared at Cody. "—and Holden."

No doubt puppy love was in the air. Hallie followed the boys everywhere these days. And it wasn't to hang out with Holden.

"Woohoo!" Holden and Cody bumped fists.

"Thank you, Chief Reyes," Hallie smiled.

"Boys and Hallie, let's put all these bags in the car before we go play." Alex motioned with his arms toward the car. "Text me."

"Will do," I smiled, and Hollie and I turned around, swinging our arms as we went back to the spa for our manicures.

I picked an orangy-red color, and Hollie picked a hot pink, to match her outfit. We both turned on the massage on our chairs and enjoyed watching a channel that showed us different nail art. I loved nail art, and sometimes on Friday or Saturday nights, I would take out our nail polish colors and attempt simple designs like a flower or polka dots.

My phone rang. My dad's name was flashing.

"Hey Dad. How's it going?"

"Good, good. I just wanted to let you know the door arrived yesterday, and I just finished installing it so we can open for business tomorrow."

"That's great, Dad. Thank you."

"Oh, and I installed the cameras and made sure the alarm is no longer silent. Now it will wake up the entire island if someone breaks in."

I chuckled. "Sounds good, Dad."

"How's the mountains?"

"Majestic. I'm getting a pedicure with Hollie while the others go play video games. Do you want to talk to her?"

"Absolutely."

I handed the phone over to Hollie. "It's your grandpa."

"Hi, Grandpa," Hollie said before she got the phone to her ear.

I was fortunate enough to have parents who treasured their grandchildren and loved being involved in their lives. I'd only met Lincoln's parents once, and they hadn't been very nice to me. The thought of them being mean to my kids turned my stomach.

"We've been fishing, hiking, shopping. Oh, Mom bought me a new outfit for school, and we got matching fish shirts."

"It's really nice. Next time, you guys should come too."

"Okay. Here's Mom." Hollie handed the phone back.

"Hey, Dad."

"Sounds like you're having a wonderful time. I'm glad you got away from Lincoln."

"I wish," I grumbled. "He showed up here. I'll tell you later."

"Shit. I hope you were with Alex."

"I was."

"Okay. Enjoy your pedicure. I'll see you on Tuesday."

"Yep. Tell Mom I said hello. Love you."

"Love you, too."

"I think Grandpa and Grandma would like it here. Can we bring them next time?" Hollie's eyes pleaded her case.

"That sounds like a fantastic idea."

After the pedicures, I texted Alex, and we met up at the ice cream store. Everyone got their favorites, and we sat at an outdoor table to enjoy our cool treat.

I sat next to Alex while the kids sat together telling Hollie about all the video games she missed out on.

"My dad called." I told Alex between bites.

"Is everything okay at home?" Alex turned toward me.

"Yeah, he installed the new door, cameras, and now we have a not so silent alarm. He's going to open the boutique tomorrow."

"That's great news."

"I told him Lincoln had stopped by, but didn't want to get into it in front of Hollie."

"I bet he loved that." Alex grumbled.

"He was glad you were with me."

Alex nodded. "Me too."

I let the subject drop as I finished my cone. "This is going to ruin our dinner."

"Nah, I'll take them for a hike or fishing and we'll eat a little later." Alex grabbed our trash and threw it away before he sat back down next to me. "What do you want for dinner? I still have some steaks in the fridge."

"Sounds good. Let's finish what we brought so we don't have to take a full cooler back home."

"My thoughts exactly." Alex smiled and squeezed my thigh under the table.

While the kids were involved in an animated conversation about video games and not paying attention to us, I asked Alex about our relationship.

"Are we going to tell the kids that we're dating?"

"I'd like to." Alex grabbed my hand and laid it against my thigh. "We could tell them tonight. Are you okay with that?"

"Yeah," I nodded. "I am."

The kids finished their ice cream, and we headed back to the cabin. True to his word, Alex took them on the back porch for some fishing. I could put a little more weight on my foot every day, so I prepped the steaks and salad. After dinner, showers, and games, the kids got in bed for their nightly story.

"Alex and I wanted to talk to you guys about something." I sat with the book in my lap. I would read the chapter if they wanted me to after I spoke to them.

"You guys know that we've been friends for several years, and I really like Alex."

"And I like Sammie," Alex said before scooting next to me.

I grabbed Alex's hand for strength as I took a deep breath and said. "So, we are going to date. I hope you guys are okay with that."

The boys stared at each other with their mouths open. The girls' hands smacked together in a resounding high-five.

"Can we still talk about Mom?" Cody whispered.

"We can always talk about your mom. I will always love her. After all, she gave me you. I think it's time we made room in our hearts for Sammie, Holden, Hallie, and Hollie." Alex got up and knelt next to Cody. "Is that okay with you?"

"I just don't want to forget Mom." Cody's eyes watered.

"We won't." Alex kissed Cody's forehead.

"Cody." I set the book down and crawled next to Alex. "Your mom was my best friend. I don't want to forget her either. We shared many wonderful moments growing up. You can talk about her anytime you want."

"Thanks, Miss Sammie." Cody sat and hugged me.

"What about Daddy?" Hollie said.

Alex crawled to the girl's bed.

"He will always be your dad. I just want to be a part of your lives along with your mom." Alex held both their hands.

"Okay." Hollie nodded and smiled at Hallie.

"Do you guys want a story?" I grabbed the book.

"Yes, please." They all replied.

I leaned back against the girl's bed next to Alex and read the next chapter.

Chapter 37

She's Perfect

Alejandro

"That went well." Sammie whispered. "Better than I expected."

"Yeah, shocker, right?" I chuckled, put on pajamas, and crawled into bed with Sammie. She wrapped her arm around my waist and laid her head on my shoulder.

"Not really. They've seen us together a lot lately. It's not like we just met."

"True. Did you know the girls were matchmaking?"

"I suspected." Sammie grinned.

"I have to keep talking about Annie if that's what Cody wants. Are you okay with that?" I ran my fingers through her hair.

"Yeah. She was the closest I ever got to having a sister. I loved her. Is that why you still have her stuff in the house?"

"Partially, yes. I loved Annie, but I should've been a better husband and father. On the day of the break-in, when you yelled at me, you were right. If I had paid more attention, maybe I could've convinced her to get treatment sooner."

"No." Sammie leaned over me. "It was wrong of me to say that. I was with her all the time, and she kept her condition a secret from me. Maybe I should have paid better attention to her. Looking back, I remember her getting tired more often and taking pain pills. But I chalked it up to being a new mother and helping me with my kids. You are phenomenal with Cody, and I know you loved Annie. I could see it every time you looked at her and she at you."

"That's kind of you to say, but you know Annie and I weren't perfect, right? We fought a lot."

Sammie scooted back down and laid her head on my chest. "That's not what I saw."

"I'm not gonna deny we loved each other, but I worked a lot and Annie didn't like that. She envied you sometimes." I murmured.

"Why? My baby daddy was the winner of the Horrible Father-of-the-Year Award."

"Lincoln's an asshole, but you are the perfect woman. You gave birth to triplets and never complained or whined about how hard it was. You not only changed diapers and fed your triplets, but you also helped with Cody. Annie never understood your inner strength to never give up. Annie wasn't as strong as you. She wanted to be taken care of, whereas you give the world the finger and march on. She loved that about you. Hell, I love that about you even though sometimes you drive me fucking crazy." I chuckled.

"Oh, yeah." Sammie pinched my side.

"Yeah,"–I grabbed her hands and rolled us over–"but I can't seem to stay away from you." I kissed the ever-loving shit out of her.

Her body yielded to me, her legs adjusting to accommodate me. Kissing her wasn't enough. I needed to be inside her body. Sitting up, I pulled my t-shirt off.

"Your turn."

Sammie smiled wickedly and sat up, struggling to take off her tank top. Ever the gentleman, I helped her and threw it toward the floor.

"Do I need a condom?" I mumbled.

"No, I'm on the pill and I'm clean."

"I'm clean, too. But I'll put one on if you want."

"No," Sammie slowly shook her head.

Her beautiful, perky nipples called out to me. I latched on and drove her down onto the mattress. I couldn't get enough of her sweetness. Her body still tasted of strawberries from her shower. *I fucking loved strawberries.* After savoring each breast, I trailed my kisses down her abdomen to her pussy.

"Grab a pillow to cover your moans because unless you tell me to stop, I'm not stopping no matter how loud you get." I grumbled against her C-section scar. I kissed from one side to the other.

I couldn't wait to taste her juices. Spreading her legs wide, I got comfortable and licked her from front to back. Her hips pushed toward my face when I played with her clit with my tongue. Sliding a finger inside, I plunged in, reaching her G-spot. Her hands grabbed the sides of my head, holding me in place.

I was relentless with my mouth and fingers. When her body trembled and she tightened, I switched positions and thrust my tongue into her while my fingers tweaked her clit unmercifully. Her moans got louder, and her legs closed around my face. Breathing was difficult, but if I died this way, I would die a lucky man. Her orgasm burst onto my tongue, and I drank all of her sweet wine.

After I lapped up every drop, I kissed my way up her body, pushing the pillow off her face so I could reach her sensuous mouth. She wouldn't need the pillow anymore. I'd cover her noises with my mouth.

"Are you okay with this?" I murmured, making sure she still wanted to make love to me.

"Yes," she gasped and reached her hand down between our bodies, stroking me several times before bringing me to the entrance of her pussy.

I slid in easily, but slowly since she'd said she hadn't been with anyone in over nine years. The last thing I wanted was to hurt Sammie, but damn she felt so good and tight. Sweat poured off my forehead with the strain of holding back to maintain a slow pace. I wanted to make it good for her. I gauged my progress by her breathing. Every time she caught her breath, I stopped and then continued when she released it.

When I finally bottomed out, I stayed still, letting her adjust to my size. Not only had she not been with anyone in a long time, but I knew I'm on the larger side.

"Alex, I need you to move." Sammie pushed up with her hips.

"Yes, ma'am." I kissed her neck and started at a slow, sensual pace. Going all the way out before driving back in slowly, rhythmically, I rolled my hips before she begged me to go harder. I rolled us over so that she was now sitting on me and could pace herself and use me however she wanted.

Sammie sat up and ran her hands through her hair with her back arched away from me. She was glorious. I held her hips tightly to mine, following her lead. She rode me like a wave determined to drag me under. Crashing onto me at varying speeds until she dropped her hands onto my chest. Her nails bit into my chest while her hips thrust and ground into me.

"Alex." Her eyes sprang open, and her mouth dropped.

I knew the next sound out of her sexy mouth was going to be a loud as fuck moan as she climaxed. I grabbed her hair and pulled her mouth down to mine while I pistoned my cock deep inside her drenched pussy. Between her nails biting into my chest and her warm body tightening around my cock, my orgasm burst over and over. I've never come so hard before in my life.

Sammie collapsed on my chest, and I ran my hands over her back, holding her against me as the pounding of my heart returned to normal. I didn't want to let her go. And much to my surprise, I hardened again.

Sammie chuckled and lifted her head, raising an eyebrow at me.

"What can I say?" I shrugged. "You feel damn good, and my cock knows a good thing when he finds it. But I'll let you relax, he can calm the fuck down." I grumbled.

"I'm okay." Sammie smiled. "How about we save some water and shower?"

"I do like to save the environment." I kissed her and scooted us over to the edge of the bed. I wasn't ready to let her go. Grabbing her ass, I stood. Sammie yelped, but I ignored her and walked us into the bathroom. I sat her on the counter before I turned on the water and returned to her for a kiss.

I led her into the shower first, and I double-checked that both the bedroom and bathroom doors were locked. The more barriers I could put between us and the kids, the less they would hear–I hoped.

As Sammie rinsed her hair, the water cascaded down her face as she tilted her head back. I helped her get the shampoo out and turned her around to apply her conditioner. I washed her; she washed me, and we had amazing sex against the tile wall before we dried off and went to bed.

Chapter 38

Distracted

Sammie

After another early-morning wake-up sex session, Alex let me sleep in a few more minutes while he made breakfast. I could get used to this. Other than my parents, no one had ever made breakfast for me and my kids.

This morning I didn't want to stay in bed. I wanted to help him, so I took a quick shower, got dressed and headed to the kitchen. Alex was on the phone, and he didn't look happy.

"Okay," Alex nodded. "Thanks for letting me know. I'll see you tomorrow."

"Is everything okay?" I rubbed his back.

Alex put his phone on the counter, hugged me, and kissed the crown of my head before releasing me.

"There was another robbery in town."

"Here or in Haven?" I inquired before grabbing the plates, one at a time, to put on the table.

"Haven." Alex flipped a pancake. "The kids can set the table so you can rest your feet."

"It's okay. My left doesn't hurt as much anymore. Now I'm only babying my right." I hobbled along.

I was sure the kids would be sick of pancakes by now, but every night they asked Alex if he was making them pancakes and bacon for breakfast. He offered to make them eggs, but they always refused. Thank goodness he bought a ton of the stuff.

"Where?" I went back for silverware.

"This time it was the bank."

"What do you mean this time?" I stopped and stared at him.

Alex ran his hand over the back of his neck. "They robbed the bookstore after you and the bank on Saturday. Lucian didn't want to tell me so I wouldn't rush back."

"Do you need to go back?" I didn't want to leave, but if Alex had to go back, I would make it up to my kids.

"No." Alex shook his head. "Lucian and my officers are taking care of it. One more day here will be fine. I'm guessing you were planning on leaving early on Tuesday?" He glanced at me.

"Yeah, I need to unpack and do laundry since I didn't do it on Saturday."

"Then we'll leave early tomorrow. I'll text Lucian and let him know when to expect me at the office. I'll take you guys home, drop off Cody and go to work."

"I can keep Cody until you finish." I grabbed the stack of pancakes.

"Uh," Alex took the plate out of my hands. "I'll take that. You, Hopalong Cassidy, can have a seat. I don't want to remake them. I'm out of batter mix." Alex gave me a quick peck.

"Okay," I grumbled and sat at the table waiting for the kids.

"Breakfast!" Alex bellowed when he placed the bacon on the table.down.

Alex was quiet throughout breakfast, and I could tell he was thinking about the robberies. The kids didn't notice. They were happy discussing their options for their last day.

"Can we go to the waterfall?" Hallie blurted.

"Cody is the kid of the day, so it's his choice." I pointed out.

Everyone turned to Cody.

"Me?" Cody's mouth dropped.

"Yep, you're on vacation with us, so you should have a day, too."

"I'm good with the waterfall." Cody smiled at Hallie.

"Yay! I love the waterfall." Hollie bellowed. "Mommy, bring a blanket and our books."

"Will do."

"Chief Reyes, should we bring the fishing rods since it's our last day?" Holden looked at Alex, jarring him from his thoughts.

"Uh, yeah. Yes, we'll bring them." Alex nodded.

I cleaned up while everyone got ready. Alex called Lucian and told him about our plan for tomorrow, then we set off on our hike. We had another beautiful day made better without a Lincoln sighting. *I'm glad Alex and Cody came with us.* I couldn't imagine this trip without them.

We ate dinner out and packed up before the kids got to bed. Alex didn't come up with me because he said he had to read his emails.

"I'm gonna read a chapter, but then I need you guys to get to bed. I'll wake you up around 4:30 am so we can get on the road because Chief Reyes has to go to work. You guys can sleep in the car."

"Is he dropping me off at my house before he goes to work?" Cody frowned.

"No, you can stay with us until he finishes."

"Okay, cool."

"Continued vacation!" Holden yelled and slapped Cody's hand in a celebratory high-five.

Once they settled down, I read a chapter, kissed them all goodnight, and went downstairs to find Alex for a little adult time. He was on his laptop. I didn't even know he'd brought it because I hadn't seen it the whole time we'd been here. I liked that he'd unplugged and wished it had stayed that way for one more night. Reality could intervene tomorrow.

"I'm going to bed." I ran my hand over his shoulders.

"Yeah, okay." He said, reading something on the screen. "I'll be in soon."

I brushed my teeth, put on pajamas, and got in bed. I read for a little while waiting for Alex, but after two hours with no sign of him. I rolled over and turned off the light. The next thing I heard was my alarm clock waking me up at four in the morning. Reaching out to tap Alex next to me on the bed, I found it empty. When I turned on the light, his side was undisturbed.

I found him crashed out on the couch with the laptop open on his lap.

I sat next to him and caressed his cheek. "Alex, it's time to get up."

"What?" he grumbled.

"It's four in the morning."

"Shit." He closed his laptop and rubbed his face with his hands.

"Are you going to be okay driving?"

"Yeah, let me take a quick shower and then I'll pack up." Alex stood and put his laptop in his backpack, turned away from me and headed to the bathroom. I didn't like this cold Alex. *Where had my "you are so beautiful", "I can't stay away from you" Alex gone?*

I packed up everything from the kitchen using the coolers and bags we brought. Because we ate most of our meals at the cabin, there wasn't much food left to pack. By the time I stepped into the bedroom, Alex was out of the shower, dressed, and grabbing his duffel bag. He didn't say a word to me as he left the bedroom.

I didn't think he was mad at me, just preoccupied with work. I remembered Annie saying his work had been one reason they had grown distant. He was a workaholic and always expected her to take care of the home life. That would not work for me. I could handle the home life, but I refuse to be with someone who ignores me. I needed to know what was in his head. Lincoln had blindsided me—no man was ever doing that to me again. He could have today since we'd been out of town, but as soon as we got back into the swing of things, we needed to have a talk about balancing work with home life.

Alex and I had brief spouts of conversation, but he answered with yes or no answers. I will give him credit. He held my hand or placed his hand on my thigh for the entire drive. Despite the silence, we were sharing a connection. The kids were out cold in the backseat, and I let them sleep while the radio played low. My mind wandered to everything still waiting for us—school started in three days, meeting the teacher on Thursday, backpacks that needed to be packed and organized. Life didn't slow down for long, but for now, I didn't mind the stillness. The kids woke up around nine, and we went to a drive-thru window for breakfast.

We pulled into my parents' neighborhood, and I texted them. They met us at the door.

"Kids, get all your stuff so Chief Reyes can get to work." I ordered before I got out of the car.

"Hey, did you have fun?" My dad came over to help us.

The kids hugged him, grabbed their stuff from the trunk and ran into the house, stopping to hug my mom on their way in.

"Thanks for going with Sammie, Alex." My dad shook Alex's hand.

"You're welcome. It was fun." Alex pulled my luggage out and placed it on the ground before shutting his trunk.

"Are you staying for a while?" Dad inquired.

"No, sir. I have to get to work."

"Cody will stay with us until Alex is done." I turned to my dad. "Can you roll my luggage in? I just need to talk to Alex for a minute."

"Sure." Dad grabbed my luggage and went into the house.

"Are you gonna be okay?" I faced Alex.

"Yeah, I'll be fine. Just have to review all the reports."

"So, I'll see you later."

"Yeah, I'll text you before I come over to get Cody." Alex pulled me in for a hug. "Thank you for letting him stay with you. I'm sorry I've been so distracted.

These fucking break-ins are messing with me because I don't think it's the same person doing them."

"Different MO's?"

"Yeah, totally different." Alex brushed my hair off my cheek. "I'll see you later. Thank you for letting us join you."

"I'm glad you came." I smiled.

"I'm glad we both came," Alex grinned.

"Perv." I leaned up and kissed his lips.

Alex blinked before he picked me up and gave me an all-consuming kiss. Setting me back down, he handed me my crutch. "I'll walk you to the door."

"So gentlemanly of you." I bowed.

Alex chuckled. "I'm sorry our vacation ended so abruptly. Thanks for understanding."

"I understand." I nodded and stayed on the porch until he drove away.

Maybe I had misinterpreted? He just needed to get to work and process all the break-ins with Lucian. Then, he'd be back in time for dinner with us tonight—fingers crossed.

Chapter 39

Robberies

Alejandro

Sammie raised her eyebrows at me, a look of surprise on her face, when I said I was going into the station. I saw the disappointment in her eyes seconds before she blinked it away. By this point, she had to understand that my role as police chief was significant, and couldn't ignore it any longer.

I'd make it up to her somehow, just not tonight. I planned to sit with Lucian and get all the information on these sudden robberies. Haven Island hadn't had a robbery in over a year. Typically, a tourist on their way out of town was usually the one to target a store or bank. Our neighboring mainland office, the Jones County Sheriff's Department, always assisted us in apprehending them.

But we never had three in a matter of a week. *What the hell was going on?* I stormed into the station, giving the front office officer a wave as I continued to Lucian's office.

"What the hell is going on?" I barged in.

Lucian was on his computer when I entered. He turned to face me with a smile on his face.

"Well, hello there, Chief. How was your trip?"

"Fantastic until you told me about the robberies. What do you have so far?"

"Uh, where's Sammie?" Lucian looked around me.

"I dropped her and the kids off. Why?"

"Cause you can still have the day off and hang out with them instead of here."

"I can't. I need to know what the hell is going on."

"I knew I shouldn't have told you," Lucian sighed.

"I'm glad you did. So talk." I crossed my leg over the other and listened to Lucian's report.

"I'm still running down the list of tourists staying at the hotel, like you asked. Whoever is doing this wears gloves, so no prints. It's the same MO, throw a brick through the glass door or break it to enter. They go straight to the register, bust it open and steal the cash. Unfortunately, the idiot hasn't realized that most people use credit now and most of the businesses, except for the bank, don't have a lot of cash."

"How much did they take from the bank?"

"Twenty grand because the bank had not locked up the rest in the main vault, which the robber didn't know about—thank fuck." Lucian spun his chair around and grabbed the reports to hand me a set with all the specifics.

I scanned them, knowing I would have to read them word for word when I reached my desk.

"Camera footage?"

"Only at the bank." Lucian turned his screen around and keyed up the footage. "We've run it over and over again, but I can only see his eyes. We're still trying to find another camera in the area that might've caught him. The fucker shoved the money into his hoodie and ran over the bridge to the mainland. I've already sent this footage to them, and they're searching for camera footage. Someone had to have seen a masked man running over the bridge, right?"

"You would think. But not everyone wants to get involved, especially if they are on vacation."

"God forbid it delays their stay on our beautiful island." Lucian rolled his eyes.

"Run the tape for me." I leaned forward.

I saw a thin, white male with a baklava covering his face and his hoodie over his head. He pistol-whipped the guard on duty before he ran to the closest teller and waved his gun in her face. She hurried along, emptying her drawer and the other teller's drawer before slipping the money through the slot under the glass to the assailant. While the assailant was watching the teller, the teller next to her slid her hand under the desk.

"Right there." I pointed to the screen. "Did she push the emergency button?"

"Yep, the idiot never noticed her hand movements."

"Was there anyone else with him?"

"Not that we can see." Lucian shook his head. "I've checked all the camera angles, and I didn't see a lookout or a driver."

"I'm glad he didn't have a lookout. With a partner, he might have grabbed a teller as a hostage and forced them to open the vault."

"He seems to work alone and likes to go in and out quickly."

"If they're local—" I liked to play devil's advocate "—wouldn't they know the bank has a vault?" I flipped through the pages searching for red flags.

"Unless you're employed at the bank—" Lucian shook his head "—you wouldn't know."

"True," I replied, my voice echoing slightly. "The evidence shows that two separate individuals committed the break-ins and robberies. In the house break-ins, the intruders didn't steal anything. Instead, they left their trash. The scattered alcohol bottles, cigarettes, and weed baggies. But in the businesses, they stole money. Luckily, no one was hurt in any of those situations, although I'm sure the tellers are all shook up."

"You've read my mind, Chief. I think we need to look for school-aged kids for the break-ins and that skinny guy for the robberies."

"Fuck! I want all patrols looking for this skinny guy with the hoodie. I'm sure he'll change his clothes, but he'll probably still wear a hoodie and face covering. I'll call Jay and ask him to send me some extra officers and to check the mainland, too."

"Chief," Lucian paused long enough for me to make eye contact. "Do you think this guy could be Lincoln? Sammie's ex."

"Could be." I nodded. "He has the same build as Lincoln, but Lincoln showed up at the cabin, so if any break-ins happened on Friday or Saturday, it wasn't him. I'll double-check the times that I saw him and get back to you. In the meantime, I'll ask Griffin to go knock on his door since he lives on the mainland. See if Lincoln has any other residences. I'll be in my office."

"Got it, Chief." Lucian turned back to his computer.

"Give me an update before you leave for the day."

"10-4."

I left Lucian's office and headed to mine. I had a lot of reading and investigating to do.

Chapter 40

Meet the Teacher

Sammie

I hadn't seen or spoken to Alex since he dropped us off on Tuesday and went to work. His mom came over and picked up Cody after dinner to drive him home. Today was Thursday, Meet the Teacher day, and tomorrow would be their first day of fourth grade. I took off more days in the summer to spend that extra time with my kids. Time was flying by, and all I could think about was having to share my kids with Lincoln now that he was back in our lives.

My kids always got excited when they got to meet their teacher, look around their new classroom, and see where it was located compared to each other. The school had three teachers per grade, and I always separated my kids. It was harder for me this way, but better for them to be treated as individuals instead of 'the triplets'. Not that they weren't called that, anyway. When we got to the school, we met with Hollie's teacher first because her classroom was the first room on the right in the fourth-grade hallway.

A vibrant dinosaur theme brought her room's door to life. Each child's name was by a different dinosaur with Ms. Angie Draper's name in the center of a bright yellow sun. We opened the door and walked into a prehistoric museum exhibit. The wall-to-wall, floor-to-ceiling poster on the back wall drew you into the scene, drawing you into their environment. The image depicted a

Tyrannosaurus, a Triceratops, a flying dinosaur and others I couldn't identify in a swampy forest. Next to each or nestled under them, were their names and interesting facts. *What a great resource!*

We shuffled along in line until it was our turn to meet Miss Draper.

"Hi." Miss Draper's smile widened as her gaze swept over all my kids. Holden and Hallie gently nudged Hollie forward.

Miss Draper didn't miss a beat. She crouched down to Hollie's level. "I'm Miss Draper. Are you in my class this year? I love your dress."

Hollie had worn one of her summer dresses. She wanted to look nice for her new teacher.

"I'm Hollie Rogers." Hollie smiled.

"Well, it's nice to meet you, Hollie. I'm so excited to have you in my class."

"I love the poster," Hollie pointed to the back wall.

"Me too!" Miss Draper put her hand over her heart. "Do you like learning about dinosaurs?"

"I like anything in nature." Hollie shook her head.

"Maybe if they were shopping in nature," Holden snorted.

"That's not nice, Holden." Hollie crossed her arms and stared at him.

"Just telling the truth," he mumbled.

Miss Draper grinned and stood. "Hello, Mrs. Rogers. I'm Angie. You look familiar?"

"Of course she does."

I heard a voice behind me and pivoted, coming face-to-face with Grace. The lady I helped before our robbery at the boutique. "Grace, so good to see you again. What room are you in?"

"This one." Grace smiled. "I'm Miss Draper's associate teacher. Angie this was the nice lady I told you about that helped me at Siren's Boutique."

"That's where I know you from." Angie smiled. "I went in there to get some work clothes, but you were closed."

"We had a little incident, but we're open now." I smiled.

"Oh no, is everything okay? What happened?" Grace frowned.

"We had a robbery, but now we have a deafening alarm and cameras, so I'm sure it won't happen again." I nodded.

"Mommy." Hollie pulled on my shirt. "Do I have two teachers?" Her eyes bugged out.

"It looks that way."

"Hi Hollie—" Grace stooped. "—I'm here to help, Miss Draper. You call me Miss Grace. If you need anything, let me know."

"Mrs. Rogers, if you have any questions about my class, please reach out. On that table," Miss Draper pointed to the table by the door. "Is a sign-in sheet for today, classroom items that we need, and if you would like to volunteer in the classroom or for field trips. I'm glad to have Hollie in my class. Are these her siblings?"

I didn't recognize Miss Draper from my time volunteering at the school, but I was friends with several teachers and heard the school hired several new teachers.

"Yes, they're triplets. Holden's with Miss Stone, and Hallie's in Miss Warrick's class."

"That's so cool!" Grace blurted. "Triplets, wow."

"Perfect. You'll love Miss Stone and Miss Warrick." Miss Draper gestured toward the rows of tables and chairs. "Hollie, walk around and find your name. That will be your seat for tomorrow. And make sure you find your cubby too—that's where your backpack and lunchbox will go. No lunchbox? Then head over to that poster"—she pointed at the laminated chart stuck to a closed door by the classrooms—"and mark your lunch option."

"Thank you, Miss Draper."

"You're welcome. It was great meeting all of you." Miss Draper smiled and was ready to meet her next family.

"I can't wait to get to know you, Hollie." Grace waved and stood by Miss Draper.

"Nice to meet you too." I nodded, and when I turned, the kids had scattered around the room checking every table for Hollie's name. Divide and conquer, the story of my life.

"Hollie, over here!" Holden shouted, and pointed to the chair in front of him at a table for six, two on each side and one on each end cap.

Hollie bounced in her seat, eyes darting around the classroom, soaking it all in. Her seat was near the teacher's desk—exactly where she liked to be. As more kids filed in, a few waved or stopped to say hi to mine. That's how it was in our town—tight-knit, familiar, the kind of place where everyone knew a piece of your story.

"Look this way, Holls." I stood before her with my phone ready to take her picture. I got part of the dinosaur poster in the back. "Okay, kids." I motioned to the door. "Hollie, let's find your cubby and head out so we can go see Miss Stone and Miss Warrick." Those teachers I knew.

On our way out, I signed in, took a picture of the classroom requests, and put my name and email down for future volunteer opportunities. I was an approved volunteer on our island. I always tried to volunteer in each of my kids' classes at least once a week and for field trips.

Holden's teacher was Miss Carly Stone, and her room was like Miss Draper's, but instead of dinosaurs, hers had a humongous world map with several country closeup maps spread throughout. Again, we met his teacher and found Holden's seat and cubby. Holden was glad to have some friends in his class, but sad that Cody was not one of them.

Across the hall we entered Hallie's room, Miss.Rosie Warrick. She was Lucian's cousin. She was the youngest of the Warrick crew. Her brothers, Sawyer, Ronin, and Roman, were all police officers in Haven Island. And wouldn't you know, there stood Cody with his dad and a tall, tough-looking man in jeans and a leather jacket. He looked like a biker dude.

"Chief Reyes," Hallie screamed out and ran to him.

"Hey, Hallie." Alex dropped to one knee and caught her hug.

"Hey, Cody," Holden followed Hallie, and they fist-bumped.

"I guess Cody is in Hallie's class." I announced when I approached the men.

"Hey, Sammie." Alex finished hugging Hallie and Hollie. "This is Griffin Riggs, a buddy of mine who works for the Jones County Sheriff's division."

Wow, he didn't look like an officer at all. "Hi." I held out my hand. "I'm Sammie Rogers. Holden is Cody's best friend."

"Hi, Sammie." Griffin shook my hand. "It's nice to meet you."

Why didn't I get a hug? My kids knew we were dating, but did he want us to keep it a secret around the community? Griffin eyed Alex in some sort of silent language. Alex blinked, ignored Griffin, and turned to me.

"Sammie also owns the boutique in town that got robbed about a week ago." Alex told Griffin.

"I heard about that." Griffin faced me. "Are you okay?"

"She's fine. Kids, come meet Miss Warrick," Alex blurted and grabbed my elbow, leading me to where Miss Rosie was talking to the kids.

"We already know Miss Rosie," Cody rolled his eyes.

"Well, come with me anyway." Alex grumbled.

Was Alex jealous? His actions were giving me whiplash. I glanced back at Griffin, but he covered the smirk on his face with his hand and looked away.

"Uh, that was rude," I murmured to Alex.

"Nah, Griffin is used to my shitty attitude." Alex stopped in front of Miss Rosie. "Hey, Rosie. I see you'll be teaching Cody this year. He's lucky to have you."

"I'm the lucky one, Chief." Rosie smiled. "I'm glad he's in my class. And..." Rosie spun around toward Hallie. "one of the triplets. Hi, Hallie."

"Hi, Miss. Rosie. I'm happy to be in your class, too." Hallie looked around the room. "I love the underwater theme. I just started fishing."

"That's great, Hallie. You can tell everyone all about your adventures when we have discussions about certain sea life." Rosie placed her arm around Hallie.

"I'd love that." Hallie was beaming up at her. "Oh, and Cody fishes too. His dad taught me when we went on vacation."

"I see." Rosie turned and raised an eyebrow at Alex.

Alex cleared his throat. "Let's not keep Miss Rosie. Cody, find your cubby and let's go. I have to get back to the station."

"I can take him with us." I volunteered so the kids could hang out. *Was Rosie interested in Griffin?* Glancing out of the corner of my eye, I saw him grinning at her, and she blushed. Holy shit, she did like him.

"Don't you have to get to work too?" Alex said.

"Uh." Alex's question snapped me back into the conversation. "No, I took the day off since it was their last summer day."

"Can I go with Miss Sammie, Dad, please?" Cody pleaded.

"Let me talk to Miss. Sammie for a minute."

Rosie included Griffin in the conversation with the kids while Alex pulled me off to the side.

"I'm sorry I haven't called. Things have been crazy at the station." Alex whispered.

"I thought you were ghosting me." I crossed my arms over my chest and stared at him.

Alex was squirming, and I knew I had hit the nail on the head. Vacation was over.

"Look, Alex," I braced myself for rejection. I'd cry later. "You don't have to date me. I get it. I helped you over the celibate hump, and now you don't want to see me anymore." I shrugged. "That's fine. We can stay friends."

"What the fuck are you talking about?" Alex leaned into my face.

"I'm giving you an out."

"What if I don't want one?" Alex quirked his eyebrow.

I hooked a finger, dragging him closer. When he bent his head, I whispered, "Next time you fuck someone, maybe don't disappear for two days like a coward."

Alex's body jerked. He straightened, looked around, and growled. "I can't believe you just said that while we're in our kids' fourth-grade class and I can't respond properly. Because the sentence that just came out of your mouth is pissing me off. We need to talk because I didn't see it as fucking."

"You know what. I have a better idea. You figure out what the hell you want, and I'll go on with my life. Text me and let me know when you are getting Cody later or if I have to drop him off." I pushed him out of my way. "See you later."

*** Alex ***

"Shit," I muttered, regretting not calling Sammie, but I was swamped at work after our vacation, from the moment I stepped into the office. I admit my response could have been more tactful. Annie always disliked my secrecy, but I couldn't reveal anything about the ongoing investigation. I had been consumed with the robberies, especially since I had a sinking feeling Lincoln was involved.

Yet, deep down, I knew I was also using it as an excuse to keep my distance from Sammie. My head and body wanted her so damn bad, but my heart was afraid to love again. A part of my heart shattered when Annie died, but if Sammie left me or died, I didn't think I would make it. It would decimate me.

For years I'd counted on Sammie after Annie died, and I was afraid to move us into a romantic relationship. But hell, I already did that when I slept with her. Sammie wasn't a one-night stand, I knew that, so why was I treating her like one? She deserved better than my seesaw attitude toward her and the kids. I wanted Sammie in my life. I had to make a change.

Sammie had walked back to Rosie and Griffin. The kids were off to the side talking with their friends.

"Griffin, let's head out."

"You got it, Chief." Griffin grinned at Rosie. "It was nice meeting you. I'm sure we'll see each other again."

Griffin stuck his hand out and caressed her hand more than shook it.

"It was nice to meet you too, Griffin." Rosie's cheeks turned red, and she glanced at their hands.

Ah fuck! Sawyer was going to have a cow if Rosie dated Griffin. So many fucking layers of shit to shift through in that relationship.

"Sammie," I waited until she glanced at me. "I'll text you before I pick up Cody."

"Okay." Sammie nodded. "Bye, Rosie." She smiled and hugged Rosie. "I'll talk to you later." Without a backward glance, she walked to the kids.

"Dude," Griffin mumbled. "You are in the doghouse, and there's no door or way out."

"Yeah." I rubbed the back of my neck. "Don't I know it."

Chapter 41

His Holiness Made an Appearance

Sammie

I took the kids out for lunch before we headed home. They all went outside to play while I finished the laundry and pulled out all the paperwork I'd collected from each of their classrooms. I had a lot of forms to sign, which they had to return tomorrow on their first day.

Taking it all to the table, I made three piles—one for each child-and dug in. Everything was easy to fill out, volunteer status, agreements to check their weekly folders, and important school info. A simple task, but my mind kept wandering to Alex.

Things were perfect—right up until that stupid work call. Then Alex slipped back into the man Annie used to worry about, the one who couldn't turn it off. She adored him, but she hated being second to his job. Maybe that's why she wanted a baby—something that was hers to love when he wasn't around.

When Annie and I met Alex years ago, he was in the military and constantly deployed. Annie thought life would slow down once he left the service, but HiPD proved her wrong. He poured everything into that job, climbing to chief in just five years—the youngest in Haven Island's history. And that was the problem: he never knew when to stop achieving.

I didn't mind Alex's work schedule. We'd made it work as friends for years. Hell, I worked too. But now that we were dating, he should at least have the common decency to call or text me after work. *Was I being realistic? It had only been a couple of days?* I didn't want to be one of those clingy females that wanted him to call me every day, but a brief text would've been nice. I didn't want our kids to believe that dating someone meant they were completely invisible. My intention was for them to understand that love and care were essential for building relationships. *Whoa, did I just admit to myself that I love Alex? Shit, I did. I've been in love with him ever since our eyes met a decade ago.*

Great. I fell in love with my deceased best friend's husband. It sounded like a made for television movie. I dropped my head onto the table. Stupid, stupid, stupid.

"Sammie?" I heard my mom's voice before I raised my head. "Are you okay?"

"Hi, Mom." I grinned at her and waved my hand over all the paperwork sprawled out on the kitchen table. "Just finishing up all this first day of school parent homework."

"I don't miss those days, and I only had one." Mom smiled. "Do you need me to start dinner?"

"What time is it?" I looked at my watch. *Holy shit, it was already five.* I needed to get my act together and feed the kids. "I didn't realize it was so late. I'm gonna make some tacos. Where's dad?" I stood and gathered the kids' paperwork, separating it so I could put it in their respective backpacks.

"He's still at work. Closing up." Mom brought me their backpacks.

"Thanks." I grabbed each one and slipped the papers inside. "We'll leave him some taco meat so he can eat when he gets home."

"Why is there an extra backpack?" My mom held it up.

"It's Cody's. He's in Hallie's class, and I brought him home with us so Alex could go back to work."

"I bet Holden didn't like that." Mom snickered. "But I think our little Hallie has a crush on Cody."

"I was wondering the same thing. Ugh," I sighed, "they grow up too fast."

"Tell me about it." Mom went upstairs, and I strode into the kitchen so I could cook the meat.

*** Alex ***

"So, you think it's the same person doing the robberies?" I asked Lucian.

We had been meeting with Griffin in my office since I got back from Meet the Teacher and my doghouse moment.

"I do." Lucian nodded. "He seems to be a step ahead of us, which sucks."

"Which places has hit so far?" Griffin sat up as I showed him a map of Haven Island.

I circled the places in number order.

"These are the ones still vulnerable." I pointed to the others.

"So he started with the boutique and hit up a different location every other night except the weekend you were out of town. If my calculations are correct, he'll be out again tonight." Griffin pointed out.

"Shit." I bolted out of my chair and stared at Lucian. "Do you think it was Lincoln, and that's why nothing happened over the weekend? Because he fucking showed up at the cabin."

"Who the hell's Lincoln?" Griffin frowned.

"Sammie's ex. The father of her triplets." Lucian answered while I paced.

"Why would he want to rob her or the other businesses?"

"Because he's an asshole with a long rap sheet." I stopped and braced my hands on Lucian's desk. "Lucian, I need you to find out where the hell he's been. I need to know where he was. Don't forget that he was at the cabin on Friday just before sunset, and he was higher than a kite. On Saturday he approached us when I was fishing with the kids."

"You got it, Chief." Lucian stood and gathered his papers.

"What time was the bank robbery?" Griffin handed him the one he'd been holding.

"Ten, as soon as they opened."

"So, he could've done it and left town immediately." Griffin stared at me.

"Yep, it's about a six-hour drive."

"What do you want me to do?" Griffin stood and took a photo of the map with his phone.

"Can you hang out and pretend to be a tourist anywhere on Main Street?"

"Uh, I'm not wearing a fucking flamingo shirt and plaid shorts if that's what you're asking." Griffin grumbled.

"I'd love to see that." Lucian snorted.

I burst out laughing. That was the last thing I wanted him to do. He would stand out like a sore thumb. "How about jeans, a muscle shirt, and your bike?" I raised my eyebrow.

"That," Griffin pointed at me, "I can do."

"Perfect. Hell, you might even get Lucian to ride with you." I pointed between the two of them.

"I love the sound of that. See you tomorrow at Hi Grill for breakfast, biker friend." Lucian slapped Griffin on the back and left the office.

"I think he's enjoying this too much." Griffin pointed his thumb over his shoulder at Lucian.

"Can you also drive around at night from sunset to sunrise and look for Lincoln? I'll text you a picture of him. As for Lucian, he likes to be outside, not cooped up in his office."

"Don't we all?" Griffin stood. "And yes, I'm off tonight, so I'd be glad to drive along Main Street and watch for a robbery." Griffin left and shut the door.

Alex sat down and turned the map around to face him. Strange that their burglar had hit the boutique first. It had to be Lincoln, but why rob the other places? He needed to find the evidence to arrest his ass and throw him in jail. *Perhaps he slipped up and left a print.*

A reminder alarm went off on his phone. The one he'd set to remind himself to text Sammie and pick up Cody.

> Alex: Leaving office now to get Cody. Can I bring over dinner?

> Sammie: Nope. Just finishing the ground beef for tacos. You're welcome to join us.

> Alex: Sounds good. See you in a few.

> Sammie: k

My doghouse door opened. *Thank fuck!* We needed to talk. She needed to know that I wanted her in my life as a partner and future wife. The hardest part for me was balancing work and my relationship, since there's nothing like seeing my love after a tough day. My love. Sammie was my love. I loved everything about her. Her smile, the way she embraced me, her sighs and moans after I satisfied her—just everything.

Sammie needs to know I'm totally into her - I love her. I've got her back, and I'm not going back to being a workaholic like I was when I was with Annie. After Annie's passing, I reduced my work hours so I could dedicate more time to raising Cody. As my anger at her death slowly hardened my heart, I felt myself retreating and fell back to depending on my parents and Sammie to take Cody. It had to stop. The demands of work were stealing away the precious years I should have been spending with my son. I can't go back to old habits. Unless I put my family first, my relationship with Sammie will suffer, and it's not fair to either of us if that happens.

Chapter 42

The Set Up

Lincoln

"**S**o, is my kid in your class?" I immediately asked Ava Grace when she entered our apartment.

"Yes." Ava dropped her keys on the counter. "Hollie is very sweet. I can see why you like her."

"I like her because she's the only one who gives me the time of day. I wish Holden would talk to me."

"It'll come. I'm sure between Hollie and I we'll help the other two come around." Ava headed to the kitchen.

"I need it to happen sooner. We're running out of money." I grabbed a beer from the fridge before dropping onto the couch.

"What are you talking about? You just got those new investment clients from your father." Ava frowned and sat in the chair opposite the couch facing me.

"They didn't pan out." I wasn't about to tell her I used part of that money to gamble and lost it. Thank fuck I kept some to buy the coke packets I added to my previously non-existent stash.

"What are you talking about?" Ava pulled out her phone and scrolled around. "Oh, my God!" She put her hand over her mouth.

I shouldn't have told her about the new clients.

"I just looked a couple of days ago, and there were hundreds of thousands of dollars. Where did it go?" Ava stood and shoved the phone in my face.

I swatted her hand, and the phone went flying across the room.

"What did you do with our money, Lincoln?" She murmured, stunned by my response.

"Forget about it. All you need to know is they pulled out."

"What do you mean, they pulled out? They asked for their money back?" Ava grabbed her phone.

"It's my business. I don't ask you about yours, do I?" I bolted off the couch and stalked to her. "Do I?"

Ava cowered. "No," she whispered.

"Then stay out of it!" I shouted in her face.

Ava took a few steps back.

"How are we going to pay the rent? I don't get paid for two weeks."

I needed to soothe Ava before I went in for the kill. That Coke was only going to last a week, and I would need another fix soon. I reached out and hugged her tightly.

"I'm sorry. I'm really stressed about my kids and my new clients. Please forgive me, Ava Grace. I love you." I kissed the top of her head. "Do you think we can ask your parents? We haven't asked them in a while."

"I could try." Ava moved out of my arms. "But we can't keep asking them."

"I know, baby. I'll get more clients, I promise." I kissed her and pushed her toward the couch. Landing on top of her, I kissed my way to her neck. "When do you think we can get the kids?"

"What do you mean, get the kids?" Ava moaned.

"Maybe bring them home after school so we can take them to meet my parents." I never told Ava I was going to use my kids as leverage to extort money from my parents. She wouldn't like that.

"Are you sure their mom will approve of that? I mean, Sammie seemed nice, but."

"I think if those kids like you, they'll follow you anywhere. You're a wonderful teacher and helper. Just keep working on Hollie."

"But I can't just bring her home. I'm not allowed to check her out. I'm not an emergency contact. Remember, you didn't want me to tell anyone that we're married."

"Well, I'm their parent. It'll be fine. Just add your name to the list." I ran my hand under her shirt and grasped her breast. She loved when I played with them.

"I don't think it's that simple." Ava moaned.

"You'll figure it out."

I went back to her mouth after that because I didn't want to discuss it anymore, and I definitely wanted no more questions. All I wanted was to fuck my wife.

Chapter 43

Policy Schmolicy

Sammie

Alex and I had a mini-talk when he came over to pick up Cody after Meet the Teacher two weeks ago, and I gave him an out.

"I'm sorry I haven't been around. I'm not trying to ignore you. I've had a lot of work since I was gone for so long,*" Alex told me when we stepped outside while Cody said goodbye to my kids.*

"I understand. No problem."

He leaned in to kiss me, but I wasn't in the mood for his lips, *so I turned my head and he kissed my cheek instead.*

"I think there is a problem." He murmured against my skin.

"I need to get the kids into a routine since school starts tomorrow, and you need to catch up on work." I took a step back and pulled the door open. "We'll reassess our relationship in a couple of weeks."

"I'm not sure I like the sound of that." Alex grumbled.

I ignored him and entered my house, not caring that he didn't like the sound of me backing off. I called Cody, and they left.

He had been radio silent since. In his mind, he must've thought I meant I needed space with no contact. Not what I was thinking. A text or call would've been nice, but I should've been clear. That was on me.

My kids were into the routine of school, homework, dinner, bedtime. I wanted to spend some time with them, so I asked my parents to close the shop so I could take them to an early dinner at Hi Grill and Yummy for ice cream. My kids didn't know I was picking them up. I wanted to surprise them when they saw me in the pickup line instead of my mom.

I pulled up along with every other parent waiting for their child and smiled when I saw Hallie and Holden. *Where was Hollie?* Holden opened the door and frowned.

"Hey, where's Hollie?" I asked and glanced in front of me. Parents and teachers got mad if you didn't move up and keep the car line going.

"We haven't seen her." Hallie got in the back.

"I thought she was with you." Holden got in the front seat.

"No, I just got here." I drove my car to Rosie.

The teachers took turns in the pickup line by grade, so they didn't all have to stand outside. Holden rolled the window down.

"Hi, Rosie, have you seen Hollie?"

"Hi, Sammie. She left with her associate teacher, Miss Grace."

"What?" I screeched.

Rosie jolted. "You didn't know she was taking her home?"

"No. Let me park and I'll talk to the front office."

"Okay, let me know if you need anything." Rosie frowned as I pulled away and turned into the parking lot.

This was weird. All my kids always sat together instead of with their own classes. Usually they sat with Cody, so why had Hollie left with Miss Grace?

"Leave your stuff in the car and let's go inside. I need to find out why Hollie left with Miss Grace without my permission."

I stormed out of the car with my two kids in tow. Glancing around, I waited for the cars to stop before I crossed with my kids. You had to make eye contact, or you could get run over. So many parents absorbed with their phones instead of the pickup line.

I looked over and found Cody talking to Rosie. No sign of Hollie. Cody looked up with a worried look on his face and pulled out his phone. Good, that meant Alex would be here shortly. One less call I had to make. The front desk lady buzzed me in.

"Hi Stacy, my daughter, Hollie, is missing. Miss Warrick said Miss Grace signed her out, but she's not on my approved list. I'd like to know why you guys allowed this?" I tried to stay calm and not yell at the poor woman in case this wasn't her fault.

"Oh, my God, Sammie." She covered her mouth and immediately grabbed the walkie-talkie. "I need Officer Spencer and Principal Cook in the front office immediately." She set the walkie and pointed to a chair. "Please have a seat."

I heard the voices on the walkie saying they were on their way. They both burst into the front office. The front desk lady pointed at me and my kids.

"Sammie," Officer Charlotte Spencer rushed over to me. "Are you okay? What happened?"

"Hi." Principal Cook came over. "I'm Principal Cook. I see you know our resource officer, Charlotte Spencer. What can we do for you?"

I stood. "My daughter, Hollie, left with her associate teacher, Miss Grace, and I want to know why. She is not on my approved list."

"Let's go into my office for some privacy. Do you want your kids to come in or hang out in the library?"

"I'm going in," Holden stated.

"Me too." Hallie affirmed.

Principal Cook had a table and chairs in the back of her office with coloring pages and crayons. "Do you kids want to sit here?"

The kids went to the table, but I sat in the chair facing her desk while Officer Charlotte stood behind Principal Cook.

"Let me access your approved list." She typed and clicked before she stared at her screen and smiled at me before turning her screen toward me.

"It says here that your husband added Miss Grace to the approved list."

"I'm not married. I'm divorced. How was he able to do this without my consent?"

"I...I," Principal Cook's eyes bulged. "All parents have a right to add to the list. It doesn't state in your file that he is not involved."

"Are you serious? Just because I listed his name as the father doesn't give you guys the right to let him do this. I have full custody. He can see them only under supervision. Does your file say that?"

"I'm sorry, no." She clicked around again, and Officer Charlotte glanced at the screen before clicking the radio on his shoulder and saying several numbers, but all I heard was missing child before my eyes teared up. *Oh, my God. My baby was missing. How did this happen? I thought she was safe at school.*

"We haven't run a background check on him because he wasn't the one who checked out your child." The principal murmured out loud before she realized her mistake.

"What!" I exploded out of the chair. My kids came to stand beside me, grabbing my body for support.

"Where's Hollie?" Hallie cried.

"Mom, what's going on?" Holden was tapping my shoulder.

"Miss Grace is one of her teachers, so no one questioned her taking Hollie home. We thought you approved it."

"Why didn't anyone call me? I have two other kids here. Didn't you think it was suspicious for her to take only one? What possible reason could she have to take one of my kids?" My voice rose with anger. I needed to calm down. I was scaring Holden and Hallie, but my adrenaline was like a runaway train with no end in sight.

"A doctor's appointment." Principal Cook winced.

"I know you are new to our school and still learning your way around, but I can assure you this school doesn't allow its teachers to take kids' home without verbal parental consent or special circumstances. Especially when they are not their children!"

Principal Cook glanced at Charlotte.

"She's right." Charlotte murmured. "That is the school's policy."

"Have you checked at home? Maybe Miss Grace already dropped her off." Now Principal Cook was picking at straws trying to save her ass.

I whipped out my phone and called my mom.

Bless my mom for answering on the first ring. "Hey, honey, everything okay?"

"Are you at home or at the boutique?"

"Your dad and I are still at the boutique, why?"

"Is Hollie with you? Or Dad?"

"No." My mom must've covered the phone because I heard her muffled voice as she asked my dad if he had seen Hollie. "We haven't seen her. What's going on?"

"The school is telling me Miss Grace, her associate teacher, took her home, but I never gave Miss. Grace those privileges."

"Your father just left to run home and see if she's there. Call me if you hear anything. I'm gonna finish with these customers and close up."

"Stay open a little longer in case she shows up."

"Okay. Where are Holden and Hallie?"

"They're with me. I'm gonna call the pol–" Alex burst into the room. "–never mind. Alex is here."

"Call me back and let me know what to do."

"I will. Love you, Mom."

"Love you, too."

"What the hell is going on?" Alex's eyes bounced around the room before Hallie ran to him. "Hey, sweetie." Alex knelt, wiping the tear tracks from her cheeks as he brushed the hair away. "It's going to be alright. I'll find Hollie."

Then Hallie burst into another set of tears and wrapped her arms around his neck. Alex hugged her back and glared at Principal Cook.

Chapter 44

Find My Daughter

Sammie

"**D**o you want to tell me what the hell happened?" His voice thundered in the room.

Principal Cook summarized the situation for Alex.

"Why don't you kids go sit out there with Cody?" He pointed to the front office waiting room.

"Mommy?" Hallie looked so lost.

I went to her and gathered her in my arms. "It's okay. Go sit with Cody and I'll let you know what's going on after we all talk.

"Okay." Hallie grabbed Holden's hand as they left the room.

Alex shut the door, spun around and crossed his arms like an angry sentry glaring at Principal Cook.

"I want to know everything about this Miss Grace person. Officer Spencer, grab your computer and bring it in here so we can run some checks."

"Yes, sir."

"Sammie." Alex pulled me in for a hug and whispered in my ear. "We're going to find her. Trust me."

I was trembling in his arms, but I knew Alex was in control of the situation and he would find my baby. We needed to go find her. I didn't want to just sit here. *Where was Lincoln?* I stepped out of his arms and began pacing. *What was happening to her? She must be so confused.* I nodded and stepped away from Alex rubbing my hands on my face to wipe away the tears.

"Why would she take her?" My voice broke as I stared at Alex.

"I don't know, but I promise you I will find out."

"I'm so sorry about this misunderstanding." Principal Cook held out a tissue for me.

I cut her off and glared at her. *Misunderstanding. What the fuck?*

"Principal Cook, a misunderstanding is the failure to understand something correctly. This was not a misunderstanding!" I braced my hands on her desk and screamed in her face. "My child is missing! How would you feel if it were your child from an estranged ex who took your child, huh!"

"Sammie," Alex whispered in my ear and held my shoulders, pulling me away from her desk. "This is not helping."

Alex turned me around and cupped my face. "Listen to me." He lowered his voice and spoke calmly. "We will find Hollie. Right now, I need you to take a few deep breaths and let me do my job."

"Sammie, we will fix the records if you could please have a seat, and we will update your family status while you are here."

I spun around. "Update my family, what? My child is missing. This school fucked up! You fucked up!" I took a step toward her, but Alex wrapped his arm around my waist. The blood drained from her face. I would not hit her, just continue yelling at her.

"Principal Cook, with all due respect, please be quiet until we get more information from Officer Spencer's computer. Now is not the time to ask Sammie to fill out paperwork."

"Of course." She placed her hands on her desk and shut her trap—finally.

Charlotte burst through the door holding her laptop. Standing next to her was Detective Lucian.

"Ryker, Judge, and I came as soon as we heard." Lucian followed Charlotte, and they set the computer on the back table. "Ryker and Judge stayed with Cody, Holden, and Hallie."

"Thank you, Lucian. My kids love hanging out with Judge."

"Everyone loves Judge, and Ryker wanted to make sure you were okay." Everyone stood facing the computer screen while Charlotte typed something in.

The screen popped up with video footage from the cameras around the school. There was a camera that faced the pickup line, several that faced the hallways, and others that faced any exterior doors. There were at least sixteen images playing at one time. My eyes bounced from one angle to the other looking for Hollie.

"Let's focus on the footage of the main exits." Lucian told Charlotte, and she closed out the interior footage.

The screen was now divided into four quarters. The front doors of the building, the back, and two side doors by the cafeteria. Even though it was still a challenge to watch four videos simultaneously, it was much more manageable than trying to keep track of sixteen!

"There," Alex shouted and pointed to one camera by the cafeteria parking. "Is that Miss Grace with Hollie?"

"That's her!" I shouted. *How the hell did he see that?*

"Zoom in on that feed and replay it." Alex grumbled.

"It looks like Miss Grace is Ava Grace Rogers." Detective Lucian's mouth dropped and he stared at Alex. "She's married to Lincoln." Then he nodded to me. "Her ex. And his prints were just identified in the robberies. The lab called me before I got here."

"Fuck!" Alex blurted out. "Is that Lincoln in the fucking car?" Alex hollered.

"Oh...my...God." I covered my mouth. "He's married?"

"She looks happy to see him." Principal Cook grinned.

Insensitive Bitch! I lunged at her, but Alex grabbed me before I could put my fist through her face.

"I suggest you keep your comments to yourself." Lucian stood blocking the computer.

"I wasn't trying to be mean?" Principal Cook cried out.

I didn't acknowledge her apology because it meant nothing to me. *How did I not know Lincoln was married?* Every time he showed up and asked to see his kids, I thought he wanted to get back together with me. I never thought of asking him whether he was married. My phone rang, and everyone spun toward me.

I held it up. "It's my dad."

"Hey, Dad. Is Hollie at home?"

"No, honey," he sighed. "What can I do?"

I shook my head and watched them all deflate like a tire that had sprung a leak. Alex grabbed the phone out of my hand and put it on speaker.

"William, it's Alejandro. Can you please stay there in case she shows up?"

"Sure, but someone has to get Eleanor from the boutique. She closed, but doesn't have a ride home."

"I'll send one of my guys to get her. Sit tight and call Sammie if Hollie shows up."

"Of course."

Alex hung up and handed me the phone. "Can you text me a photo of Hollie?"

"Yes." I scrolled through my phone as a rush of tears slid down my face. So many photos of my little girl, smiling and laughing. *How could Lincoln do this?* I found a beautiful photo of her looking head-on at the camera with her sweet smile from our vacation. She was standing in front of the waterfall, splashing water up into the air.

"Sammie," Alex brushed my hair behind my ear. "Do you think Lincoln would harm Hollie?"

"I...I don't know." I stared at him. *Would Lincoln harm our daughter?* I hadn't seen him in so long. "If he was on drugs, maybe?" I shrugged. It was possible.

"Text me that photo." Alex pulled me into his arms and said over his shoulder. "Issue an APB, a BOLO, and an Amber Alert for Hollie," Alex commanded, his words echoing in my ears as I dropped my phone and I wept, clutching onto him. Where had Lincoln taken my baby?

"Lucian, get her phone and text that photo to me and yourself. Send it out with the alerts. Then get me Lincoln's address so we can go to his location."

"I want to go." I fisted Alex's shirt and pulled him toward me.

"No."

"That's my daughter!" I screamed in his face.

"I'm sorry, Sammie," Alex shook his head and released my hands from his shirt. "I'm gonna take you home, and I need you to stay put. We don't know what his endgame is, and I will not risk your life or your kids when we confront him."

"If you don't let me go, I'll follow you." I crossed my arms and cocked my hip. I meant business.

"Chief, I'll go to his location. You stay with Sammie."

"Fine." He growled.

"Men!" I threw my arms up and stomped out of the principal's office. She tried to pacify me again. I'm sure she was afraid I would sue her or have her job, but that wasn't on my mind right now. Right now, I just wanted my baby girl found safe and in one piece away from her asshole father.

Chapter 45

The Con

Lincoln

Ava Grace did exactly as directed. I waited with my car running by the cafeteria back door. As soon as the bell rang, Ava stepped out with Hollie. I could see the frown on Hollie's face, but as soon as she saw me, her face brightened, and she ran to the car.

"Hi, Daddy. What are you doing here?"

Ava opened the back door and helped her buckle in. I left as soon as Ava sat in her seat. We had to hurry off school property before anyone caught on.

"Don't you want to wait for Hallie and Holden?"

Looking through the rearview mirror, I saw Hollie looking out the window at the pickup line.

"No, it's our special day." I smiled at her.

"Mommy said our visits should be supersized."

"You mean supervised," I chuckled. "They are. Miss Grace is here with us, and she's one of your teachers."

"Okay." Hollie smiled at Ava.

"Do you like Miss Grace?" I glanced at Hollie to gauge her reaction.

"I do."

"I bet you didn't know that Miss Grace is my wife, your stepmom." I dropped the bomb because I needed her to know before I introduced her to my parents.

"Really? Why didn't you tell me, Miss Grace?" Hollie frowned at Ava Grace. "This is so cool. Wait till I tell Hallie and Holden."

I continued to drive straight to my parent's house on the mainland while Hollie questioned Ava on how we met and married. I wasn't stopping until

I reached my destination. Hollie needed to meet my parents and melt their hearts before Sammie figured out where we were. I was running out of time. The bookie had already sent a guy to our apartment to threaten me. If I didn't give him fifty grand by the end of the week, I would pay for it with broken bones—a different one per day. Not sure how he found me, but the last thing I wanted was to have broken bones or worse—truly kidnapped kids.

I know I'm not winning any Father of the Year awards, but even I draw the line at a bookie's henchmen taking my kids and hurting them to get to me. I called my mom before I got Ava Grace and Hollie to let her know I had a special surprise. It would've been nice to introduce her to all three kids, but for a quick payout, one kid would do.

I pulled up to the monitored gate and hit the buzzer. After I'd taken some of my parents' valuables and gotten caught, they had me buzz in before visiting.

"Master Lincoln, your mother has been expecting you. Come through."

"Thanks, Benjamin." My parents had several security officers, but when they were walking the perimeter—I'm not sure why; they weren't Mafia—Benjamin, their butler, answered the gate call. My parents had a shit ton of money, but they didn't keep any of it at home, as far as I knew.

"Wow," Hollie's voice whispered from behind me. "Who lives here?"

"Your grandparents. This is the house I grew up in." I smirked.

From the outside, the house was an architect's dream, a monument to innovative design. The decor inside was pristine, but the house's chilling atmosphere came with strings attached. My mom was always busy with her social engagements, and Dad was working or golfing. It suited me perfectly. They left me with funds to "have fun" and plenty of time to enjoy them. If they had known I was using it for drugs and gambling, I'm certain they would have reconsidered their decision. After I graduated high school, they stopped the flow of easy money until I went to college. As they say, "C's get degrees." I graduated, and they helped me get my business started. I followed their rules to keep my inheritance.

Then I broke their last rule. I was supposed to marry a woman who came from a family that had significant wealth. That had not been Sammie. Really, they were the ones that forced me to leave Sammie and my kids. It was all their fault they didn't have grandkids, but I was going to help them out. They should thank me and fall at my feet for granting them their wish.

We stood by the front door, and I rang the doorbell.

"Master Lincoln." Benjamin opened the door to allow us in. "Good to see you. Your mother is in the den."

"Thank you, Benjamin." I motioned with my arm for Ava and Hollie to go ahead of me.

"Hi." Hollie bounced up to Benjamin and put her hand out for a handshake. "I'm Hollie. It's nice to meet you."

Benjamin grinned and shook her hand. "Nice to meet you as well, Hollie."

I took Hollie's hand and put my hand on Ava's lower back as I led them into the den. My mother was sitting in her favorite straight-backed chair watching the news.

"Mother, it's good to see you." I led the girls to her, and she stood for her air cheek to cheek kisses. I never understood why she did dual kisses. We weren't European, at least not that I knew, and the air kisses were so fake, they annoyed me.

"Hello, Mrs. Rogers." Ava repeated the nauseating double kisses.

"And who might this be?" My mother frowned at Hollie.

I laid a hand on Hollie's shoulder and squeezed before she said anything. Hollie was so quick to introduce herself to anyone, I wanted to be the one to introduce her.

"Mother, this is Hollie, my daughter." I stared at my mom, watching several reactions appear on her face. Confusion to joy, to anger, and finally acceptance with a dash of disappointment.

"Your daughter?" She enunciated every letter in slow detail.

"Hi." Hollie extended her hand like she did with Benjamin. "I'm your granddaughter. It's nice to meet you."

"Uh...Hi Hollie." My mother's eyes softened, which shocked the hell out of me. I don't remember her ever looking at me like that. "Please sit with me and tell me all about yourself."

Mom led Hollie to the loveseat and sat next to her, absorbed in everything Hollie said.

I leaned over and whispered in Ava's ear. "This is going better than I expected."

"Did you think she would close the door on a child's face?" Ava snickered. "Your mom can be cold, but not even she would treat a child like that, especially if said child was family."

"I guess." Still shocked by how well they were getting along.

"Lincoln, do be a dear and ask Benjamin to bring us tea. Your father will be home shortly."

"Are we going to have a tea party, Grandma?" Hollie's mouth dropped.

"Indeed, a proper one with delicate porcelain cups and the inviting aroma of delicious English tea."

"Wow, can Miss Grace join us?"

My mom pointed at Ava. "You mean Ava Grace?"

"Yes, she's my second teacher. I have two."

I heard Ava explaining to my mom how she was Hollie's associate teacher this year as I left the room to find Benjamin.

Chapter 46

Where's Hollie?

Sammie

Alex followed me and the kids home in his patrol vehicle.

"Dad!" I hollered as soon as I entered. "Have you heard anything?"
My mom and dad walked into the living room simultaneously as we came in.
"No." My mom was wringing her hands. "We were hoping she was with you."
"No," I sighed. "How did you get home?"
Mom pointed at Alex. "One of his officers helped me lock up and drove me home. I didn't want to stay there by myself when I could be here with my family."

"I get it." I hugged her. "I wouldn't want you to stay there alone either."

"Mommy, where's Hollie?" Hallie cried.

"Uh, I think she's with your dad."

"Then call him and tell him to bring her home," Hallie whined.

"We're trying."

"Did Dad kidnap her?" Holden's angry voice boomed over mine.

"We don't know everything yet, and we're gonna find out. Why don't you guys go to Holden's room and play?" I didn't know how much to tell them because if Lincoln ever got custody, he could accuse me of brainwashing the kids. I'd heard horror stories about custody battles.

"I can call my parents, and they can come get them." Alex whispered after the kids left.

"That's nice, but I'm guessing they'll want to stay here waiting for Hollie to show up. Do you want to take Cody to their house?"

"If I know my kid, he'll want to stay here with Holden."

"Follow me." My mom spun around and led us into the kitchen. "I just made a pot of coffee."

Mom and I got busy pouring cups and setting everything on the table.

"Have you heard from any of your officers?" I sat next to Alex, my leg bouncing under the table.

"Not yet." Alex reached over and placed his hand on my thigh. "They'll follow every lead they can and let me know as soon as they find out something."

"Have they gone to his house?" I relaxed my leg and sighed.

"They did. No one was there." Alex took a sip before grabbing his ringing phone.

"What do you have for me?" Alex answered. "Yeah. Okay. Motherfucker, how did we miss that?"

"What?" I shook Alex's shoulder. "What's going on?"

"Yeah, okay. I'm at Sammie's house. Send me the address and we'll meet you there."

It killed me to watch Alex's facial expressions and not hear the conversation on the other end. *Who was he talking to? What had they found?* He should have put the call on speakerphone so we all could hear it. The minute he hung up, I pounced.

"Who was that, and why did you curse?" I brought my cup to my lips for a sip.

"That was Detective Lucian. He just found out that Miss Grace has been married to Lincoln for the past five years."

"What? Five Years?" My coffee cup crashed to the table. "She could have introduced herself as his wife when we met at the boutique." My mom jumped up and grabbed paper towels. I couldn't move as hot coffee dripped onto my lap. *Had they been trying to trick me this entire time?* He had set all this up.

"Sammie, Sammie." Alex pulled me out of the chair while my mom continued to clean the coffee spill.

"Go to the living room. I'll pour her another cup." I heard my mom tell Alex while he led me to the couch.

"Sammie, I need you to look at me."

I blinked and gazed into his eyes. "Alex, how long has he been planning to take my kids?"

"I don't know," Alex rubbed my back. "But they sure as hell planned to have Miss Grace in one of your kids' classes."

"But why?" My body trembled in fear of what he could do to my baby.

"We haven't connected all the dots yet, but Lucian thinks it's got something to do with money. He found out that Lincoln has several outstanding gambling debts."

"But why not just ask his parents? They're loaded." I shook my head. "Why take my baby girl?"

"We'll find her."

"Oh, my God!" I screamed and exploded off the couch. "You don't think he's going to sell her, do you?"

"No, no," Alex grabbed me and pulled me into his chest. "He might be a loser and a scumbag, but he's not a child molester or into human trafficking."

"That you know of?" I leaned back to look at him.

"True, but he's never even remotely shown any signs of anything to do with kids."

Then I remembered the end of the conversation about going somewhere.

"Where are we meeting, Detective Lucian?"

"They have an address for Lincoln's parents, and they were going to see if they had seen him."

"Okay," I pulled out of his arms. "Let's go."

"Whoa, are you sure you want to go? Do you know his parents?" Alex grabbed my arm and spun me around.

"Yeah. I met them once. They didn't approve. My parent's boutique wasn't to their liking. Apparently, they needed to own a specialized boutique for the rich that sold expensive merchandise for them to approve of me and my family."

"So they're snooty?"

"Oh, yeah." I grunted.

"If I let you come with me, promise me you'll do exactly what I say, and if I tell you to stay in the car, you will stay put."

"Okay," I said but crossed my fingers behind my back. I never intended to fulfill that promise if Hollie was there.

*** Alex ***

Did my sneaky girlfriend cross her fingers behind her back? I grinned, knowing she didn't realize I'd caught her when she turned around to leave the house. I'd be mad, but I couldn't dredge up any anger toward her. I couldn't wait to find Hollie. She was like a daughter to me. The thought of her with that asshole brought a sense of urgency.

In my head, I begged and pleaded with every god imaginable that Hollie was at her grandparents' house so I could put a smile back on Sammie's face and rid her of this horrible heartache. I prayed that nobody had a weapon and that the situation would not escalate. Right now, Miss Grace and Lincoln could face kidnapping charges if their intention was to keep Hollie. However, taking her to his parents' home for a meeting could be interpreted as interference with child custody. That was a civil charge, and even though Lincoln hadn't taken Hollie during a supervised visit, all Sammie could do was file a motion for civil contempt or a motion to enforce custody and visitation with the court. None of which was a felony that would put Lincoln behind bars for scaring the shit out of Sammie and her family. *Asshole that he was.* Alex wasn't sure what the charges to Lincoln would be until he arrived at the location and assessed the situation.

Several police vehicles lined the street, with Lucian's car leading the caravan. I drove up to Lucian and rolled Sammie's passenger window down.

"Has anyone tried to go in?"

"No, we were waiting for you." Lucian pointed to the gate. "Lincoln's car is in the driveway. We decided not to scare Hollie if she is with him and to let you guys go in first. But if it gets dicey, call us and we'll storm our way in."

"Sounds good." I rolled up the window and approached the call box for the gate.

"Hello, can I help you?" A man's voice came.

"Yes. Is Lincoln Rogers here?"

"Who may I say is asking?"

"I'm Chief Alejandro Reyes with the Haven Island Police Department. I have Sammie Rogers with me."

"Just a minute."

Sammie's leg bounced, and I pressed my hand on her thigh. It didn't take long for the disjointed voice to say, "Come on in."

The gate opened, and I drove up to the house. "Nice mansion. You weren't kidding when you said they were rich." I mumbled.

"Lincoln's dad is a financial advisor to several millionaires and a couple of billionaires."

"Okay." I squeezed her thigh after I turned off the car. "You can come in with me, but stay behind me in case it gets crazy. Do you know whether they own weapons?"

"Not while I was with him. They abhor guns. Only common folk, country bumpkins, and hoodlums have guns."

"Well, alrighty then." I shut off the car and waited for Sammie before I went to the front door.

We rang the doorbell, and a butler came to the door.

"Master Lincoln, Miss Hollie, Miss Ava Grace, and Mrs. Rogers are in the den. Follow me, please." The butler shut the door behind us and led us into a Victorian-decorated room full of cherry antique furniture and flowered couches.

Wow, it looked like something out of Homes of the Rich and Famous. Hollie sat on a loveseat with an elderly woman while Miss Grace sat across from them. They were all drinking tea with their pinkies up. Not what I was expecting, and I was glad the rest of my officers were outside.

"Oh my God, Hollie!" Sammie screamed and ran to her daughter, dropping to her knees for a tight hug.

I stayed back and observed everyone's reaction. Grandma was frowning. She clearly didn't know what the hell was going on. Miss Grace ducked her head and stared at the floral carpet on the hardwood floor. *Busted Bitch!* She couldn't look at Sammie or me in the eye.

"Hello dear," the elderly woman smiled at Sammie. "It's good to see you again. Thank you for letting Lincoln bring our grandchild to us. Are you okay?"

"Am I okay?" Sammie stood. "Are you serious?" Her voice rose, tinged with emotion.

Sammie was so lost in her anger, she wasn't reading the room. She was directing her anger at the wrong person. Grandma was clueless.

"I've been worried sick wondering where Hollie was. And you—" Sammie pointed at Miss Grace. "—have a lot of explaining to do. You lied to me, and you're not allowed to take my child out of school without my permission."

Miss Grace looked up, her brow wrinkled. "But I'm her stepmom. Lincoln said it was okay for me to add my name to her emergency contact."

"I'm her mother!" Sammie yelled. "Didn't you think you should have asked me first since he doesn't have custody of our kids? You met me. I thought we were friends."

Either Miss Grace was an idiot or she was an exceptional liar. My vote was for the latter. Miss Grace had met Sammie before and never told Sammie she was married to Lincoln. Something fishy was going on, and I planned to get to the bottom of it. Sammie released Hollie but ran her hands and eyes around Hollie's face and body.

"I'm okay, Mommy. This is Grandma Aggie, and we're having tea."

"I see that." I could tell Sammie was trying to control her temper in front of Hollie, which I totally understood because I was about to lose my shit on Grandma Aggie, did she say, and Miss Fucking Grace for taking her out of school with a trumped up approval. Fucking Lincoln, wait until I get my hands on him.

I glanced around looking for a place to take Hollie while Sammie spoke to Grandma Aggie and Miss Grace. Behind the sheer curtain of a window, I spotted a garden.

I walked up to Hollie, bowed, extending my hand with my palm facing up. "Hollie, milady, would you show me the garden?"

"You're silly, Chief Reyes." Hollie giggled. "Grandma, can I show him the pretty flowers?"

"Of course."

Hollie placed her hand in mine, and I kissed her knuckles before I led her toward the doorway leading out of the den. I texted Lucian to come around back and take Hollie the hell out of this fucking three-ring circus.

Chapter 47

Help Acquired

Lincoln

"**D**ad, you've gotta help me. How am I supposed to raise triplets when the stock market crashed?" I pleaded while Albert Mason Rogers the third sat behind his desk in his study like the Godfather. He'd been angry at first for not telling him about my triplet children, but then he met Hollie and changed his tune just as I suspected.

"Did you not invest in my suggestions? Your mother and I didn't lose any money."

"I'll admit I made some risky moves." Like not investing their money in anything except myself so I could live the high life, buy some coke, and gamble—but he didn't need to know that.

"I'll help you because of the kids. That little girl out there," —dad pointed out the door— "should not suffer due to your incompetencies." Finally, after telling me what a waste of a human being I was, who never listened, he pulled out his phone and Zelle'd me several hundred thousand dollars. "You need to make better choices, Lincoln. I can't keep bailing you out forever. Come into work with me tomorrow and let's discuss your clients' portfolios so I can see what we can do to salvage this fiasco. After all, those were my clients."

Pompous ass.

"What is going on out there?" My father threw his phone on his desk and stood so abruptly, the force of his movement sent his chair rolling back to slam into the bookshelf.

Sammie's screaming voice boomed through the walls. Dammit, if my dad hadn't taken so long to convince, I would've returned Hollie well before

Sammie ever found me. I checked my account, and the money was showing as deposited. Time to get the hell out of dodge. I followed my father out of the study and came face to face with Sammie.

"You had no right." Sammie screamed at Grace.

"Dear, please have a seat." Mother pointed to a chair.

"No! I'm not sitting down and pretending this is all okay. You took my child without my permission! How could you do that to me?"

"Young lady." Mr. Rogers screamed from the doorway. "Stop yelling at my wife and daughter-in-law. You do not come into my house and make demands."

Sammie spun around so fast I thought she was going to lose her balance and land on her ass. "I can make all the demands I want. Your son and daughter-in-law took my daughter from school without my permission."

"Well, of course he has permission. He's the father." Mr. Rogers' eyes widened.

"How could you do this to me, Lincoln?" Sammie rounded on me.

Oh shit! Just what I wanted to avoid. Good thing the deposit had come through because my well just ran dry.

"He didn't do anything to you." My father growled at her. "Look what you did to us!" He walked to my mom and held her in his arms. "You kept our grandchildren away from us for all these years. Lincoln did nothing wrong."

This was the first time my father had ever stood up for me. Granted, he was really standing up for his grandkids, but I was included in that circle now. I stood up straighter, knowing I would finally be financially secure as long as I waved the kids at him.

"Didn't do anything wrong?" Sammie's face was getting redder by the minute. "He left me after I gave birth. Not once has he reached out to me to see if the kids and I were okay. Hell," Sammie threw up her hands, "he never even met them until a few weeks ago!"

"He would've had he known you were pregnant."

This was taking a wrong turn because I told my dad Sammie never told me about her pregnancy, we'd broken up because she wanted to move back home and I wanted to continue to build my clientele and prove to my dad that I was worthy of taking over his company one day.

"What the hell are you talking about?" Sammie's eyes ricocheted between my dad and me. "He knew I was pregnant with triplets before we ended our relationship."

My dad turned to face me. "Is that true, Lincoln?"

Busted.

"She was trying to stop me from pursuing my career. How did I know she was telling me the truth? You know the lower class is always trying to sink their teeth into our money." I knew Sammie wasn't with me for the money, but I also knew my family hated a gold digger. My dad nodded, and I knew I hit the mark.

"If you had bothered to see me anytime after I told you, you would've seen I wasn't lying about being pregnant. I was as big as a house a month into my pregnancy." Sammie retorted.

"How would he have known it was his? Many women do that in order to raise their status." Dad huffed.

"I don't give a shit about your status," Sammie growled. "I just wanted the father of my babies to help me."

"Well, we are going to step in now." My father pulled out his phone. "How much?"

"How much of what?" Sammie frowned.

"How much for you to give us our grandkids so you can live your life with your boyfriend?"

"Are you shitting me right now?" Sammie's jaw dropped. "My kids are not for sale, and neither am I."

"Everyone has a price." My father typed in an amount on his phone and showed it to her. "How about this?" Damn, that was a lot of fucking zeros.

"No. You are all a real piece of work." Sammie stared at all of us with anger-filled eyes before she pointed at Ava Grace. "Hollie will be removed from your class unless they remove you. I'm taking my daughter, and I'm going home."

"For now." My father blurted out. "But you'll be hearing from our lawyers. You're gonna wish you'd taken the money."

Chief Alejandro and a shitload of officers busted through the front door and into the den, guns up at the ready.

"Lincoln and Ava Rogers," Alex hollered. "You are both under arrest for kidnapping. Do not fucking move."

Fuck! Sammie stood a foot away from me. I pulled the knife out of my pocket, grabbed Sammie, and put her in front of me with the knife at her throat.

"What the hell are you doing?" she gasped.

"If you move anywhere near me. I'll kill her." I walked backward, pulling Sammie with me. I could go out the back and make a run for it. "Ava, come to me. We're getting out of here."

"Lincoln!" my father shouted. "What the hell are you doing? You stupid boy, you're only making this worse."

"Albert!" Agatha screamed from the couch. "Do something!"

"Where's Hollie?" Sammie asked Alex while I stared at Ava and motioned my head for her to come to me. If I had Ava, I could still get money from her family.

"She's safe with the officers in a car." Alex's eyes bounced between Sammie and me.

"Ava, come here. Let's go!" Lincoln shouted.

"No, I will not be a part of this. You said it was okay. I never meant to take that little girl from school if it was against the law. I'm not going anywhere with you." Ava stood and stepped next to an officer.

Fucking bitch! In my anger, my hand tightened around the knife, and it cut into Sammie. Startled, I looked down at the knife and saw red on the blade. *Shit!* I didn't want to kill her. I just wanted to get away from everyone.

*** Alex ***

I was waiting for the right moment to rush Lincoln. For him to drop the fucking knife away from Sammie's neck so I could arrest his ass. My waiting paid off, but not before he cut her neck out of his anger toward Ava. The minute he pulled the knife away and stared at the blood, I grabbed his arm and pulled it around his back. Lucian took Sammie away from him.

"You son of a bitch!" I hollered and shoved him against the wall, causing a nosebleed on Mrs. Rogers' ornate Victorian-flowered wallpaper. "You are also now being charged with attempted murder." I pulled his arms up high on his back so it would be uncomfortable as hell and cuffed him. "Let's see what else we've got."

I started my quadrant search on his right side. His phone came out of his back pocket first, then I spun him around to check the rest. One by one, I emptied his pockets until a small, clear bag tumbled free—sealed tight, filled with white powder. Jackpot.

"Well, what have we here?" I handed the baggie over my shoulder to Griffin. "Test this, would you?" Being an undercover narcotics deputy, he always had drug test kits in his unmarked car.

"It would be my pleasure." Griffin took the baggie and stepped away.

"Let's see if it turns a pretty blue for me, asshole."

"Benjamin! Call Morty." Albert Rogers screamed out.

"Who the hell is Morty?" I asked because we didn't need any more clowns in this circus.

"My attorney. He will sort this all out. It is clearly a misunderstanding."

"A misunderstanding?" I squinted at him. "He took a child, withheld information about her whereabouts from her mother, and held a knife to her. You call this a misunderstanding?" What the hell was wrong with this guy?

"He...He was confused. Besides, he's the father." Mr. Rogers said indignantly.

"Un-fucking-believable," I mumbled.

"It's blue, Chief!" Griffin hollered and held up the field kit.

"And there you go, add possession to those charges and now you get to stay at the lovely Jones County Green Roof Inn. Take him away, boys." I nudged him toward the deputy closest to me from the Jones County Sheriff's Office. Because our police department was part of the Jones County Sheriff's Office, and they had the jail, they had to keep him there until his trial or he was bailed out.

"You got it, Chief." The deputy grabbed his arm and escorted him out of the house.

"Albert, help him." Mrs. Rogers ran to her husband.

"I already called Morty. What else do you want me to do?" Then he turned to Sammie. "You'll be hearing from my lawyer."

"About what?" Sammie gulped.

"Custody, my dear." Albert wrapped his arms around his wife.

I reached Sammie just as her legs gave out and carried her out the door.

Chapter 48

I Need a Lawyer—FAST

Sammie

I came to while Alex carried me to his car.

"Hollie, my baby." I jumped out of Alex's arms.

"Dammit, be careful." Alex hollered behind me. "You're going to re-injure your foot."

I didn't care about myself. I just wanted to hug my daughter. Hollie was sitting on the grass with Lucian, coloring in a book far away from the car Lincoln was being placed in.

"Mommy?" Hollie stopped and looked up. "Why is your neck bleeding?"

Dammit, I forgot all about that. I pulled my shirt and placed it against my neck. *Oww, that fucking hurt.* The cut was deeper than a paper cut.

"Sammie, stop." Alex grabbed my wrist. "Let the paramedics clean your neck."

"Ma'am," the paramedic next to Alex said, "it will only take a few seconds unless you want to go to the hospital?"

"No, I'm fine. Let me see my daughter and make sure she's okay."

"We already checked her out. Not a scratch on her." He smiled at Hollie.

"Mr. Trey was really nice, Mommy." Hollie stood up and ran to me. "He even gave me a lollipop." Hollie pulled it out of her pocket. "I didn't eat it since it's close to dinnertime."

I turned to the paramedic. "Mr. Trey, I presume."

"Yes, ma'am. You have a sweet little girl. Please come with me so we can stop the bleeding?"

I hugged Hollie. "Are you sure you're okay?"

Hollie shrugged. "Why wouldn't I be? Everyone was nice to me. Mommy." Hollie pointed behind me. "Why are they taking Daddy and Miss Grace away in police cars? Are they in trouble?"

Not what I wanted Hollie to witness. "They took you out of school without permission, but we'll get it sorted out. I'm gonna get them to put a Band-Aid on my neck, and I'll be right back. Lucian, will you stay with Hollie for a few more minutes?"

"Of course, I love coloring with her. She lets me go outside the lines." Lucian winked at Hollie.

"Officer Lucian." Hollie propped her arms on her hips and glared at him. "You know you're not supposed to."

"Come on, let's get that cut cleaned out. Lucian won't take his eyes off her."

"Fine," I sighed and followed them to the ambulance.

A car drove through the gates and skidded to a halt by the front door. Mr. Rogers led inside the man who hauled ass out of it with a briefcase in tow.

Great, just fucking great—the lawyer. I winced as the cut on my neck burned from the antiseptic. They wrapped my neck and sent me on my way.

My mind was reeling on the ride to my house. How was I supposed to fight Lincoln and his father for custody when I couldn't afford to hire a lawyer? Hollie kept up the conversation, telling me all about her new grandparents, their house, and the delicious tea. I tried to ask the right questions and give acceptable answers to Hollie while she talked, but inside I was dying. I'd never thought I would hear from Lincoln again, much less his parents.

Alex's hand was on my thigh. He squeezed it, and I glanced at him.

"I called my officers and your parents as soon as Hollie and I went outside. They all know she's safe, but not the details. I couldn't say much with her next to me."

"Thanks," I mumbled.

I'd only met Lincoln's parents once. They'd been so condescending and rude, I was glad we never went back to their house. I remember Lincoln asking them for money that night. *Was that what he was doing today? Did he need money? Was he going to parade my kids in front of his parents for a payoff? How did I not see this coming?* Alex had said he had gambling debts.

"What did Lincoln's father mean by they'll be seeing Hollie soon?" Alex grumbled.

"Let's get inside, away from the kids?"

"Okay."

Hollie ran into the house as soon as the door opened and hugged my parents. By the time we made it inside, she was already down the hall looking for her siblings, screaming about how cool it was meeting their new grandparents.

"What is she talking about?" My mom stood with her arms wrapped around her body. My father's arm draped over her shoulders. "What happened to your neck?"

"Lincoln took her to his parents' house, and they are going to hire a lawyer to take my kids away." I word-vomited before I turned to Alex, grabbed his shirt, and cried.

"Hey, hey." Alex ran one hand over the back of my head. His other hand applied soothing strokes to my back. "No one is taking your kids away from you. Over my dead body."

"Let's go have a seat in the living room." My dad motioned to us. "Honey, get Sammie a shot of brandy. I think she'll need it."

My dad solved everything with a shot of brandy. He swore it soothed the soul. I hated the taste, but always humored him. Alex sat on the couch and settled me on his lap. I rested my head on his shoulder while he played with my hair and rubbed my back. This was the longest we'd been together in several weeks. I wanted to depend on him, but what if he got scared again and bolted or, worse, put his work before his family again? It would be awful to be with someone who was never there, emotionally or physically. For that, I'd rather stay alone.

A small glass appeared in front of my face.

"Here, drink this." My dad swirled it around. "It'll make you feel better."

I doubted it, but I took it anyway and lifted my head from Alex's shoulder. I tried to move off his lap, but his other arm tightened around my waist, keeping me right where I was for the duration of this conversation.

"What exactly did he say?" My mom sat next to us on the couch.

"First, he tried to buy me off." Alex's hand made a fist in my hair, causing a slight tug before I gave a little moan and he released it. "He offered me five million dollars to walk away and leave him my kids. I obviously said no. Then Alex arrived with the cavalry, and all hell broke loose. Lincoln grabbed me and threatened my life at knifepoint. Alex arrested him. And I ran to Hollie."

"Oh, no! Did Hollie see all that?" My mom gasped with her hand over her mouth, her eyes bulging from her face.

"No." Alex shook his head. "I took her outside and handed her off to Detective Lucian as soon as I could before going back in for Sammie."

"In the end, Alex saved me. Lincoln and Miss Grace were arrested, and Mr. Rogers said he was getting a lawyer and suing me for custody."

"He won't win. He can't get away with this." My father drank the rest of his brandy and slammed the glass on the coffee table. "We'll help you."

"I don't know, Dad. Lincoln's family is loaded. They can afford the best lawyers in town. Hell, the lawyer had already pulled up as we were leaving. We don't have that kind of money."

"We can go talk to the bank and take out a loan. Put the boutique up as collateral." My mom and dad nodded to each other.

"No!" I downed the brandy. It burned all the way down. "We are not doing that. I will figure something out."

"Give me a minute." Alex slid me off his lap and onto the couch. "I need to make a call."

"Now?" I glared at him. We were having a serious conversation. My life was falling apart, and he had to make a damn phone call. What the hell?

"Just—" he put his hand out. "—give me a minute."

Unbelievable. Alex took out his phone and stepped outside the front door. I couldn't hear a word he was saying, but he was certainly going to hear me when he came back in. My head was about to explode. Alex had left me alone with those lunatics when he went outside with Hollie. Why didn't the officers storm the house? What had taken them so long? Had they been outside smelling fucking daisies in the backyard? I was grateful they took Hollie out, but why didn't he come back in quicker?

"I'm gonna go check on the kids. I need a hug right now." I stood and walked down the hallway.

Alex had closed the front door when he stepped out onto the porch. I couldn't hear him. Fine. All the kids' voices were coming from Holden's room, and it sounded like they were fighting.

"Whoa," I said as soon as I opened the door. "What's going on in here?"

"Hollie needs to stop telling us about how great our 'dad's—" Holden used exaggerated air quotes "—parents' are. Why should we call them our grandparents? We've never even met them before. I don't want to meet them. Tell Hollie to shut up."

"Holden." I strode over and sat next to him on the bed. "We don't tell people to shut up. You know better. Now apologize."

"Sorry," Holden grumbled. "Please stop talking about them."

"Hollie. I know you want to tell your brother and sister all about your trip to your grandparents' house, but now is not the time if they don't want to hear it. They were so worried about you. Let's just be glad that you are home safe."

"Okay," Hollie muttered. "I'm going to bed."

"Brush your teeth, and I'll be in shortly for a story."

"I don't need a story tonight. I'll think about my tea party with Grandma and Miss Grace."

All the other kids groaned, looked at me and pointed at her. This was going to be a tough one because it was clear to see the Rogers had won her over. Dammit, I could lose my kids all because that asshole wanted money. A little late to think about why I shouldn't have dated Lincoln even after my parents and all my friends warned me about him. Then again, if I hadn't been head over heels for him, I never would've gotten my three wonderful children. Life took some wicked turns. I listened to my kids' complaints before I turned to Cody. Alex had told me Cody texted him as soon as I pulled out of that pickup line without Hollie.

"Hey, big guy." I scooted closer to him and put my arm around his shoulders. "How are you doing?"

"I'm good, Miss. Sammie," he mumbled while he stared down at the floor.

"Your dad was making a call, but he'll be in soon to take you home."

"Can we stay home from school tomorrow?" Holden blurted. "Can Cody spend the night?"

""How about," I sighed, "you can stay home tomorrow, but you have to go on Friday. I'll ask Chief Reyes about Cody."

"Ask his dad what?" Alex said from the doorway, startling me and the kids.

"Can I have a sleepover?" Cody begged while still sitting next to me.

"Sure, but you'll need to come home with me and grab some clothes."

"He can borrow mine." Holden insisted. "Plus, Mom said we don't have to go to school tomorrow."

"Uh..." Alex frowned.

"Cody went through the craziness with us, maybe he can have a day off too?" I glanced at Alex. "As far as clothes, he and Holden are the same size."

"Yeah, okay." Alex rubbed the back of his neck. "I can come get you tomorrow because you are not missing school on Friday, too. Maybe we can all go do something together like fishing on Saturday."

"Fishing?" Hallie stood and placed her palms together facing Alex.

Alex was smart and deferred to me. "Up to your mom, but why not?"

"Mommy, please?"

How could I say no to that after the shitty day we had today?

"Sure, why not?"

"Where's Hollie?" Alex glanced around.

"She went to her room." I kissed Cody's temple. "Thanks again for helping us out today."

Cody blushed and mumbled, "No problem."

"Goodnight, Holden." I kissed his temple too. "I'll be back after I read to your sisters."

"We'll go with you so you only have to read once, Mom."

I held Hallie's hand, and I pulled her out of the room. "Okay. Brush your teeth and get ready for bed. Come to their room in ten minutes."

"Okay." Holden nodded.

"Wait for me?" I whispered to Alex on my way out.

"Yup. I'll come with the boys in ten for the story."

Chapter 49

Priorities

Alejandro

I helped the boys get ready for bed, and we knocked on the girls' door.

"Come in." Sammie shouted.

The boys and I sat on the floor while Sammie read a chapter from the second book in the Harry Potter series. They must've finished book one after vacation. These past few weeks without Sammie had been horrible. I wasn't lying to her about my absence. I had work to do. I wanted to nail Lincoln for the burglaries. One more charge to be added to his already growing arrest sheet for today.

I missed coming home to Sammie, eating with her and the kids, making love to her, and our pillow talk before falling asleep. Every night we slept in the same bed, whether she faced me or nestled from behind, her warmth against my chest lulled me into a peaceful sleep. I wanted to talk to Sammie, but I'd never been good with words, and avoiding her wasn't working. Annie ignored things and pretended everything was okay. Sammie wanted to talk. Forcing me to look within myself and figure out what the hell I wanted. Her—I wanted her, dammit. Now that Hollie was home, I was going to suck it up and talk to her. Lay my feelings on the line and promise to change.

I had already spoken to Lucian about taking on more responsibilities as my assistant and promoting Sean O'Reilly, who had passed his exam, to full-time detective. Not sure why I didn't think of this sooner since Lucian was already in that role, but not receiving the extra pay. He'd been training Sean, so it was the obvious decision.

Sammie finished reading, we kissed the kids goodnight, and the boys headed to their room.

"I'll be down in a minute." She whispered after she shut their girl's door.

"Okay. I'll wait in the living room."

I sat on the couch with Sammie's mom, waiting for Sammie while we watched old show reruns.

"How are the kids?" Eleanor glanced at me.

"They're good. Sammie is letting Cody sleep over. I'll come get him tomorrow when I get off work."

"Will Lincoln stay in jail overnight?" William looked up from his drink.

"Yes, but his father was already at the station yelling and screaming to let his son out because he was posting bail for him and Miss Grace. Unfortunately for them, the judge won't be in until morning. But I'm sure as soon as he sets bail, Mr. Rogers will pay it."

"Even though he took our granddaughter and held my daughter at knifepoint?" William guffawed.

"It all depends on the judge." I sighed. I'd seen everything during my law enforcement career, and I hated to give Sammie's dad false hope.

"Well, let's pray the judge has a daughter and a soft heart."

"Sorry, it took me so long." Sammie sat between me and her mom. "I wanted to make sure all the kids were okay. Cody is spending the night."

"Alex told us. I'll cook a big breakfast for everyone tomorrow. Your dad can open the boutique with Lindsey."

"Thank you, both."

"We're going to go to bed. We've had a long day. Let us know what you want to do about a lawyer." Sammie's mom kissed her cheek and stood, leaving with Sammie's dad.

"I will. I'm gonna look into it tomorrow." Sammie grinned.

"Goodnight," they both said.

"Alex," Sammie pulled a knee onto the couch and faced me at the same time I said her name.

"You go first." I leaned against the armrest of the couch.

"I'm gonna be in the fight of my life for my kids, and I think we need to cool off." Sammie looked down at her fidgeting hands.

That was not what I wanted her to say. I wanted her to ask me about the phone call, yell at me for not being around, hell throw something. But this Sammie looked defeated and tired. Leaning over, I grabbed her hand and intertwined our fingers.

"No." That got her attention. Her face jerked up, lips in a straight line, and fire burning in her eyes.

"What do you mean, no?" she said between gritted teeth.

"I don't want us to cool down. I want to help you. I want to be with you. I...," Sammie put her free hand up to stop me from talking.

"I don't have time for this right now. You're hot and cold. After we came back, you haven't even called me. I know you get busy, but not even a booty call?"

I grinned because she was so mad she didn't even know what she was saying. A booty call was off the table. She wasn't that kind of girl—not to me.

"You wanted a booty call in the middle of the night?" I raised my eyebrow knowing the answer, or so I thought.

"Maybe." She sat up straighter before deflating. "No, I wanted my boyfriend to at least want to come see me, text, or call. But all I got were two-word texts or nothing. I can't live like that. I understand that you still love Annie. I miss her too, but I need someone who needs to be with me and not with the ghost of their deceased wife. I can't measure up to that."

"You don't have to. I...," Sammie cut me off again.

"I deserve to be happy after what Lincoln did to me. My kids and I deserve to have someone who loves them like a father should." Sammie pulled her hand out of mine.

"Sammie, stop, please." I cupped her face and turned it to me. "I'm not pining for Annie. I haven't been in quite some time. If I'm being honest, I count the hours, minutes, seconds that we are apart. I just wanted to bring Lincoln to justice and thought it would be best to keep working to help you. I crave being with you and talking to you. You are my best friend and helped me so much after Annie's death, but I'm ready to move on—with you. You," I kissed her softly on her lips, "are the only woman on my mind. I want to spend my days and nights with you. I love you."

"What?" Sammie said breathlessly, her eyes roaming my face.

"Exactly what I said. I love you." I smiled and wiped the tears streaming down her cheeks. "I've loved you for a long time. I just didn't want to admit it to myself because you were Annie's best friend, and I didn't want to betray our memory. But after the cabin trip, and losing Hollie." I took a deep breath. "I don't want to live without you. I want to marry you and join our families once and for all."

"Oh...my...God," Sammie's tears came rushing down her cheeks. "Are you serious?"

"Absolutely." I leaned in and kissed her, pouring all the love I had into that kiss, making sure she felt it.

"I love you, too." She murmured against my lips. "I've loved you from the moment I saw you, but I couldn't stand in the way of Annie. That love grew into friendship only strengthened by your support after I moved back. I don't want to live without you either, but you must promise me that when something comes up, you'll talk to me and not let your job come between us. I understand your job is important to you. I love you for who you are and how you take care of all of us. I don't need you to always be next to me, but these past few weeks with no communication have been brutal."

"I understand. I've spoken to Lucian about becoming my second in command so we can divide the work. It's about time since he's been my right hand for some time now. Not sure why I didn't promote him sooner. Anyway, I promise to be home after work as often as possible, but if there is an emergency, Lucian and I will share the calls."

Sammie smiled. "That sounds good. Thank you." Then she sat back and sank into the couch with a frown. "What am I going to do about Lincoln's parents?"

"We are going to talk to a lawyer."

"I can't afford one. I have some money, but not a lot since I spend it all on the kids and helping my parents."

"I have plenty of money, but we won't need it."

Sammie sat up. "What do you mean?"

"That phone call earlier," Sammie nodded. "It was to a friend of mine whose wife is a family lawyer. She will take your case pro bono."

"Alex, no." Sammie shook her head. "That's not right. What if she gets in trouble with her job?"

"She won't. They do a certain number of pro bono jobs a year, and she is more than happy to take on a rich family that is trying to take the kids away from a hardworking, loving mom. Besides, she owes me. I saved her sorry ass husband while I was in Iraq as a Ranger and never cashed in my favor. It's all good."

"Okay. When can I talk to her?" Sammie laid her head to rest on my chest while I held her.

This was the life I dreamt we would share. She and I sitting on a couch holding each other as we discuss our problems and come up with solutions. I could live like this for the rest of my life. I was given a second chance at love, and I sure as hell would not blow it this time.

"She's going to come over to my house tomorrow at ten. We'll leave the kids here. I'll come get you so I can get Cody when I drop you off after our meeting."

"Sounds good." Sammie threw one leg over mine and sat on my lap facing me. "Thank you."

"You don't need to thank me. We're a team, right?"

"Yes," Sammie wrapped her arms around my neck and kissed me, pouring her love into my soul.

"Now and forever. I love you, Sammie."

"Now and forever, I love you too, Alejandro."

Chapter 50

Epilogue

Alejandro

After we declared our love to each other, Sammie and I met with Janice Butch, our lawyer, the next day and went over everything that happened with Lincoln from the moment Sammie met him. Janice wanted both of our sides since Sammie and I had both had encounters with Lincoln.

I wholeheartedly agreed with Janice's statement that Sammie would look like the better stable parent if she were married. Sammie and I went down to the courthouse the following Saturday, along with our parents and kids, and got married instead of going fishing. We celebrated with lunch at Hi Grill with our families. Sammie and I didn't care where we ate as long as we could go to my house for our weekend honeymoon while the kids stayed with Eleanor and William. We would do a proper honeymoon at a later date. Several of our friends and fellow officers showed up to congratulate us. We promised to throw a badass party on our one-year anniversary.

The following weekend we moved the kids into my house—our house. It was a little cramped. We would either have to expand or move into another house.

We had a trial early because of Albert's connection with judges in Jones County. He threw everything he had at Sammie. But I also had connections within Jones County, and the judge couldn't overlook Lincoln's rap sheet. He was going to jail. He received five years for possession of cocaine, fifteen years for attempted kidnapping, and five years for attempting to harm a hostage—totaling twenty years. The judge took pity on him since Lincoln and his family threw themselves at the mercy of the court, letting them know that Lincoln never would've harmed Sammie or his kids—he just wanted the money. The judge bought it. Twenty years was better than nothing, although with good behavior, he would get out sooner.

Albert was smart in filing for custody instead of Lincoln, but in the end, after all the dirty laundry was aired and Sammie got full custody of her kids. The judge did award Albert and Agatha supervised visits, which was fine, but I was monitoring those motherfuckers. I didn't trust them. They had enough money to leave the country on a dime. I was upset with the judge for that, but they were the kids' grandparents—I had to get over it.

We settled into a routine. Sammie hired on extra help at the boutique, and we both came home around five to eat dinner as a family. The kids were ecstatic, and Sammie and I watched Hallie and Cody to make sure their crush stayed a crush. Hell, the boys were over the moon to have sleepovers every day since they shared a room. My three-bedroom house was brimming with laughter and noisy as hell. I loved every fucking single minute of my life.

Sammie and I were in bed after a satisfyingly exhausting hour-long round of sex. Her breath warmed my chest while she lay sprawled out on my chest. She came down off of her third orgasm. I loved giving them to her. The look on her face, her flushed body, and sexy sounds—they were the highlight of my day.

"I love you," she groaned into my chest.

I rolled us over and bent over her, leaning on my elbow. My hand brushed her hair off her beautiful face. She was my angel come to save me from a lonely life.

"You are my light at the end of every day and my sunshine when I wake up in the morning. I've never known so much peace as when I'm in your arms, in our bed." I caressed her cheeks. "I love you more today than I did yesterday, if that is even possible. I'm honored and proud to call you my wife. I look forward to growing old with you, rocking our grandbabies on the front porch. I love you now and forevermore."

"Ditto," Sammie pulled the back of my head down to her lips, and we sealed the deal. Together forever!

Chapter 51

Special Thanks

Thank you to all my readers. You are the BEST! I am beyond grateful for all of your continued support.

I am grateful to Michelle K and Michelle Z, who offered their valuable time to read my manuscripts and improve my books.

Without the help of many individuals, this book would never have been written. Any mistakes or imaginative liberties taken are entirely my fault. Thanks to their insightful feedback and extensive knowledge, my story was transformed into something much more captivating.

I feel blessed and honored to know the following first responders. As I write my chapters and questions arise, I reach out to them via text, email, or phone call, and they ALWAYS respond with answers as quickly as they can. The Best Men and Women in Blue Support Team ever: Sgt. TJ Williams, Sgt. Stacci Sastre, K9 Deputy Bryan Wright, and Corrections Deputy Nathan Lebon.

As always, to all the first responders out there, the ones I'm blessed to call my friends and those I haven't met, please stay safe out there. It can be a little crazy. Thank you, thank you, thank you, for what you do for all of us in your community daily.

I know my books are hard to find because I lack reviews, but if you follow me on Amazon as one of your favorite authors, you'll receive alerts when I release a book. While I value your feedback and reviews, I realize your time is valuable.

Happy Reading and Thank You!
Neri

Chapter 52

About the Author

Neri

Neri Lopez is a two-time Global Book Awards winner, celebrated for her Romance–Action & Adventure novel *Red Path* and her Romance–Suspense novel *Deputy Sean*.

Her stories blend emotional depth, high-stakes suspense, and heartfelt romance, often rooted in cultural history (the Path Series) and character-driven drama.

A lifelong creative, she has been a stay-at-home mom to triplets, a graphic designer, and a high school teacher of Spanish, 2D Art, and Digital Design. She now writes from her home in Florida, where her two rescued cats—Salem and Sabrina—dutifully assist by walking across her keyboard at crucial moments.

Neri loves to hear from her readers. You can email her at: nerilopezauthor@gmail.com or join her mailing list by going to her website: **nerilopez.com**

(When you sign up for her newsletter, you will receive a FREE downloadable bookmark of Red Path.

Please consider writing a review on Amazon and/or Goodreads after you read Neri's books. It helps other readers find her books on Amazon.

Or follow her on:

facebook: Neri Lopez - Author

instagram: Neri_Lopez_Author

(She is most active on facebook)

Reading Order:

Haven Island PD: Protecting Paradise

Book 1: Deputy Sean (Sean and Cassie)
The Path Series (entire series is available on Amazon)
Book 1: Red Path (Thunder and Isa)
Book 2: Unconquered Path (Alex and Tori)
Book 3: Wagering Path (Holt and Freya)
Book 4: Unexpected Path (Mark and Maggie)
Novella Book 4.5: Double Trouble Path (Maggie and Freya's weddings)
Book 5: Twisted Path (Barrett and Angel)
Book 6: Blue Path (George and Lizzy)

Turn the page for part of the first chapter in the next Haven Island PD: Protecting Paradise, Book 3: Detective Lucian.

Chapter 53

HiPD: Protecting Paradise Book 2 Teaser

Detective Lucian

"**J**osie!" I hollered as soon as I opened the door.

I drew my gun and scanned the front hallway, my heart pounding in my chest. The piercing sound of sirens blared behind me, growing louder with each second. I requested backup but rushed to the location as soon as dispatch reported the caller as being Josie Hale.

"Dammit, Josie! Where the hell are you?" I entered the living room and listened for any noise. *Where the hell was she?* Her car was out front. She had to be here somewhere. If anyone hurt her, there would be hell to pay.

Officers Sean O'Reilly, Charlotte Spencer, and Hudson Shaw burst through the front door.

"Charlotte, Hud, finish checking the downstairs. Sean and I will check the upstairs." I motioned my gun toward the stairs.

"When Ryker gets here with Judge, have him sniff every fucking thing in this house."

"Got it," Hud mumbled and motioned for Charlotte to follow him.

Sean followed me up the stairs. The first bedroom we cleared was empty. We slithered along the wall into the next one. They were all empty. The last room at the end was a bathroom.

"Josie!" I banged on the door. "Open the door. It's Detective Lucian. Are you alone?"

I heard crying behind the door and motioned to Sean to kick it down. I braced my gun ready to shoot if anyone other than Josie was behind the door. Sean kicked it open, and I stepped in. Josie was alone, sitting with her knees up to her chin, arms wrapped around her. I put my gun away and crouched down in front of her.

"Josie, it's me. You're okay now." I ran my hands over her arms, but she cringed at my touch. *Had they hurt her?* "Josie, I need you to look at me," I whispered.

"Lucian!" Several boots stomped in the hallway, making their way toward me. "The house is empty."

Josie was shaking so hard her body looked ready to crack.

"Stay out there. Close the door. I'll be out with Josie in a second."

The sound of the door clicking shut raised Josie's tear-stained face toward me. Her mascara ran down her face.

"Is...I...Is he gone?"

"Yes, who was here, Josie? Let me help you." I murmured.

She looked at me, and the hurt in her eyes was a piercing plea.

9 781963 995275